THIS SIDE OF
Yesterday

ANGELA D. MEYER

Darlene Books
This Side of Yesterday
Copyright © 2020
Angela D. Meyer

ISBN 978-0-692-89634-1

Cover design by Roseanna White Designs
Cover images from Shutterstock
Formatting by Polgarus Studio

Scripture taken from the Holy Bible, NEW INTERNATIONAL VERSION®, NIV® Copyright © 1973, 1978, 1984, 2011 by Biblica, Inc.® Used by permission. All rights reserved worldwide.

This novel is a work of fiction. Names, characters, places, and incidents either are the product of the author's imagination or are used fictitiously. Any resemblance to actual events, locales, organizations, or persons living or dead is entirely coincidental and beyond the intent of either the author or the publisher.

Printed in the United States of America

To Kevin, whose constant love, support, and understanding made this possible.

Welcome to

THE MOSAIC COLLECTION

We are sisters, a beautiful mosaic united by the love of God through the blood of Christ.

Each month The Mosaic Collection releases one faith-based novel exploring our theme, Family by His Design, and sharing stories that feature diverse, God-designed families. All are contemporary stories ranging from mystery and women's fiction to comedic and literary fiction. We hope you'll join our Mosaic family as we explore together what truly defines a family.

If you're like us, loneliness and suffering have touched your life in ways you never imagined; but Dear One, while you may feel alone in your suffering—whatever it is—you are never alone!

Subscribe to Grace & Glory, the official newsletter of The Mosaic Collection, to receive monthly encouragement from Mosaic authors, as well as timely updates about events, new releases, and giveaways.

Learn more about The Mosaic Collection at
www.mosaiccollectionbooks.com

Join our Reader Community, too!
www.facebook.com/groups/TheMosaicCollection

Books in

THE MOSAIC COLLECTION

When Mountains Sing by Stacy Monson
Unbound by Eleanor Bertin
The Red Journal by Deb Elkink
A Beautiful Mess by Brenda S. Anderson
Hope is Born: A Mosaic Christmas Anthology
More Than Enough by Lorna Seilstad
The Road to Happenstance by Janice L. Dick

Coming soon: novels by Sara Davison, Johnnie Alexander, and Regina Rudd Merrick

Learn more at www.mosaiccollectionbooks.com/books

CHAPTER ONE

Ginger looked around the dining room of the Jukebox Café which had been in her family for generations. When her dad passed away she took the reins, and enjoyed running the café as much as her mother had enjoyed it. Wiping the menus free of stickiness, she recalled how much of a stickler her mother had been for cleaning them. But she had managed to make even that task fun for Ginger. The last menu cleaned and stacked, she was satisfied that they were ready for the supper rush.

Ginger grabbed a mug of coffee and headed to the corner booth for a quick break. The only other occupants of the dining room were Grandpa and Pastor Mike battling it out over their weekly chess game. The place was quiet. The seat cushion swooshed softly as she sat and rested her feet up on the opposite bench. Holding her mug next to her lips, she enjoyed the warmth of the steam before she took a sip.

A loud clatter jolted Ginger out of her peaceful moment of relaxation and yanked her attention across the room to Grandpa and Pastor Mike. Grandpa's beloved chess pieces were scattered across the floor. He glared at Mike.

"Want to play tomorrow?" Mike bent to pick up the pieces.

"I don't know what I'll want tomorrow." Grandpa's gruff tone mirrored the look on his face. With a stonewall expression, he marched away from his friend, and out through the kitchen. He was probably going to their house across the alley out back.

Ginger knelt and helped Mike pick up the scattered chess set. "What happened?"

"Walter was taking a long time to make his move and I ribbed him a bit like usual. This time..." Mike swept his hand toward the chess pieces spread across the floor.

Ginger focused on the white and black pawns at her knee to hide the moisture gathering in her eyes. She didn't want Grandpa to change. He had always been her rock. But lately, he had been growing more easily agitated. Add his forgetfulness and she was afraid of what it might indicate. He was a strong ninety-eight-year-old man and she never expected to lose him to anything besides death when it came his time.

She sat back on her heels and swiped a stray tear.

Mike touched her arm. "You're not alone."

"I feel like I'm losing him."

Mike waited.

The bell over the door jingled and Ginger looked down at the chess piece in her hand. "I better get back to work."

"If you need to talk, you know where to find me."

"Thanks." She handed the piece to Mike and got up from the floor.

"Want me to take his chess set over to him?"

"We might want to let him cool off. You can put it in my office for now." Both men were veterans, Grandpa with the Army Air Corps in War World II and Mike more recently retired from the Marines. Several years ago, when Mike first came to town as their pastor, they had knocked heads for over two months till they made peace during a Christmas Eve snowmobile ride. They formed an unexpected friendship and now, at least once a week between the lunch and dinner rush, Mike paused from his pastoral duties and played a round of chess with her grandfather.

Ginger went back to hang the Help Wanted sign lying forgotten on a table near the door. Sandra, one of their waitresses had been late several times over the last couple weeks. Ginger attempted to talk to

Sandra about it, but the young woman's response had been vague, and her tardiness had continued. Ginger had no choice but to find someone she could count on.

Mike followed her. "Need any help?"

She laughed. "I think I can hang a sign." Ginger paused. Moments ago she had felt such heaviness when thinking about her aging grandfather and now she was laughing. Somehow it didn't seem right to move from the weighted emotion so quickly. But she was thankful for friends to keep her mind in a better place. Grandpa had an appointment later in the week with the doctor. She would talk to him about the changes in her grandfather.

"Here. It's a bit crooked." He pointed at the top right corner.

She swatted his arm. "You're getting ornery like Grandpa." She stopped and closed her eyes. Even a few months ago, that would have been something to laugh about. Grandpa had always hidden his tender heart underneath his gruffness. Not anymore.

"I know what you mean, Ginger. Count on me for whatever help you need with Walter."

"I appreciate you always looking out for him. You're a good friend."

He stuck his hands in his jeans pockets. "I better get back to my sermon prep. See you Sunday."

Ginger picked up a rag to wipe down tables as she watched him leave. Mike was considered quite the catch with the matchmakers at church. They had set Mike up on plenty of dates over the years with nieces, granddaughters, or daughters of friends. Ginger had gone out on one date with him in the early days, but she had no desire to be involved with anyone. Life kept her too busy for a romantic relationship. Yet, Mike had become a part of the fabric of her life through their conversations over early morning coffee at the Jukebox. The kindness and friendship he gave to Grandpa and the love and care he had for the church endeared him to her. His friendship was a blessing.

She added a stray menu to the stack on the counter, then pushed the swinging doors open into the kitchen. She stopped near the cook. "Harry, hear from Sandra yet?

"Nope. Looks like she's going to be late again." He eyed her from where he worked at the stove.

Ginger hoped this wasn't going to be the second waitress in the last six months she had lost to the new mega store on the west side of Preston Hill. "I wish Sandra would talk to me about what's going on. She really is a sweet girl. We might be able to work something out."

Harry leaned against the counter. "The right waitress will come along. At least we still have Shelby. Remember what Pastor Mike says."

"'Take one day at a time. Jesus has this.' He's right."

"Yoo-hoo." Betsy sashayed through the back door of the kitchen. Dark shoulder length hair swung back and forth with each step. Her bling-drenched red tunic hung over black tights that ended in red stilettos.

The outfit reminded Ginger of a young collegiate out on the town for the night. What would Betsy do when she got too old to wear those types of outfits? Ginger snickered. She would keep wearing them. Back in high school, there hadn't been much the two of them agreed on, especially fashion. But over the years, they had stood by each other through enough of life's difficulties that the differences no longer mattered.

"You ready for that cup of coffee yet?"

"Have to take a raincheck. Waitress didn't show. Tomorrow?"

Betsy plopped her fists on curvy hips. "If I didn't already have a commitment tonight, I would grab an apron and help, you know I would."

"If I could clone you for a waitress, the Jukebox would be set." After a quick hug, Ginger scooted Betsy out the door.

After changing into fleece pants and a sweatshirt, Ginger reclined on the sofa. She stretched and wiggled her toes. Nothing like freeing her feet from shoes after a long day.

Grandpa sat in the easy chair across from her, a mug of something hot cradled in his hands.

"Long day?" Ginger sat up and tucked her feet underneath her.

"You could say that."

A heavy pause draped around them, snuffing out any hope Ginger held that he would be up front with her. "Grandpa?"

"Today was one of my better days."

"Yeah?" How he considered this afternoon a good day was beyond her.

"Taught that boot a thing or two about chess. Hung out with Bo and Eugene over at the Custer's community room. The usual." He took a sip of his drink, dipping his eyes away from hers.

Never knowing how far to push, Ginger debated about what to say. Grandpa's bad days were happening more often, but there was no use upsetting him tonight. "I'm going to call it a night. See you in the morning." Ginger headed down the hall toward her room.

"That's it? No twenty questions?" Grandpa called after her.

"I can oblige."

"No, no. You're right. It's time to turn in. See you in the morning."

She watched Grandpa from the doorway of her room. His posture slumped and he shook his head. Lifting a hand, he swiped his face. Her breath caught in her throat. He never cried. Resisting the urge to go to him, she allowed him his privacy.

CHAPTER TWO

"Time to go." Ginger tapped her foot.

Grandpa sat with Bo and Eugene in their regular booth at the back of the Jukebox Café. Most days of the week, you could count on them spending a portion of their day huddled around their coffee. If only she knew what they talked about, she could probably write a book.

"Don't need to go to no doctor." Grandpa winked at his buddies as though she wasn't standing there.

"Fine." She started to leave.

"What are you up to, young lady?"

Ginger enjoyed his good days when the banter was light-hearted and teasing. Plastering her best no-nonsense look on her face, she turned around. "You remember what the doctor said last time?"

He scowled. "Course I remember. That interfering young whippersnapper."

The new doctor had a way with Grandpa. From the first visit the young doctor had made time to hear the war stories. Talked about his own great-grandfather who fought for America. The two bonded, much to her relief, and the doctor had proved helpful in convincing Grandpa to cooperate with her. She remembered his mutinous expression when the doctor instructed him to take his meds and make it to his checkups. But when the doctor told him a change might be in order if he didn't cooperate, Grandpa had changed his demeanor. Until recently, most days he was a model of cooperation.

"I'm leaving in five minutes. With or without you." As she left the dining room, Walter spewed out a few new cuss words. Ginger

6

clamped down a reprimand. His swearing was getting worse, but it did no good to say anything. Besides, she didn't want to start a fight.

Striding to the car, Ginger's thoughts turned to Grandpa's forgetfulness and his agitation of late. She had hoped his moods were the normal frustrations-at-getting-older type of forgetfulness, but her mind leapt to the stories about elderly relatives of people at church who had been diagnosed with dementia at a younger age than Grandpa. She often overlooked his age because he still got along so well, but truth was, they were fortunate he was still able to live in their home. Eventually, the changes of age would catch up, and hopefully she could keep with them. What would happen to him if something happened to her?

Lord, keep Grandpa strong. Keep me safe so that I can care for him. Help me to be faithful. Be my strength, because lately I'm too tired to deal with it.

"Wait up."

Halfway to the car, Ginger turned and smiled at Grandpa. "How about we stop at the flea market on the way home?"

Grandpa's countenance brightened. "Now that's worth a trip to the doc's."

Grandpa sat with his arms crossed as he listened to the doctor.

"At your age, forgetfulness can be a normal part of aging. And there are stressors and illnesses that can bring on episodes of forgetting." The young doctor studied the chart on the computer. "I want to run a couple tests to rule out those possible causes." The doctor rolled his chair over and stopped directly in front of Grandpa. He folded his arms and put on a stern face. "Listen to Ginger. She's not your enemy. Exercise and make those changes to your diet that I recommended."

"Hmph. I'm not eating kale or skipping pie." Grandpa stood.

The doctor laughed and handed Ginger a slip of paper. "Here's the number for the nutritionist. She'll help you figure out something you can both live with." He handed her another piece of paper. "This is a list of things to watch for between now and your next visit as well as the titles of a few books that might be helpful. Any questions?"

Grandpa grabbed the paper and scanned it before shoving it at Ginger. Lifting his chin, he marched out of the examining room.

The doctor stopped Ginger on her way out. "You need to prepare yourself. This is most likely dementia. Make an appointment for a consultation with the seniors specialist before Walter's next visit. You need to know what to expect. Don't ignore the signs but try not to worry. If this is dementia, it's in the early stages and there's medicine that can slow its progression. He might have good years ahead of him. Focus on that."

"Thanks." She tried to process what he told her as she caught up with Grandpa, already outside waiting next to the car. His scowl set her on edge. Refusing the tension that crawled through her body, she picked up her step and determined to focus on one day at a time and the hope of still having good years ahead.

"What did that whippersnapper say to you when I left? I know there was something he didn't want me to hear. He told you the truth, didn't he? I'm finally going to forget everything."

Ginger unlocked the car. "He encouraged me to not worry, and he wants me to schedule a consultation with the seniors specialist."

Grandpa climbed into the car and slammed the door.

Ginger walked around to the driver's side and got in.

"I don't want to forget Irene."

She touched his hand. "You could never forget your wife."

He jerked away from her touch. "Whatever." Grandpa stared out the window.

Ginger sighed and started the car. "Grandpa, you know I want you to live with me, right? That isn't going to change." She knew from other friends whose parents were older that being left alone was a fear that needed to be addressed up front.

"That's what you say now, but what if I do forget everything?"

"Let's take it one day at a time. You ready to go to the flea market?" Ginger turned on the radio and lifted a prayer of thanks for the new doctor and Grandpa's cooperation at the appointment.

Nearing the light in the middle of town, she slammed on her brakes and swerved into the turn lane to avoid an oncoming car turning left in front of her. More often now since that mega store opened up on the west side of town, some joker passed through Preston Hill who thought they owned the road. It was enough to make her want to swear. She clamped her lips together as swear words tumbled out of Grandpa's mouth at a faster rate than usual. Hopefully he was releasing some of his pent-up agitation and this increase in swearing wasn't becoming a new habit.

She turned on her wipers as mist coated the world. A sheen of sparkles brightened the view as the sun peeked out from behind the clouds.

Ginger's phone played the tune she had assigned the Jukebox. She pulled onto a side street and parked.

"Let's keep going to the flea market."

She wavered at the plea in his voice. "You know I can't do that to Harry." Ginger swiped to answer. "Can this wait? We're headed to the flea market."

"That depends."

Ginger groaned inwardly. *Not today.* "On whether I want happy customers?"

"Pretty much. Sandra called in and quit. Got a new job at that mega store. I called Shelby. She can help close."

"See you in a few." Ginger ended the call. "Sandra quit and I have to go in to work. I'm sorry." Expecting a taciturn response, she held her breath.

"Do what you need. We can do the flea market another time." He patted her hand.

Surprised, Ginger pulled back into traffic. Tomorrow she would place an ad in the *Preston Chronicle*.

Within ten minutes, Ginger arrived at the café. Grabbing an apron, she encouraged kitchen staff on her way to the dining hall. The young man she had hired a couple weeks back to assist Harry grunted in response to her words and appeared to be deep in thought. She started to leave, but his knife clattered to the counter and he let out a loud expletive. Startled, she turned, expecting to see him injured.

He wiped his hands on a towel and threw it down. "I can't do this one day more."

"Am I missing something?"

"I don't want to be a cook."

"You're the one who came to me for a job."

"My mother says I can do anything I want then makes me work here to help the family."

Understanding flooded Ginger, and she offered a brief smile. "Maybe you need to have a talk with your mother."

He nodded and took off his apron. "I won't be coming back."

She cleared her throat. "Perhaps a two-week notice?"

He paused and gave her a sheepish look. "Yes, ma'am. I wasn't thinking." He donned his apron and reached for the knife.

Ginger went to her office for a moment's reprieve. She closed the door and rested her forehead against the cold metal of the door frame. The responsibility of the café and taking care of Grandpa weighed heavily on her. The Jukebox provided a living but not much more. And lately, not only was her staff shrinking because the mega store offered higher wages, her income had declined due to lost traffic. A fast food place had sprung up next to the store and it was drawing people away from the Jukebox with the promise of a quick in and out. How would she be able to afford more care if Grandpa needed it?

Some months, she barely made the mortgage payments, and the last two payments were late. The Jukebox was all they had. She had to find a way to keep it going. *One day at a time.* Ginger closed her eyes. *God, this is all feeling a bit overwhelming. I need help.* If only she was part of a larger family, she wouldn't be alone in this. After a few moments of stillness, she went back to work.

CHAPTER THREE

Ginger had posted the Help Wanted sign in the window and put an ad in the paper two weeks ago. Until she hired a new waitress and cook's assistant, double duty fell to her. She helped Harry with prep in the kitchen and backed up Shelby out in the dining hall. Betsy stopped by on occasion to help. Between them, they managed to cover the shifts. Ginger's eyes watered as she chopped onions.

"Corned beef and cabbage up." Harry slid a plate full of their current most popular dish onto the ledge of the pass-through window. "Ginger, we need more cabbage chopped." The cook grinned at her. "Kinda like bossing you around for a change."

She shook her finger at him across the counter. "You be careful." Harry had worked in the café for her parents since he was a freshman in high school and had made his way to head cook by the time he graduated. He exhibited a natural talent with food and could have gone anywhere if he had attended culinary school. Instead, he married his best friend and stayed in Preston Hill. He had considered moving after his wife passed away a few years ago, but Ginger was thankful he chose to stay. She needed his steady presence in the restaurant.

Sliding a large bowl of cabbage his way, she checked the clock. "I need to get off my feet. What's it like out there?"

"Caught up for the moment. Go ahead. I'll holler if I need help."

Ginger took advantage of the respite and grabbed a plate of food to eat in the office. A few bites into her meal, Grandpa's voice rose above the din of restaurant noise. What was going on?

When she entered the dining area, he stood toe to toe with a young teenage boy whose right arm was covered in tattoos. Grandpa pointed a finger at the kid. "That's not the way you treat people, young man."

The kid shrugged. "Whatever." He tried to move past, but Bo and Eugene joined Grandpa, barring the way.

Behind them, Greg Jordan from church corralled his family's two youngest foster children. An upside-down plate had shattered on the floor and milk spread across the table. One of their own kids snuggled next Greg's wife, Megan. Greg latched onto the errant youngsters, who tugged against his hold like two ponies ready to bolt from a starting gate. The Jordans' two older kids sat glued to their chairs.

Greg's jaw muscles twitched. Managing six kids was no easy task, and it had to take a lot of self-control to maintain his calm in the middle of this chaos. At least it wasn't the height of rush hour. Motioning for Shelby to help, Ginger took a deep breath and waded into the stream of confusion.

She grabbed a rag and stopped the flow of milk heading for Megan's lap. "We'll clean it up. Let's move you guys first."

Megan scooted the chair away from the table. "We need to go. This isn't going to work."

"Come on kids." Greg tilted his head toward the door.

"Rachel." One of the younger foster children broke free from Greg's hand and ran for the young woman entering the café.

Rachel knelt and opened her arms. "What are you running from in such a hurry?" She wobbled on her heels when the child plowed into her.

Ginger let out a sigh of relief. Rachel, a waitress who had worked at the Jukebox last summer, was back after all. When she had left at the end of last summer, she hadn't planned on returning.

The little boy pouted.

"That bad, huh?"

He nodded.

"You hungry?" Rachel worked her magic like she had last year.

The boy nodded.

"Then let's get you some food." She reached out her hand, and he allowed her to lead him to the table. She stopped in front of Megan. "Need some help?"

Megan's stiff posture relaxed as the other kids hurried over and clamored for hugs from Rachel.

Ginger's eyes met Shelby's. "Take care of the other customers. Rachel's offered to help with the Jordan kids." She grabbed the crayons and coloring pages.

Rachel led the parade of kids to the new table.

Ginger caught up with Rachel. "How long are you here for?"

"Till the end of summer, if you'll have me."

Ginger laughed. "I don't have to think twice about that."

"Sorry for all the mess." Greg set one of the youngsters in a chair. "I thought a meal out would be nice for a change."

"No apology needed. I'm glad you came in." Ginger jutted her chin toward the tattooed youth still talking to Grandpa. "Is he the new foster kid you were telling me about?"

Megan nodded. "Josh."

"He's a great kid, but he has a few rough edges." Greg scratched the back of his neck.

"With a grudge a mile deep." Megan sighed. "Not sure how we'll get through to him."

"One day at a time." Ginger led them to a table away from the kids. "You guys are doing a great job. Taking in foster kids is hard and takes a lot of love." While Rachel occupies the kids, you two enjoy some time off."

"Thank you." Megan gave Ginger a hug before sitting across the table from Greg.

"I'll be back in a jiff with some of your favorite pie." Nothing like a slice of the Jukebox's chocolate deluxe pie to bring a smile to a tough day.

"Yoo-hoo." Betsy's bracelets jangled like wind chimes as she walked across the dining room floor. "Are you going to be able take a break?"

"Today, yes. Look who's back." Ginger pointed over at Rachel engaging with the kids.

"It will be a good summer after all. Let's go while we can. I'll catch up with Rachel later."

Ginger grabbed a plate of food for Betsy before they headed to Ginger's office for a much-needed girlfriend chat.

The next day, Ginger's head pounded as she worked on placing an order after the breakfast rush. Her focus was hit and miss. Some pain reliever was necessary before she faced any customers, but she was out.

Rachel stopped by the office about half an hour before she needed to clock in. "Knock, knock."

Ginger gave the young woman a hug. "Walk with me while I start some fresh coffee. We never did get to catch up yesterday. Tell me what's going on." Last year, Rachel had come to Preston Hill to live with a friend from college for the summer but ended up living with Beth, the girl from the flea market, before the summer was out. Ginger hired her, and the only regret she had was that Rachel had needed to leave.

"I finished my associate degree, but I have no clue what to do with it. I don't want the debt from going into a four-year college program, so Beth urged me to come back for a while and take a little time to figure it out. I would have called, but I wasn't sure how long I would be hanging around. But there's something about this town. It felt like the right place to be."

"You're staying with Beth again?" Ginger measured the coffee grounds and poured them into the filter.

"At least for now. She might have to move before the end of summer, though. Family stuff."

"I'm glad you're here. We need the help. Things are a bit more challenging than last year." As they walked to the kitchen, Ginger caught Rachel up on the challenges brought about with the opening of the mega store. "Shelby opens. You'll both need to work lunch and then you'll close. I'll pitch in where needed, but there might be a bit of overtime."

"Perfect. It's an answer to prayers. I'm saving up for a better car."

"Are you comfortable if I run a quick errand before the noon rush? Shelby will be here soon."

"It's like riding a bike." Rachel clapped her hands. "It's good to be back."

"I'm thrilled to have you back. And not just because we need a waitress. You always brought joy to this place." Ginger gave Rachel another hug. "I'll see you in a bit."

Ginger turned to leave and bumped into Mike. When she stumbled back, he caught her by the arms before she lost her balance. She slipped away from his hold. "How long have you been standing there?"

His eyes revealed a mischievous glint. "Long enough. Hey, Rachel. Welcome back to Preston Hill."

"Thanks, Pastor." Rachel snagged an apron. "I'm going to make sure things are ready for lunch."

Mike waved before turning to Ginger. "Can I give you a ride? I stopped by to check up on Walter, but we can talk while I drive."

"Thanks." Ginger grabbed her purse from the office.

"Where to?" Mike led the way to his SUV.

"The Corner Pharmacy. Need something for my headache."

"Your chariot awaits." He held the door open while she climbed in, then walked around to his side and got behind the wheel. "Rough day?"

"More a culmination of things." She rubbed her temples. "It never stops."

"I get that." He drove in silence for a couple blocks. "How did Walter's doctor's appointment go?"

"The doctor needs to run some tests to rule out other causes of forgetfulness, but he's pretty sure it's dementia. He didn't tell that to Grandpa yet. For now, the bottom line is that we need to make some lifestyle changes. Diet, exercise, and lowering the stress."

"How can I help?" Mike made a right-hand turn.

"I've got it covered."

"Ginger. You're doing it again."

"Fine." It irritated her when he called her on her propensity for self-reliance. She ran through a mental list of things that needed to change. "Make sure he gets out for more walks?"

"Done." Mike came to a stop at a red light.

"If you can make sure he eats well, you might get a prize." Ginger snickered.

"Right. Not sure anyone can manage that."

Ginger sobered. "I have to try." What would her life have been like if her fiancé had chosen to come to Preston Hill with her after her father died instead of throwing everything they had away? It would be incredible to have someone to help carry the load of life. But her fiancé had been more interested in his trajectory toward his pre-planned future. With a different woman for his wife.

When she returned to Preston Hill she found a new normal where she was content. Without the complications of a relationship. Ginger loved Grandpa, and it gave her pleasure to serve those around her in their community. Even though she had good friends, she hated to rely on them too heavily. And she was afraid that was looming ahead of her.

"Penny for your thoughts?" Mike slowed as they approached a stop sign.

"I'm thinking about Grandpa. Not everyone gets to his age as healthy as he is."

"He's lived a lot of good years."

"True." Beyond health, would Grandpa consider the years good? Or did he have regrets?

"He's been talking about Irene more often lately."

Ginger angled her head toward Mike. Was he reading her mind? "Why do you think that is? His wife disappeared right after Pearl Harbor."

"He's been talking about her as though she's still alive."

"There's no indication she's still living."

"How much do you know about her disappearance?"

"Only that she left their young daughter Patricia, my mother, behind with Grandpa's parents. He tried to find Irene for a while."

Silence cocooned them for the last two blocks to the pharmacy. Mike pulled into a parking spot. "How are you holding up?"

She was overcome by an urge to pour out her heart, to share her fears about Grandpa's future, and to lean on him for the support he offered. That's what friends did, wasn't it? But it felt like an imposition. She could handle this. "I'm not the one in danger of losing his memory."

"That doesn't answer my question."

Ginger chuckled. "Really, I'll be fine."

"You'll tell me if you're not? Ginger?" He placed his hand on her arm.

His touch flooded her with comfort and a sense of belonging. With him. She tensed. Filling him in on the facts was one thing, but the thought of opening up that empty place in her heart felt like being at the top of a hill on a rollercoaster, waiting for the bottom of her stomach to drop.

She must be more on edge than she realized. This headache wasn't helping. A sigh escaped. Unnerved, she rubbed her forehead, pressure tightening around her head. "Sorry. My head is pounding. I need to get back to the café soon. Be back in a minute." Ginger got out of the car and hurried into the pharmacy.

CHAPTER FOUR

Ginger woke the next morning before sunrise with a heaviness in her head left over from her headache. Her emotions had fluctuated up and down yesterday, throughout one of the café's busiest nights of the week. Clean-up kept her from rest until late. And now, the busyness was starting all over again. She fell back in bed and went to asleep.

A thumping on her door startled her. Light hurt her eyes, and she covered her face with her arm to shut out the morning sun.

"Ginger?"

Sunlight. She sat up straight in bed. The café.

"You sick?"

"Be right out, Grandpa."

"Rachel called and said everything is okay at the Jukebox and not to worry. I'll eat breakfast at the café."

Ginger sat on the edge of her bed and pulled on her jeans and a T-shirt. After making herself presentable, she relaxed into the idea of extra time this morning. Rachel was a gem.

The front door slammed, and she jumped up. Opening the door to her room, she looked out.

Grandpa stomped down the hallway, a scowl on his face. "I've never seen the like."

"What happened?"

"See for yourself." He stomped back out of the house.

Ginger grabbed a jacket and followed him. She stopped on the porch while Grandpa continued his angry march across the alley and into the café. Graffiti splayed across the whitewashed walls of the café—hateful words dispersed between beautiful colors and images. She sank down on the steps with her mouth gaped open.

Mike exited the café and contemplated the wall. After making a call, he jogged over and sat next to Ginger. "The sheriff will be here soon to take a report."

Ginger nodded. "Why would someone do this? Why the café?

"People who destroy property don't need a reason."

"First Grandpa. Then the waitress. Now vandalism to my property. What next?"

"Hey. It's not the end of the world."

She glared at him. "Please. No platitudes or clichés."

"You're right. This is awful." He steepled his fingers together and gave her a serious, no-nonsense look. "But you really do need to stop crying over spilled milk."

Ginger narrowed her eyes at him.

"It's better when you look on the bright side."

Ginger reached for the pillow on a nearby lawn chair and threw it at him, which he caught and threw back. Ducking, she grinned and grabbed the dripping water hose where it still hung from last night's watering. Mike dashed off the porch when she sprayed him and she laughed at his antics to get away from the water. "That's what you get for making light of my situation."

Mike stopped, his shirt soaked. "My nefarious plan worked." His belly laugh rang out across the yard.

She laughed along with him. If she had met someone like Mike in college, he wouldn't have trampled her heart like her fiancé had. Not on purpose. But unavoidable outside elements often tore at the fabric of life leaving a gaping hole. Elements such as health and mortgages and destruction. Ginger sobered at the thought but, not wanting to dwell on the realities of life, she turned her mind away from her conundrum. For this moment she chose to laugh.

She dropped the hose. "Thanks. I needed that." Mike had a way of helping her look past her troubles and be more positive. Of course, that's what pastors did. Well, maybe not water fights. Ginger had to admit that lately his intentions felt more like a man interested in something deeper than their simple friendship. The evidence was spoken to her here and there, sometimes in words, sometimes in actions, and sometimes not quite hidden in his eyes.

"Good thing this is a warm spring day." Mike gave her a playful punch on the arm.

One day at a time. Ginger breathed in the fresh morning air. "I guess there's nothing for it but to move ahead."

Ginger sent Mike an occasional sideways glance as they examined the wall together. What would it be like to have more than a friendship with Mike? Reminding herself that she didn't have time or energy to think about a relationship of that nature, Ginger refocused on the wall.

"Some of those images are good." He pointed out the one on the far right. "That's a nice depiction of an angel."

"Maybe I should only paint over the hateful words."

"A free mural. Great idea."

The sheriff parked his car and joined them. He looked at Mike's appearance and shook his head. "I don't even want to know."

"Wise man."

"Ginger, you ready to make a report?" The sheriff pulled out his notepad.

An hour later, report and pictures in hand, the sheriff gave them the okay to paint over the graffiti then left with promises to investigate. By the time he drove out away, word had spread, and Ginger decided she should charge a fee for people to gawk at the back wall. Maybe it would help pay the mortgage.

In the kitchen, she stopped at the island where Betsy chopped veggies. Always ready to help out, her friend went above and beyond most days. "Harry bossing you around?"

"Hey, girlfriend. Sorry about your wall."

"I'm thankful it wasn't worse."

"Ginger. You're falling down on the job." Harry called to her from the stove.

"Funny. How's breakfast going?" Ginger took the bowl of chopped veggies from Betsy and walked it over to Harry.

"That Rachel is something. Jumped right in calling the shots. Things running smooth as butter."

Rachel pushed through the swinging doors and set a pile of dirty dishes next to the sink. "Hey, Ginger. I'm glad you aren't sick."

"Sounds like you're doing a great job running things."

"It's fun. I could do it more often to give you a break."

"Listen to her." Betsy pointed the knife in Rachel's direction.

"Better be careful, Ginger. She might take your job." Harry's spatula flew through the air when he waved it at Rachel. "Oops."

Rachel retrieved the spatula and tossed it in the sink. "No harm." She handed him a new one.

Ginger covered her casual garb of the day with an apron. "Rachel. You keep running things today. Let me know if you need me to fill in somewhere."

"Really?" Rachel did a mini dance without moving her feet.

"Absolutely. Do your thing. You can even boss Betsy around." She elbowed her friend, who scowled at her in response.

Ginger made her way through the dining hall. She stopped at a few tables to check on the customers, pleased to hear several nice things about Rachel's ability. Maybe Rachel would consider staying longer than summer.

Mike sat with Walter and his buddies at a back table. Ginger joined them. "What's the topic du jour?"

"We're going to find out who made that mess on our back wall." Grandpa tapped his finger on the table.

Ginger straightened the condiments as she listened to Grandpa's tirade about young people and their lack of respect for people and property these days. No use trying to calm Grandpa down. That would only serve to fire him up more.

"Walter, I brought you fresh coffee." Rachel poured the brew into his mug while he continued talking. Catching Ginger's eye, she sat in a nearby chair. "Walter, would you be able to help me with my car?"

"Hmph. Able? I was a mechanic on airplanes during the war. Of course I'm able. Where is it? What's wrong with it? I can look right now."

"Oh. Now? Sure." Rachel dug in her pocket for her keys. "I have to jump start it all the time. I got here this morning, but one of these days, I'm sure it won't start at all. I parked out back."

Walter took the keys. "No worries. I'll have it figured out in no time. Come on boys, we have work to do."

Rachel moved to the seat vacated by Walter. "He can be a handful. How do you keep up with him?"

"I don't think anyone can. Distraction is the only way to move him off a topic. And I've heard all I want to today about that wall. Thanks for shifting his focus."

CHAPTER FIVE

Rain pinged against the side of the metal building housing the old flea market. Dampness chilled the late spring air, and Ginger shivered, rubbing her upper arms as she breathed in the musty scent of second-hand memories.

Thankful to be out with Grandpa and away from the stress of the café, Ginger followed him as he meandered through the vendor stalls. The weather had stirred up his arthritis and he was using his cane today. She meandered around the full of eclectic treasures. This flea market held her interest more than most. Non-pretentious, it offered unique finds at a bargain. Childhood jaunts to this same location had always made a bad day better. The place had changed ownership a few times but maintained the same charm she remembered as a kid.

She glanced across a table of collectibles at the man who had always been larger than life to her. Her father hadn't been a patient man, and after her mother died, Ginger's buffer between her and her dad was gone. She cried a lot those first few months, as she missed her mama something fierce. Her dad would tell her to buck up when he caught her crying—they had work to do. As soon as she could get away from whatever task he gave her, she would run to her closet and pour her heart out in desperate prayers. Something had to be wrong with her, because she felt so much hurt while her father carried on as though nothing had happened and expected her to do the same.

Grandpa was different though. Always ready with a hug, he listened and let her cry. In his arms, she grieved for her mother.

When she hit puberty, her dad didn't have time for the drama. But

Grandpa never got mad at her bouncing hormones. Over the years, she learned how to control her emotions. The trouble with stuffing feelings, though, was that they eventually found a way out. Grandpa didn't flinch when he was on the receiving end, only witnessed her worst and loved her anyway.

Now it was time for her to return the favor. If Grandpa did have dementia, Ginger couldn't bear thinking about her loss. She watched her grandpa as though memorizing everything about him.

"What are you staring at, child?"

She rolled her eyes heavenward. "Why must you call me child?"

He slapped his thigh and laughed, then headed down another row of tables.

Ginger fought the urge to laugh. It was useless. Her laughter joined his as she trailed behind him. If only everyone knew him like she did. His teasing sarcasm, often spoken with a scowl, and his tendency to be abrupt convinced many that he was a harsh character. His love and his loyalty ran deep, though.

She almost tripped into him when he halted at a table. "A little warning, please."

He ignored her plea as he stared at the mismatched items in front of him. Pushing aside a bouquet of silk flowers, he looked up at her.

Ginger wrinkled her brow at the tears glistening in his eyes. "What is it?"

Her grandfather pointed at an intricately carved jewelry box that stood about a hand's breadth tall, balanced atop legs shaped like the claw feet of an old bathtub. The walnut finish, scratched and dented, hinted at the stories hidden within its past. The hinged lid opened to reveal various compartments for jewelry, and the inside of the lid touted a mirror. Miniature flower carvings, accented with paint, covered its sides. It was beautiful. She reached out to run her fingers over the flowers. Grandpa swatted her away. "No touchy, young lady. I don't need your help."

Ginger backed off. Looked like cantankerous Grandpa had returned. Why the attitude? It was just a box. Ginger bit back the temptation to get offended.

He lovingly wiped away the dust layered on top before he pulled it into his arms as if he was hugging it. "We can go." He stood tall, as though he had found a priceless treasure.

They stopped at the cashier and Beth, the young woman Rachel was staying with, reached for the jewelry box. Grandpa held on tight.

"Grandpa, Beth needs to check the price."

He narrowed his eyes at the young woman. "It's not yours."

Ginger cleared her throat. "Actually..."

The girl waved off Ginger's protest. She looked Grandpa in the eye. "Mr. Gipson, did you serve in World War II?"

Grandpa narrowed his eyes at her. "You been spying on me?"

"I saw you in the Fourth of July parade last year. My great-grandpa served in the war, too."

Grandpa nodded. "Those were tough years. Lots of lives lost." His fingers loosened their grip.

"Thank you for serving."

Grandpa tightened his lips. "So much was lost."

The young woman nodded as she traced the flowers with her fingertip. "It sure is pretty. I need a bit of information before you take it home, though. See?" She turned the box upside down and pointed out a yellow sticker. "I'll give it right back."

"I suppose." He relaxed and let her take the box.

She copied the information before straightening and returning it to him. "Thank you."

Walter grabbed his prize and headed toward the exit.

Ginger grimaced. "Sorry."

"Don't worry, my great-grandpa gets agitated, too. I imagine there's a lot going on in their minds we have no clue about." Beth put her notes in a drawer. "Does he have a pet?"

"No. I can't handle one more living thing to take care of."

"My grandpa doesn't have one either. The nursing home won't allow a pet to live there, but I take my dog over to visit whenever I can. All the residents love Mustard. He's a golden retriever and has such a sweet way with the older folks. Seems to calm them down. I visit the Custer Retirement Home as well." She reached for a piece of paper and pen. "If you like, I can meet you and your grandpa at Center Square Park in Preston Hill sometime and bring Mustard. Mr. Gipson might like it."

Ginger sighed. "Maybe. I'll think about it."

Beth handed her the slip of paper. "Here's my number."

Ginger took the piece of paper Beth offered and glanced down at it. "Maybe this would be good for him. Thanks."

Ginger spotted Betsy walking down Main Street. Pulling over to the curb, she rolled down the window on Grandpa's side.

Betsy leaned down to where she could make eye contact. "Stopped by the café. Where have you been? I needed to talk to you about that... thing."

Ginger bit back a grin and held up her hand.

"Hmph." Grandpa settled back in his seat. "Secrets. Are you planning on shipping me off somewhere or something?"

Ginger rolled her eyes. Why Betsy insisted on keeping their book club a secret, she had no idea. "We're headed back to the café now. Stop by later, and we can grab coffee."

"Maybe. I need to go to the post office first."

Ginger laughed. That explained the outfit. George must be about to take lunch break. "See you when we see you."

Betsy dashed across the road as though it were the autobahn.

Ginger looked in her rearview mirror. Fields stretched out behind her on this end of town. Much like any direction out of town, except where the new mega store took up space. Pulling away from the curb, she caught a movement out of the corner of her eye and slammed on the brakes. A cat scrambled up a nearby tree.

"Whoa, Betsy."

Ginger glanced at her grandpa. He grinned from ear to ear and slapped his leg. She laughed at the phrase he had been using as long as she could remember, though it never made sense to her. Still, she enjoyed seeing his lighter side.

He patted her arm. "Trust me. That was funny. But I don't think Betsy would like it. The guys are old enough to appreciate it. Let's go. Giddy up."

CHAPTER SIX

Ginger entered the still, quiet sanctuary. She wished Grandpa would come to church with her, but she had to admit these were the best moments of her Sunday. Just her and God. She sighed and set her things down on a chair close to the front and knelt on the floor nearby. Stilling her thoughts, she prayed until she felt a nearby presence and rose from the floor.

Rachel waited. "Can I sit with you?"

"Sure." Ginger pointed to the row where she and Betsy usually sat.

"Yoo-hoo!" Betsy sauntered down the aisle. "Hey, girlfriends. Love your hair, Ginger."

Ginger reached up and touched her hair, now cut to her shoulders. She hadn't had it this short since college.

"You look great, don't fret. We still doing lunch today?"

"Sure. And you, too, Rachel." Ginger glanced at their young friend.

"I'd like that." Rachel's face lit up as she smiled.

Betsy set her diaper-bag-sized purse on a chair. "Lillian will be there, too. That might be best for the first meeting of..." Betsy paused as though concerned the secrets police might be watching, and then whispered, "...our book club. You can come, too, Rachel. Don't tell anyone, though."

Ginger laughed at Betsy's melodramatic notions. This wasn't a secret society. They had been trying to get a club started for a while, and spring seemed like a good time to start. She wasn't sure about the sanity of adding one more thing to her plate. But, it made Betsy happy.

Ginger moved her belongings to a chair next to Betsy's. "Is Lillian coming this morning or just meeting us for lunch?"

"There she is." Betsy pointed out the window at Lillian walking toward the front door. The flowing paisley skirt she wore gave her the appearance of a flower child from the sixties. But she also knew how to pull off a power suit when it fit her needs or a little black dress when her husband Nick had a black-tie event to attend.

"Along with half the congregation." Rachel nodded toward the crowd of people entering the building along with their friend.

Lillian joined them after a few minutes, and they huddled to make plans for their afternoon as the sanctuary began to fill up. Their laughter spilled down the aisle and attracted glares meant to shush them. Betsy ignored them and continued her tirade against some perceived cultural misconduct by the masses. A loud throat clearing interrupted her groove.

Mike stood in the aisle, arms folded, watching them with a deep frown. His tattoos alone would intimidate someone who didn't know him. "You ladies need to settle down." The corners of his mouth twitched upwards.

Betsy put her hand on her right hip and stared him down. "What? Are we being too loud?"

Pastor Mike laughed.

Betsy stomped her foot. "You got me again, didn't you?"

"Good morning ladies. A pleasure as usual." He bowed, almost imperceptibly, and changed his tone to a bit more serious one. "I thought you all might want to know that Megan's feeling a bit overwhelmed today."

"Seems to be the norm with the new kids." Betsy picked up her purse. "We're on it."

Ginger, Lillian, and Betsy left the sanctuary as worship began. Megan, a pile of wadded-up tissue next to her, sat on a bench near a window.

"Megan?" Ginger sat down next to her. "Another rough day?"

Megan nodded as she burst out in tears and melted into Ginger's waiting arms. Lillian and Betsy gathered around and began praying. A deep groan escaped the young mother's throat as she allowed herself to be cared for.

The sound of worship ended in the sanctuary, and Mike's voice drifted through the doors. The tears slowed as Megan reached for the box of tissues. "I'm sorry for interrupting your worship time."

"Don't give it a second thought." Betsy patted Megan's knee.

"We've all needed friends around us like this at one time or another." Lillian handed the young mother a fresh box of tissues.

Megan nodded. "Thank you." She blew out a deep breath. "Sometimes I doubt we're cut out for this foster thing. I'm so tired, and lately...I feel alone all the time."

"Marriage taking a hit?" Betsy met Megan's gaze.

"How...?"

"Six kids in the house and half of them aren't even your own? No-brainer."

Ginger looked over at Betsy and motioned downward with her hand to encourage her to bring it down a notch. Anything that brought Betsy's past marriage to her mind called out the less tender nature of the woman. Betsy had softened since she was left a widow but had asked Ginger to remind her when she was headed to a darker place in her heart.

Betsy nodded. "Greg's a good man. You'll find your rhythm." She reached into her purse. "Anyone want chocolate? I have fudge."

Ginger stared at Betsy as she switched the direction of the conversation like someone pulling the track switch for a train. Betsy had a heart of gold, but sometimes, her abruptness left Ginger's mind spinning

"Not the right time?" Betsy stuck it back in her purse.

Megan laughed. "Actually, I'll take a piece. Can I call it breakfast?"

Betsy lit up and pulled out her treats. "I have enough for everyone." She passed the bag around and everyone took a piece. Giggles ensued as they enjoyed the decadent bites through the tears of shared burdens.

The door to the sanctuary opened and people trickled out into the foyer. Megan stood. "Thank you, ladies. I really needed this, but I better get my kids." She grabbed another tissue. "I don't even know what we're doing for lunch."

"I do." Ginger grinned. "You're joining us." The book club would have to wait for another day.

Megan shook her head. "I couldn't do that to you guys. Not again."

"Do what? Let us be your friends? Besides, you know I only open on Sundays for private parties, and no one has made reservations. It will be us and the leftovers."

Megan managed a weak smile. "Fine. I'm too tired to fight you on it." She wiped her eyes again. "I don't usually cry this much."

"Sounds like you've been holding those tears in too long, and they exploded."

Betsy's words struck a chord in Ginger, even though they were meant for someone else.

"That's a gentle way of explaining it." Megan blew her nose.

Betsy pressed her lips together. "I mean well."

Megan threw her arms around Betsy's neck and gave her a hug. "The best kind of love is real, not perfect."

"Now you're going to make *me* cry." Betsy rubbed Megan's back.

"Megan." A deep voice littered with frustration interrupted them. "The kids are hungry."

Greg held on to the toddlers. Josh stood nearby, arms crossed, earbuds in, shutting out the world. Their own three children sat on a bench against the wall, staring at the floor.

"You're all eating at the Jukebox for lunch." Ginger picked up her purse and Bible.

"I appreciate the invitation Ginger, but we really need to head home."

"I don't have anything ready at the house. We'd need to go shopping." Ginger threw her ball of tissues in the waste basket.

Greg's jaw muscle twitched as he turned to Ginger. "It looks like we're taking you up on your offer. Thank you. I'll get the younger ones buckled in while you get the other kids." He pulled out Josh's earbuds.

"Hey." The young boy rose to his full height and glared at Greg.

"It's time to go."

"Fine. But stop yanking on my buds." He spun on his heel and headed for the door, yanking it open before disappearing outside. Greg followed with the two toddlers and the other kids.

Betsy and Lillian helped Megan pick up the middle-aged children from their classes while Ginger hunted down Mike to invite him to join them for lunch. He typically did when she had guests from church on Sunday afternoon and today was no exception. Happy to avoid his own cooking, Mike promised to be there.

CHAPTER SEVEN

"Ladies. Please. Keep it down." The librarian shushed them with a smile before returning to the circulation desk.

"Kind of like being back in school." Betsy giggled.

"We do need to get down to book club business." Ginger pulled out her pad and pencil. It helped her to think if she doodled. Taking a couple hours away from the restaurant wasn't ideal, but Rachel and Shelby would be fine for a couple hours. Making time for her friends apart from work would be good for her as long as Betsy hadn't chosen some deep, intense read.

"What are we starting with?" Lillian scooted her library books stack to the side.

Bracelets jangling, Betsy put an Agatha Christie novel on the table between them.

Ginger read the back cover before handing it to Lillian. "You good with this one?"

Lillian took a moment to look over the description then handed it to Betsy. "Sounds good."

"I went ahead and ordered yours. Hope you don't mind." Betsy pulled two more books out of her over-sized bag.

"Not at all. Now we don't have to wait to start reading." Lillian clapped then added the book to the library pile next to her.

"Perfect." Ginger took her book.

"We need a name." Lillian tossed her braid over her back.

"I like that idea." Her cell phone vibrated, and Ginger scanned the screen. "Sorry. Message from the restaurant. No rush on it." She set it back down.

"What about Lonesome Valley Readers? There is that valley outside of town."

"Only because the hills on either side are manmade." Ginger doodled circles on her pad.

"Anything beyond flat is manmade around here." Betsy scowled.

"What do you think of Cherry Creek Readers?" Lillian held her hands up as though offering a platter of questionable hors d'oeuvres.

"What cherry? The one on top of the ice cream shop that sits next to the creek running through town? Like that's any better than Lonesome Valley Readers." Betsy snickered.

"What about Prairie Land Book Club?" Ginger looked up from her scratch pad full of doodles.

"More accurate with the description, at least." Betsy popped a piece of fudge into her mouth and offered some to the other women.

Lillian took a piece of fudge. "What about the Preston Hill Book Club? We do live in Preston Hill."

"Perfect. Let's vote." Betsy looked at the other two ladies, who each gave a thumb-up. "Perfect. Preston Hill Book Club is it. What's next? Ginger? I know you have something else on that list of yours. Always do." Betsy elbowed her friend.

"But we're thankful for your lists, aren't we, Betsy?" Lillian squinted her eyes at Betsy.

They had been teasing Ginger about her lists since they became friends. But she would be lost without the lists. "We better be quiet before we get shushed again." She turned to a page full of writing in her pad. "Before I mention what's on my list..." She nibbled on the end of her pen as she laid her pad down.

"What is it, girlfriend?" Betsy popped another piece of fudge in her mouth.

"Grandpa."

"Did the doctor find something?" Lillian's focused gaze relayed her concern.

"Something curious happened, is all."

"And?" Betsy and Lillian spoke in unison.

"We went to the flea market on the north side of town, and Grandpa found an old jewelry box he insisted on buying. He won't let me touch it, and he won't say a word about why he wanted it. I can't figure out for the life of me what's so important about it. I guess I'm a bit concerned. It's like he's obsessed about it. It's probably nothing, but...if you guys happen to hear anything, could you let me know?"

"We will for sure." Betsy offered the others another piece of the fudge. "Maybe Mike could play detective for you. He would do anything for you."

Ginger rolled her eyes. Betsy had been playing matchmaker between her and Mike every chance she got since she found out that Ginger had gone out on that one date with him. "Betsy, you know how I feel about this."

"He's crazy about you."

"He's a good friend to Grandpa and me."

"Ha. You call all the repairs he does at your house, the early morning conversations over coffee and cinnamon rolls, the invitations to hang out at church activities, and his general willingness to help you out in any way you need 'just being a good friend'?" Betsy made quotation marks in the air with her fingers.

Betsy saying out loud what Ginger had been thinking confirmed it wasn't her imagination. The thought made her happy and uncomfortable at the same time, but Ginger refused to say the words herself. "And a good pastor."

Betsy smacked Lillian's arm with the back of her hand. "Can you believe her?"

Lillian chuckled. "Love is blind."

"Really blind." Betsy shook her head.

"No one said anything about love." Ginger's defenses rose.

"But what about a date or two?" Betsy's bracelets jangled as she gestured with her hands to make a point.

Ginger grimaced. Truth be told, there were moments when she had been surprised by thoughts of what-ifs with Mike. But between her schedule with the Jukebox and all the other places she served, when did she have time to think about dating anybody? And that didn't take into account Mike's job as pastor in a small town where every life event—even your child losing a tooth—was something to involve the pastor in.

Lillian shushed Betsy. "I think you're starting to badger the witness."

"Too much?"

Lillian and Ginger nodded.

"Sorry. I know that jerk of a fiancé hurt you when you had to leave college. I want what's best for my friend."

"But you can't make it happen for me."

"Message received." Betsy held up her hands. "Where were we before I sidetracked us?"

"Getting ready to talk about my list." Ginger ran her finger down the list in front of her. "I think we need to help out the Jordans." She handed them each a piece of paper. "Make a list of everything you can think of that might be helpful." Quiet settled around them while they scribbled ideas.

"This is a job for more than the three of us." Betsy laid her pen down.

"Yep. Not enough hours in my day." Lillian gave her attention to Ginger. "Thoughts?"

"Mike is already helping with the house repairs. I'm sure he would be happy to recruit more men to help. Can one of you check with Maggie and Millie about the Bible study ladies helping?" Ginger scanned the lists. "They could organize weekly meals to give them at least one break each week."

"I'll do that now." Betsy pulled out her rhinestone-covered phone. "I'm so glad those ladies are up on the tech." She started texting.

"Lillian, can you check with the youth department about babysitting? Maybe in teams of two, since there are so many kids."

"I'll call the youth pastor when I get home. And what about Charlie? Maybe he could help with car repairs when they need them. Or maybe your grandfather could help."

"Perfect. You never know with Grandpa, but I'll talk to him. You talk to Charlie. We've got a good start. I'm going out to visit them in the next couple days and take over the first batch of food from the restaurant. I'll let Megan know what we're up to. Maybe there's something we haven't thought about."

Ginger gathered her things into a pile in front of her. "Did you hear about the vandalism last night over at the grocery store? Same hateful stuff that was on the café."

Betsy shook her head. "Who would do that kind of thing?"

"Sounds like someone is very angry. It makes me sad that a person would stoop to dealing with what's inside them like this." Lillian rested her chin on the stack of books in front of her.

"Let's pray." The three bowed their heads, and Ginger lifted a prayer for the culprit that, beyond getting caught, Jesus would soften his or her heart and that no one would be hurt.

When she finished, Lillian stood and picked up her books. "I need to get back to the shop. I have a student stopping by at two. Later 'gators."

CHAPTER EIGHT

Harry lugged the last box of food from the kitchen and lowered it into the trunk of Ginger's car. "That should be it. The Jordans will eat well tonight."

"Are you sure you're okay without me here for the rest of the day?" Ginger closed the lid to her trunk.

"Those two ladies from the church who volunteered to play waitress today will do fine. Rachel is here to tell them what to do, and my nephew will be in around three to help me in the kitchen. I think we can handle it."

"You realize I'm never going to let you quit. Right?"

Harry chuckled. "The good Lord provides what you need when you need it."

"Are you trying to tell me something?"

"What would I be trying to tell you? You know I don't make plans further out than I can see. Now scoot."

"I'm coming with you," Grandpa shouted from the doorway of their house. "Don't leave without me. Hear?"

Ginger gave him a mock salute. "Yes, sir." Why he was coming? He'd had nothing but complaints about the kids' noise last Sunday at the café.

"It'll be good for him to help." Harry bumped Ginger's shoulder with his own.

"Are you reading my mind again, Harry?"

"Who in their right mind would try and do that? No one could chase those thoughts fast enough to figure them out."

Ginger laughed. "Thanks for the reminder. I have to keep looking past the tiredness of this life."

"And look to the one who is enough." Harry headed to the back door of the café.

"Awful quiet for a family of six." Grandpa studied the passing bushes lining the drive as though kids might start popping out any minute. "You sure they said they would be here today?"

"You didn't have to come, Grandpa." Why was he getting agitated at such a small thing? Ginger reminded herself that it meant he was tired or frustrated. And probably not at her. God, *help me to be gracious.* "Let's go check it out. Mike's truck is here." She parked next to his beat-up green model gifted to him by someone in the congregation, since he was always hauling things around for people. His SUV had started showing it, too. "You can wait here..."

He jumped out of the car. Grandpa would do what Grandpa wanted to do. It made things easier when she didn't voice her suggestions. She picked up her purse and followed him, already halfway to the door. She was surprised by the speed at which he moved and tucked the fact away in her mind. All that shuffling he did must be for her sake.

Ginger followed the sound of voices coming from around the house. Grandpa returned to his slower gait behind her. In the middle of the yard, a water fight raged, Mike and Greg in the middle of it. From the patio, Megan laughed and waved Ginger and Grandpa over. "Pastor Mike showed up today with a load of water guns. Promised the kids after a morning of hard work they would stop for a major water battle." She pointed at the group of kids tackling Mike. "They've been needing this. I wish Josh would have joined in."

"He'll warm up. Don't worry." Water splashed on Ginger. She

yelped and turned to see the kids aiming water guns her way. Mike tossed her a weapon. Not one to back away from a challenge, she kicked off her sandals and ran after the second oldest, the nearest suspect for involving her in the battle. Firing away, she found herself quickly surrounded and drenched. "I surrender." Out of breath and laughing, Ginger bent over as the kids dropped to the ground around her.

"You did good, lady." One of the middle kids gave her an exaggerated grin.

"I've been trained by the best." Ginger pointed with her thumb toward Grandpa.

"Him?" The other middle kid stared at her grandfather with gaping mouth.

"When he was younger, he could run a mean water fight." Ginger squealed and turned around when water hit her back.

"Still can, young lady." Grandpa stood with a water rifle on his hip. A serious glare changed to a chuckle then a full out belly laugh.

Ginger shook her head. "What am I going to do with you?"

"Battle." The kids all yelled together and proceeded to drench her grandpa.

Ginger held her breath, but Grandpa fired back. Relief mingled with joy at the life she saw on his face. Thankful this was turning out to be a good day for her grandfather, she joined the other adults on the back patio. "What's on the agenda after everyone dries off? Oh, that reminds me, I have your supper in the car."

Megan's face lit up. "Really? I don't have to cook for this crew tonight?"

"No, ma'am." "Mike, would you and Greg unload everything? It's unlocked."

Megan tossed Ginger a towel. "The kids are supposed to help deep clean their rooms after they are sufficiently dried off to come inside.

Now that I don't have to cook, I can work on cleaning other parts of the house. It's been needing it, but I'm bad at laying out a plan and implementing it."

"I could help you come up with one." Ginger wiped dripping water off her face.

"Would you?"

"Absolutely. But till this water fight is over, let's sit and enjoy the sunshine." Ginger hung the towel across the back of a chair.

"I'm going to grab my tea first. Want something?"

"I'll take a glass of water. Thanks."

A few minutes later, Megan returned. "You brought enough food to feed an army."

Ginger accepted the glass of water and pointed at the kids battling in the yard. "I think you have an army."

"True. We'll have enough leftovers to lighten the load for a few days."

"Speaking of which, what else do you need to lighten the load? Betsy, Lillian, and I are getting together some people who understand how hard it is to be a foster family. We want to help."

Megan's eyes watered and she met her husband's eyes. "Really?"

"Not even our own families are supportive." Greg shook drops of water out of his hair. "What you all have done today is more than they have even offered. They keep bad talking our choice to take in foster kids, suggesting we need to focus on our own. But this is the kind of family we've chosen." He squeezed Megan's hand. "God has given us so much."

"We've invited them to come visit anytime they like, but they never take us up on the offer." A look of defeat settled over Megan's features.

Ginger handed Megan a notebook flipped open to a blank page. "Make a list. Anything you can think of that would lighten your load."

"We couldn't ask you to..."

"There will be plenty left for you and your family, but we want options for how people can help. Anything you want to put down." Ginger handed Megan a pen. "From taking the kids to the park so you can have a nap to putting a new roof on the house. While you and Greg put your heads together, Mike and I will round up the kids and get them dried off. Got any Popsicles in your freezer?"

"Great idea. I'll grab them." Megan started to get up.

Ginger stopped Megan. "Point me in the right direction. Mike, can you round up the kiddos?"

Mike gave her a thumbs-up.

Ginger waded through the pile of shoes in the mud room before entering the kitchen. It had been a while since she had been inside this house and was again surprised by how spacious it was. A large window above the sink to her left flooded the room with natural light. The avocado-colored walls made her cringe. Perhaps it was time for a color change. She would suggest it to Megan.

The refrigerator stood against the right wall between more cupboards and counter space. She skirted the island in the middle of the kitchen and made her way toward the café-style counter straight ahead. On the other side of the counter, a table large enough to seat the whole family separated the living room from the kitchen.

Ginger spied Josh planted in front of the television in a gaming chair with earphones on and game console in hand. Images of a more serious looking battle than what raged outside flashed across the screen. Animated human-type forms with unnaturally proportioned shapes warred against each other.

The things kids like these days. "Hey, Josh." She walked over to stand behind him. "Josh." She tapped his shoulder. He kept playing. She moved to his peripheral vision. "Josh."

His slight head movement her direction indicated he saw her. After a brief maneuver or two, he took off his earphones. "What's up?"

"Come join us." She ignored his look of utter dismay at the suggestion. "If you want to talk to a real war hero, you should have a conversation with my grandpa."

"For real?"

"World War II."

He jumped up out of his chair and joined her at the freezer. "He wouldn't mind talking about it?"

"He likes bragging." Ginger grinned at Josh's newfound enthusiasm.

"Sweet." He took the box of Popsicles and headed out the door ahead of her. By the time she caught up with him, he was already at Grandpa's elbow.

"What did you do to Josh?" Megan offered a Popsicle to Ginger.

"Told him Grandpa was a real war hero."

"I didn't realize Josh was into history. Of course, he rarely shares anything with us. He's been resistant to connect on any level. His attitude with adults doesn't help. I believe he's a good kid under all that bravado, I see it in how he treats the younger children, but I'm afraid that if we can't get through to him, he could get off track fast. Hopefully, it will be harder to find trouble out here than in the city."

"I feel like my list is too long." Megan handed Ginger the list of ideas for people who wanted to help them out.

Ginger waved off her concern. "Let's head into the house and go over some of these in more detail. Grandpa has the kids entertained with his stories, and Greg and Mike are sorting through that junk in the old shed." They slipped away unnoticed.

A couple hours later, Mike yelled for help. From the open window, Ginger and Megan saw Greg was lying on the ground, Mike bent over him. They hurried out of the house, and then Megan took off running toward the men.

Ginger called for Grandpa to keep the kids away from the shed as she ran to catch up with Megan.

"What happened?" Megan squatted on the ground next to the still form of Greg.

Bending over the prone form, Mike listened for Greg's breathing and felt for a pulse. "He fell backward off the top of the shed." Mike pointed to where a portion of the roof had broken through.

Megan gasped. Ginger knelt beside her and prayed.

Mike checked Greg's bones. "His arm is broken, but he's breathing. I'm going to call the trauma clinic."

Everyone remained quiet while Mike made the call and listened for instructions. "The ambulance will be here in about twenty minutes. We need to make sure he doesn't move. I'm going to get my medic bag. Be right back."

Ginger was relieved that Mike had taken charge of the situation. He had been trained as an emergency medical responder and worked for the volunteer fire department in town. She relayed these assurances to Megan.

Within minutes, Mike returned and checked Greg's vitals. Reconnecting with the clinic, he reported Greg's stable condition. Sirens wailed as he hung up. "Ginger, I'll take Megan to the clinic. Can you stay with the kids?"

"I want to go, too." Josh spoke up from behind Ginger.

Mike glanced at Megan then nodded at Josh. "You would be a support for Megan."

Josh rested his hand on Megan's shoulder from behind.

"Grandpa can help with the kids. We'll take care of things here." Ginger moved out of the way for the paramedics.

Ginger handed a glass of lemonade to Grandpa when he came out from under the hood of Greg's old truck. "Mike called. Greg is going to be okay."

46

"Sounds like God sent some angels to soften that landing of his."

"It's a good thing. I don't think they could have handled one more thing."

"When are they getting back?"

"Anxious to get home?"

"Hmph." He set the glass down and went back to working under the hood.

"Greg has to stay overnight. Mike's going to stay at the clinic. Megan will be back to care for the kids."

"Guess that means we're staying. When they get here, send Josh to me."

"What do you want with me, old man?" Josh stood next to Megan at the corner of the house, watching them with his arms folded.

"Josh." Megan covered her mouth with her hand.

Grandpa looked over at Josh.

"Sorry." Josh kicked the dirt with the toe of his sneaker. "Sir."

Grandpa narrowed his eyes, nodded, then went back to work. "Know anything about cars?"

Josh shook his head.

"What's that? I may have hearing aids, but they don't help the back of my head see what you're saying."

"Sorry." Josh raised his voice. "Not much. Don't know anything actually."

"I'm not deaf either."

"Sorry."

Grandpa came out from under the hood. "You say that an awful lot."

Josh shrugged. "Seems to keep me out of trouble."

"Hmph. Didn't your dad teach you about cars?"

Josh tensed. "He wasn't around enough to teach me anything."

"Can you stand on old man showing you a thing or two?"

"Yes, sir."

"Okay, then, let's get our hands dirty." Grandpa disappeared under the hood again with Josh close behind. "This is the engine."

"I know that much."

Their conversation lowered to a murmur. Megan turned to Ginger. "Josh needs men teaching him how to do life."

Ginger slid an arm around Megan. "Talk to me."

Megan led the way to the patio chairs. "They're doing a scan to be sure there aren't any internal injuries. He does have a mild concussion, but the doctors were flabbergasted he had no more injuries than that and a broken arm. Greg wanted to leave without the tests, but they refused to release him."

"That sounds positive."

"It is." Megan sat in the chair closest to the house.

"But...?"

"You can tell, huh?"

Ginger waited.

"He's supposed to start his new job next week. But with a broken arm?" Megan rested her elbows on her knees. "We've got a bit of savings, but I don't know how long that will last. What will we do?"

"I'm afraid the practical suggestions I might offer would fall short. Let's talk to God about it." Ginger held out her hand and led them in prayer for provision, peace, and strength through the days ahead.

CHAPTER NINE

Ginger locked the café doors during a lull in the afternoon and hung the "Back in an Hour" sign on the door. She pulled down the shades so no one would knock on the window and disturb her meeting with Betsy and Lillian. They had invited Rachel to join them, but she needed to run an errand.

Betsy pulled a mallet out of her purse.

"What's that?" Lillian pointed to the tool in Betsy's hand.

"It's our gavel."

"We don't need a gavel."

Betsy tapped the mallet and smirked at Lillian. "Will this emergency meeting of the Preston Hill Book Club come to order?"

"What have we created?" Lillian lowered her forehead to the table in a display of great melodrama.

Ginger fought the urge to escape and start prepping for supper.

"Let the minutes read it is Monday afternoon at three o'clock p.m. on the..." Betsy looked across the table at her friends. "Who's going to write all this down?"

"I'll do it." Ginger went over to the counter and found a yellow tablet and pen them wrote down the date.

"We are meeting to discuss how we can help the Jordans while Greg is recuperating. What are their needs?"

"Depends on what happens with Greg's work." Lillian pulled out her pocketbook-size purse and thumbed through its contents. "Randy gave me a card for one of his clients looking to hire someone. Here." She handed the card to Ginger. "In case his current employer isn't patient with his recovery."

"That's great. Ginger, do you know the start date for Greg's new job?"

"They're giving him a three-week grace period, then seeing what his doctor releases him to do before they make a permanent decision."

"Sounds—" A knock interrupted Lillian's flow.

Pastor Mike peeked into dining area from the kitchen. "Heard there was a meeting about the Jordans." He looked around at the women. "But do I dare enter, is the question."

Betsy banged the gavel. "Let's take a vote. Be sure and put this in the minutes, Ginger."

Mike raised his eyebrows. Ginger and Lillian laughed.

"I'm serious. All in favor of letting Pastor Mike join our emergency meeting, raise your hand."

Lillian raised her hand. Ginger tapped her lips with her pen. "I don't know. This is a girls-only meeting."

"Funny." He wiggled his eyebrows in a comical Groucho Marx imitation. "I do come bearing a gift." He pulled his left hand from behind his back, then took a pie out of the bag he held. "My humble offering."

"Is that..."

"My mom's turtle pie."

"Well then." Betsy set the gavel down. "Why didn't you lead with that?"

"That would have been too easy." Mike handed out napkins, paper plates, and plastic forks. "And not nearly as much fun."

The ladies accepted their pieces eagerly as Mike served them.

"You haven't made this in a while." Lillian bit down on the decadent blend of chocolate, nuts, and caramel.

"It's delicious. You're getting better in the kitchen." Ginger elbowed Mike. "When are you going to share the recipe? I still want to put it on the menu."

"I would be honored to have it on the menu. But it might come with a price tag." He dug into the piece of pie in front of him.

Ginger coughed and reached for her glass. If that wasn't a hint of his intentions, she didn't know what was.

"What, you want royalties or something?" Betsy ate the last bit of her piece of pie.

"Or something." Mike lowered his voice and spoke to Ginger. "What are you doing Saturday? There's an outdoor movie at Town Center Park down in Kearney—*Princess Bride*. There's a group going from church. Thought you might want to check it out."

Ginger hesitated.

Betsy whispered in her ear. "You're overthinking it. Say yes."

Ginger squinted at her friend. Maybe she should. Besides, they had gone out and done things as friends before. This didn't have to be any different. "Sounds like fun, although I'll have to check my calendar. Now, dish me up another piece of that delicious pie."

A smile lit Mike's face as he gave her the biggest piece in the pan.

"Wait a minute. I wanted that piece." Betsy eyed Ginger's plate.

Lillian tossed her napkin on her empty plate. "Take two pieces."

Betsy banged the gavel. "Fine." She passed her plate to Mike. "Let's bring this meeting back to order."

"I second that motion." After dishing out more for Betsy, he served a piece for himself. "I can help round up men to finish the house repairs. Greg said that they have to pass the inspection by family services, or the kids will be sent to who knows where."

"What about help with the kids?" Ginger waited for the others to speak up.

"I'll schedule some sitters, so she has some sort of relief every day." Lillian scooted her now empty plate to the center of the table.

"I'll organize the meals." Ginger spoke as she wrote. "And Grandpa said he would get their second car running."

"That will help when Greg is ready for work." Betsy looked around the table. "Anything else?"

"With all the excitement, did anyone invite Megan to join the book club?" Lillian scooped up the last bite of pie on her plate.

"I can do that." Betsy banged the mallet. "And that brings our meeting to an end." She stuck her mallet in her purse and stood. "Hate to rush, but I need to go on a walk or something. As wonderful as that pie is, I'm feeling it."

"Let's go to the park." Lillian looped her arm through Betsy's. "You guys want to join us?"

"Before you ladies disband, I did want to bring up this matter of vandalism around town." Mike stretched his legs out in front of him.

Betsy and Lillian sat back down.

"There are rumors that Josh is the one who's painting the graffiti." Mike scooted his plate to the center of the table.

"That's so off course." Betsy tapped her red fingernails on the table. "Sometimes this town embarrasses me with its ego. Point the finger. Blame the one who doesn't quite fit. At least the church isn't—"

"Actually..."

"Seriously? The church is blaming them?" Ginger looked at Mike.

"Mainly one couple. Seems they had a bad experience when they lived in the city. They had a neighbor who took in an older foster child who was quite rebellious. The police even got involved. But one person can be enough to influence an entire crowd. I pointed out how far out of town the Jordans live and their lack of transportation, but several persisted in pointing fingers at Josh. When people are determined to see things the way they want, it's hard for them to see reason."

"What is the sheriff doing about it?" Ginger contemplated what they could do to help the situation. Was there anything?

"Whoever is doing this isn't leaving behind evidence. Any proof of innocence or guilt is purely circumstantial." Mike sighed. "It's frustrating."

"Ladies. We need to be praying that the truth becomes evident and the young foster kid doesn't get railroaded." Betsy pulled the mallet out and banged it on the table. Glasses jumped. She lifted her shoulders. "Sorry."

"I'll mention it from the pulpit tomorrow. Should have done it already." He ran a hand through his hair. "As the church, we need to lead the way in grace and be careful not to pass judgment."

"That's a wrap. And I'm off. Still need that walk." Betsy tossed her mallet into her purse and slung it over her shoulder. She and Lillian left through the kitchen.

Mike linked his fingers together behind his head. "I'm stuffed."

"Your fault." Ginger licked her fork. "Seriously, let me put this on the menu."

"One of these days." Mike's phone chirped, and he glanced down at the number. "Hmm." He furrowed his forehead.

"Everything okay?" Ginger scraped the last of the chocolate off her plate.

"Yeah. It's a number from California I keep getting calls from. Probably marketing." He stuck his phone back in his pocket.

"There you are, young man." Grandpa burst into the dining hall from the kitchen, Bo and Eugene trailing after him. "Ready for that rematch?" He set the chess set on their usual table.

"The question is, are you ready?"

"Ha. You better watch your king's back. I'm all over it today." Grandpa started setting up the chess pieces.

"Looks like I'll be leaving you to dream about my mom's turtle pie on your menu someday." He winked then joined the older men.

CHAPTER TEN

"You guys are doing great." Ginger admired the new look on her café back wall as she came across the alley from her house. The morning sun poured down the alley and lit up the painting.

"Mike wasn't sure you would go for the blue." Grandpa dipped his brush into the paint bucket.

"I voted for pink."

"Not really a pink gal. Grandpa nailed it with the turquoise." The hateful words were painted over with a solid turquoise color, creating a blank space for new words to take their place. New words that would take beautiful images meant to mar and turn them into encouragement every morning as she walked across the alley. Breathing in the aroma of fresh blooms on her lilac bush, she closed her eyes and thanked God for the day and making old things new.

Mike held out his brush. "Want to help?"

She backed away. "I'm already in my going-to-work clothes."

"Nice excuse." Mike dipped his brush in the paint. "Did you decide what words you wanted?"

"Surprise me."

"You trust me?" Mike raised his eyebrows.

"That's debatable." She laughed. "But I'll take my chances with words on a wall."

"Walter's been telling me about Irene."

"Do tell." Ginger felt the familiar pinch of frustration. Or was that jealousy? Grandpa refused to talk about her grandmother any time she asked and yet freely talked to Mike? She wanted to know about her family. Especially the woman Grandpa had never let go of in his heart.

"She is the gentlest woman I know." Grandpa set his brush down and took on a dreamy expression as he gazed off into space. "Kind. Understanding. And what a beauty."

"Tell her about the time you met."

Grandpa gave a wave of his hand. "Later."

Ginger listened to the volley of words back and forth as Mike attempted to convince Grandpa to share what was on his heart. Something niggled at the back of her mind. He was talking about Grandma in present tense. Mike had mentioned that earlier.

"Ginger?"

She shook off her thoughts and realized her gaze was centered squarely on Mike. Looking through him, not at him. "Sorry."

"Penny for your thoughts?"

"It'd take more than a penny to get those out of me." She hurried over to the café door.

"What about *The Princess Bride* this weekend?"

Ginger shook her head. "Sorry. I checked my calendar. I promised Megan I'd watch the kids."

"Need any help?"

"I don't know if you would be more help or more work." She backed toward the door.

He dipped his brush in paint and started toward her, pointing his brush at her as though he had plans to teach her a lesson. She made a face at him and hurried inside.

CHAPTER ELEVEN

Ginger gave a quick stir to the eggs on top of the stove then grabbed the ketchup from the fridge. "Grandpa?" She heard him shuffle down the hall toward his bedroom. The jewelry box sat unguarded on the coffee table. Setting the ketchup down, she pulled her phone out of her purse and swiped the screen. She snapped several pictures from different angles before turning the box upside down and taking a picture of the tag.

A bump down the hallway alerted her to Grandpa's return. She placed the box back where he had set it and returned her phone to her purse before going back to the kitchen. "Grandpa, your breakfast is on the table. You going to church this morning?" She stacked her breakfast dishes in the sink.

Her grandpa entered the kitchen dressed in suit and tie, relying heavily on his cane.

She paused and stared at his attire. From what her mother had told her, after the war he showed no real interest in God beyond sitting in a pew once a week. Ginger figured he only went to keep them happy. He hadn't been to church much since his parents died and, when he did, he didn't dress up.

"Don't look at me that way. I have something to talk to God about." He straightened his posture and tilted his chin in the air. "I thought it might carry more weight if I went to church." He inspected himself in the hall mirror. "Do I look okay?"

"You look dapper."

He smiled and nodded. "Hurry up or we'll be late."

"Don't you want to eat?" Greeted by his silence, Ginger grabbed her purse and followed him out to the car. She had learned a long time ago not to argue with Grandpa when he wore that determined look on his face.

After a time of worship, Mike rounded the pulpit and sat on the edge of the stage. "It's time for a family meeting." He shared about the vandalism rumors and encouraged the congregation not to rush to judgment based on people's opinions or on their personal assumptions of people's character. He told them to wait and let the authorities do their job. "The Jordan family needs our help, not our judgment. Betsy, Lillian, and Ginger have started several serve teams to come alongside them with as much help as each of us are able to offer."

Mike stopped talking and turned the time over to discussion. Many in the congregation were love personified, reiterating a willingness to be on a serve team to help the Jordan family on their fostering journey.

Led by the couple who'd had a bad experience with foster kids, a few people argued about the lack of respect foster kids showed. Grandpa shifted in his seat and tapped his cane on the floor. Sam, one of the most outspoken in the crowd, added his opinion about the foster kids' disrespect. In the back, Megan rose from her seat and turned toward the door.

Ginger stumbled past the legs of those sitting between her and the aisle. "Wait, Megan. He doesn't speak for all of us."

Megan stopped with a hand on the door.

"Sam, you should be ashamed of yourself." Grandpa's voice rang clear. Megan turned and Ginger followed her gaze. The audience waited in silence as Grandpa made his way to the front where Sam sat.

Grandpa used his cane like a pointer and poked the air toward Sam. "Don't you remember what it's like to be taken from your home and interned with only a satchel full of belongings during World War II and then being an orphan after that war? Foster kids are orphans."

Sam slumped in the chair.

"Do you remember not being accepted because of the nationality of your parents and having to hide who you were so people wouldn't bully you? You relied on the graciousness of the family that took you in and risked their own well-being."

Sam covered his face in his hands. Gentle sobs shook his body. A gasp rippled through the audience at Grandpa's boldness. Ginger held her breath to see how Sam, a man who always took a stance of pride, would respond.

"I forgot." He raised his head and faced Grandpa. "I was wrong." Sam cried.

Grandpa pointed back at Megan, watching from the back.

Sam got up and faced Megan. With the back of his sleeve, he wiped his face. "Please, forgive me? I was out of line."

Megan nodded and dabbed her eyes with a tissue. One by one, women gathered around her. A gentle buzz rose from the group. Betsy grabbed a notepad and hurried to join them.

Mike waited at the front and took names of those willing to come out to help with repairs at the Jordans'. He also reminded them of the serve day coming up at the local shelter, Sunrise.

Ginger watched the miracle that Grandpa had inspired and wished other matters were so easily resolved.

Ginger pulled up to Sunrise, which Preston Hill called their start-again shelter. It was a haven for people who were in a tight situation. They could live there while they got back on their feet.

Mike met her at the car and took the box of sandwiches she handed him.

"How many showed up to help with repairs?" Ginger grabbed a basket of supplies.

"We started with fifteen, but after lunch we'll be down to six or seven." Hillside invested more than money into the shelter. Every quarter, they brought a team of men to make whatever repairs were needed. One year, they even helped replace part of the roof.

Mike dropped off his box and grabbed a couple more guys to bring in the rest of the food while Ginger set up. Hammers pounded in the background. A few of the residents wandered in and made themselves comfortable in a gathering corner of the dining hall where a few comfy chairs were situated. A couple ladies offered to help. Mike stuck around to assist too, once lunch was in from the car.

Ginger noticed a young woman watching her from a corner of the room. Her frame was more like a young man's, but the way she moved reminded Ginger of a woman. Hiding behind a hoodie, her head moved in sync with the Ginger's steps. Trying to watch out of the corner of her eye, Ginger noticed how much of a loner she was.

Ginger spoke in a low volume to Mike. "Don't be obvious, but do you see that girl in the hoodie?"

"Yeah, she's been shadowing the workers from church today. Almost like she wants to be around people but doesn't want to interact."

"Kind of the vibe I got. Here, can you empty those bags of apples into that big basket?"

Mike tried to open the bag. "Have you thought about the words you want on your wall yet?"

"Haven't had time."

"Help." The bag Mike held busted, and he attempted to catch the apples while still holding on to the half-full bag slipping out of his hands.

Ginger chuckled. "Perfecting your act for the circus?"

"Ginger. Help a guy out."

She hurried over and took the bag. He caught a few apples in his shirttail. The hoodie girl picked up a couple apples that had rolled her way and brought them over to the table, keeping her eyes lowered.

"Thank you. What's your name?" Ginger reached out as though to touch the girl's arm.

She jerked back. Looking up briefly, she glared at Ginger before leaving the dining room.

Mike stopped behind her. "That was strange."

"Don't know what I did to make her angry."

"When they're practically on the streets, there's no telling what fears they fight."

CHAPTER TWELVE

Ginger tossed her keys on the entry table and kicked off her shoes. It had been a long day with serving lunch at Sunrise and a busy dinner hour at the Jukebox. Her supper had consisted of a few bites of sandwich when she was able to sneak off to the office.

She stretched her back and headed to the kitchen for a bowl of leftover soup. In the doorway, she stopped short and stared at the piles on the kitchen table. A hat box, scrapbook, two thick manila folders, several women's handkerchiefs, a small box that looked like it might hold a piece of jewelry, a stack of letters held together with ribbon, and a few other odds and ends. What was Grandpa up to now?

Fingering one of the handkerchiefs edged in lace, she opened the old scrapbook. He had never allowed her a peek inside his memories before, yet here they lay, unguarded. Was it temptation or invitation?

She ran her fingers over the image staring back at her. A picture of Grandpa and Grandma welcomed her into their story. A tear dampened the corner of her eye. The image was too blurry to see facial detail, but she could tell they made a handsome couple.

Sighing, she turned the page. A news article threatened to fall away from where it had been attached, the yellowed tape having lost its holding power. She smoothed out the curling newsprint.

Ginger widened her eyes when she read the article headline: "Woman Missing." She skimmed the article about World War II ending and vets returning. Her eyes rested on the name Irene Gipson. Grandma. The article was about her grandmother.

"I leave the room for two minutes, and you have to snoop."

Grandpa stood in the doorway between the kitchen and living room.

"I'm sorry." Ginger closed the album and stood, handkerchief still in hand. "You left it out and I—"

"Hmph." Eyes shimmering, he grabbed the lacy piece of cloth that Ginger held and rubbed it between his gnarled fingers. "I can't find her."

"Do you know what happened?" Hopefully this time the question might supply some real answers.

"If I knew, we wouldn't be having this conversation."

"I'm trying to understand."

"Who asked you to?"

"We're family."

He marched out of the kitchen and down the hall to his room. Ginger jumped when the door slammed. The pictures rattled on the wall.

Letting out a pent-up breath, she ran a sinkful of soapy water and dumped the breakfast dishes beneath the suds. Grandpa exasperated her when he treated her as though she didn't matter. As his sole caregiver, she felt the weight of dealing with his issues when they reared their heads. It always worked out, though. No doubt in a few minutes Grandpa would be back with a different attitude. Mike's admonition to take one day at a time fit well when dealing with Grandpa.

Ginger put the last dish in the drainboard and then poured herself a cup of hot tea. She stared out the window while sipping her favorite brew and watched as darkness cloaked the yard and the stars begin to shimmer.

Grandpa cleared his throat from behind her. "All my research is here on this table. Maybe it can help you."

Ginger almost spewed the tea out of her mouth. "Help me?" She set her cup down on the counter.

"Help you find Irene."

"Hold on. No one said anything about me finding Irene."

"You have to."

"You haven't allowed me to be privy to any of this for how many years now? Ever. And all of the sudden you think it's time to turn it over to me without even asking?" Ginger reminded herself that it would only feed the flames if she kept this up.

"Who else is there?"

Ginger believed that her grandma had died long ago. Now, with Grandpa's massive treasure hunt laid out before her, fear rose in her heart. If they solved this mystery, how would it affect their lives? She didn't want Grandpa to be hurt.

She grasped for a reason to excuse herself from the hunt. Searching her grandfather's eyes, she felt the stirring of possibilities. *No. I can't take time for this.* "Grandpa, I've got the café to run, responsibilities at church and—"

"Think about it?"

"I can't right now, I..." At the look on his face, she stopped. She didn't want to start another argument. "Okay, I'm not promising anything, but I'll look at what you have and then decide. Leave it there for now."

He stood in the kitchen doorway as though waiting on something.

"What is it?"

"You need to get started."

"Grandpa. I had a long day at the restaurant. I barely had time for a few bites of sandwich and I'm hungry. Can you give me a little space?"

He narrowed his eyes at her, pivoted on his heels, and walked out the front door.

Ginger breathed a sigh of relief. Thankful that Grandpa would be at the café with his friends for a while, she looked forward to a bit of silence. A few moments to rest.

After changing into her comfy sweats and reheating a mug of soup she had in the fridge, she settled into her favorite cozy chair near the window. She opened her book but, unable to engage with the story, she allowed her mind to roam while she ate.

They had hired a new assistant for Harry yesterday, and he appeared to be a quick study. He would be a great help, although they still needed to hire another waitress. *Lord, I can't run the restaurant and wait on tables, too. I don't have enough energy. Please send someone I can rely on. Someone who is trustworthy and won't run off at the first idea of something better.* She eased against the back of her chair and drifted into an uneasy sleep.

Images of her mother flitted through Ginger's mind. Another woman, older, faded into the distance. Ginger ran after her but couldn't catch up. Jewelry boxes fell from the sky and she ducked and ran for cover. She began weeping as a longing for family overwhelmed her. Finally, she fell to the ground as darkness covered the images dancing in her mind.

Ginger jerked awake at the sound of a slamming door. Disoriented, she looked up to see Grandpa watching her, jewelry box in hand. An immense dislike for this box that he had latched onto rose in her. "Why do you lug that thing around all the time?"

He turned on his heel and headed back to his room.

"Why are you ignoring me?" She got up and followed him.

"You wouldn't understand." He turned and faced her.

They glared at each other. Why wouldn't Grandpa say what was so important about the jewelry box? But even as she thought it, a warmth crept up from her feet through her body as if the box was filled with immeasurable importance. This was crazy.

She waved her hand in dismissal. "Do what you want. You obviously don't want me to be a part of it."

"I want to know where my wife is."

Overwhelmed, Ginger stopped in her tracks. "I don't know how I'll have time."

Tears slipped down his wrinkled cheeks.

"I need to hire a waitress before I can do anything."

Grandpa held out the jewelry box. "You might need this."

"How can that help?"

"I think it was hers."

Ginger took the jewelry box. "Grandma's?"

He nodded.

"What makes you think that?"

"I just know."

He seemed so confident. The longing from her dream to have a family filled the space between them. Could it be that after all these years they might find her? She didn't dare allow room for hope. "I'll do what I can."

"Thank you." Grandpa placed a kiss on her forehead. "Maybe the boys and I can help wait on tables." A brightness in his eyes hinted that he joked.

"That might not be a bad idea."

"I wasn't serious. Who would want old men waiting on their table?"

"Think about it. It would be more like being a host. Get people seated, serve water and coffee, make them feel at home. That sort of thing."

"I'll talk to the boys about it." He headed toward his bedroom. "Right now, this old body is tired. Talk to you in the morning."

Ginger took the jewelry box to her room. Why had she said she would investigate this? She didn't have time and didn't know where to start.

Taking a deep shuddering breath, she prayed. "Lord, with You guiding my way, I can do this for Grandpa."

Ginger forked a bite of cinnamon roll into her mouth as she watched Mike across the counter. She liked this coffee habit she and Mike enjoyed together most mornings before he headed to the church to work on his sermon or to some other ministry-related duty. Often shared in silence, it brought a continuity of sorts to her day. He would arrive when she opened the door at five for coffee and cinnamon roll service only. Sometimes the ensuing talk was brief. Other times they lingered until the morning crowd began to gather. Over the years, they had built a solid friendship.

"How were the Jordan kiddos last Saturday?" Mike wrapped his hands around the mug of coffee sitting in front of him.

"Piece of cake. Once I had them in bed." She chuckled. "How was *The Princess Bride*?" She took another bite of her cinnamon roll.

"Not as much fun without you."

"I'm sure someone would have been willing to go with you."

Mike picked up his mug of coffee. "I didn't ask you to come because I wanted just anybody's company." He took a swig of his coffee and set it down.

"Oh." She scooted a bite of cinnamon roll around on her plate, covering it in excess icing.

Mike used to tell her about some of his blind date adventures set up by the matchmakers in his life, but somewhere along the way he had stopped sharing, and she had been relieved. The hint of jealousy she felt when he mentioned going out with someone annoyed her.

She bit her lip. It had been several months since the matchmaker grapevine had mentioned one of those set ups. "I haven't heard about any of your crazy blind dates lately. Did the ladies run out of eligible young women?" She shoveled the icing-drenched bite into her mouth.

"I ran out of patience for blind dates. I told the ladies I would find my own dates from now on."

"And do you?"

"All in good time. For now, I enjoy not having to go out on dates to keep little old ladies happy."

"I can see that." She sipped coffee as her thoughts turned to her grandfather. She stabbed the next icing-covered bite.

"What's got you riled?"

"Nothing." She gulped her coffee, which was hot enough to burn her throat. She followed it with a drink of water.

"Now I know something is wrong."

"I'm frustrated at Grandpa."

"I'm listening."

"It's all this talk about his wife. Has he said anything to you about trying to find her?"

Mike shook his head.

"Last night he asked me to find her."

"He's been missing her a long time."

"She left."

"Still." Mike picked up his mug.

"He's asking for heartache."

Mike raised his eyebrows.

"What will he find? Betrayal? What if she moved on?"

"What if she's waiting on him? Would you have him miss out on all the good a relationship offers?"

"Why wouldn't I want to protect him from getting hurt?"

"Ginger, love isn't about protecting yourself. If that's all you do, you'll never really love."

Ginger poured herself another cup of coffee and warmed up Mike's cup as she mulled over what he'd said. "But doesn't love sometimes protect others from yourself? I would probably disappoint anyone I went out with. That's been the case so far in my life." She lowered her eyes. Why did she even go there? She was just asking for him to pick up the thread.

The bell over the door jingled and they watched as a couple regulars filled their coffee mugs and sat in the back.

"Is that what you've done with me all these years? Protect me?"

"How did you jump to us? We were talking about Grandpa."

Mike looked at her and waited.

"Fine. No. I mean...maybe." Ginger sighed. This conversation was highlighting the loneliness she often felt. She longed for a relationship she could count on.

"Even friends disappoint each other from time to time. That doesn't end the friendship."

"But..."

He put his hand on top of hers. "You are a kind, compassionate woman. You love and serve everyone around you. You're beautiful inside and out." He raised his hand when she opened her mouth. "Why do you think I stop by for conversation every morning? I know you're not perfect. None of us are. But you're an amazing woman. Stop selling yourself short. And stop trying to protect others from you. Don't you think that's the other person's decision?"

She pulled out of his grasp and picked up a rag. "I should get to work."

Mike offered her a smile even though a sadness seemed to fill his eyes. "I'm going to finish this." He nodded at the food in front of him.

She watched him as she wiped tables. He gulped down his coffee, which was no longer steaming with heat, and took the last bite of his cinnamon roll.

A few minutes later, he was gone. A chill swept into her heart where a few moments ago warmth had kept her company. Something was shifting between them that she felt powerless to stop.

The phone rang and pulled her attention back to reality. She hurried to pick up before Harry had to leave his station at the stove.

"Good morning at the Jukebox Café. How can I help?"

"Mrs. Mooreland? This is Shelby."

Ginger glanced at the clock over the door. Already fifteen minutes late. She dreaded what was coming.

"I'm sorry. But I got a new job."

"You really need to give me two weeks' notice."

"They said that if I didn't start today, they would hire someone else."

"When did they tell you this?"

Silence echoed across the phone lines.

"Long enough you could have given me fair warning?"

"I have to go." Shelby ended the call, and Ginger hung up. Today was going to be a full day. At least she could count on Rachel.

CHAPTER THIRTEEN

Ginger flipped the lights on in the kitchen and pulled together the ingredients for her signature cinnamon rolls. Weary from a restless night of sleep, she found herself lost in thought as she kneaded the dough. This quest Grandpa had assigned her was too big for her to handle alone, and she fought against the tentacles of overload threatening to entangle themselves inside her. Pressing her lips together in determination, she set the dough aside to allow it to rise.

Cracking eggs kept her busy as she mulled over who she could get to help. The back door slammed, and Grandpa marched through the kitchen and out into the dining hall. Ginger heard him slam coffee-making supplies around as he made a pot of coffee.

What was he upset about? No sense trying to guess. He would inform her when he was good and ready. She whisked the eggs and set them aside. Betsy and Lillian would be game to help her with a bit of sleuthing. They would think it so romantic. Maybe Rachel, too. Of course, with her workload increasing, Ginger wasn't sure how much Rachel could manage. She said a quick prayer for a new waitress.

Noting the time, she started the large dispenser of coffee in the dining room then returned to the kitchen to roll out the dough. After another half hour, the rolls were in the oven and she went out to pour herself a cup of caffeine. She would have requested a couple extra shots this morning if this were a coffee shop.

The bell over the door jingled and she looked up, expecting to see Mike. The owner of the shop across the street glanced her way before grabbing his mug of coffee. The bell jingled again and a couple more regulars entered and waved on their way to the coffee.

"Rolls will be up in a few." This time of day, paying was on an honor system. With only two items on the menu, the math was simple and she didn't need anyone in to help her. Harry arrived around six to take over the cooking. Now that Shelby had quit, Rachel had agreed to longer hours. Bless the girl.

Ginger was bussing tables when Mike entered the café mid-afternoon with the chess board under his arm. He glanced her way and waved, then headed straight to the back table, appearing preoccupied.

Two hours later, Mike still hadn't spoken to her beyond asking for coffee. She went over to their table. "Refill?"

"No. Thanks." Mike gave her a quick smile then turned his concentration back to the chess game in front of him.

"Don't interrupt." Grandpa narrowed his eyes at her.

Fine. Leaving the men to their game, Ginger told herself the way they were acting didn't sting. But it did. It must be her lack of sleep last night. She needed a break, but still had a couple more hours left before heading home. First thing in the morning, the "Help Wanted" ad was set to go in the paper.

Grandpa left the café and holed up in his room before she arrived home. Hardly a word to her all day. He didn't even challenge her about moving his stuff and then let her explain. Not the best day of their relationship. But, unwilling to spend any more time on a subject she could do nothing about at the moment, she planned to take care of herself tonight.

She shuffled into the living room, fuzzy slippers encasing her feet in a cocoon of comfort. After she sat down, she kicked off her slippers

71

and stretched her feet. Trading her cup of steeping hot tea for her book on the nearby coffee table, she squished herself into the corner of the sofa and pulled the cozy blanket up around her.

It was a breath of fresh air to be able to enjoy another world even for a few minutes here and there. Whether or not the book club ever got around to discussing the book didn't matter to her. It was an excuse to read and spend time with friends.

She flipped the book over and reminded herself of the storyline. Maybe reading a bit of Agatha Christie would help her think more like a detective. Ha. She opened to the bookmarked page. The title sounded negative at best. Betsy liked some pretty strange things, at least by comparison to Ginger's taste.

Ginger put on her reading glasses. Comparison only led to discontent. She'd learned that lesson long ago when she gave up on having a life of her own separate from caring for an aging grandparent. But lately she had been falling back into that old habit far too often. Perhaps that was part of her feeling overwhelmed. She took a sip of her chai tea. The warmth relaxed her and took her mind to more pleasant places. She set her cup down on the coffee table.

After several pages, she began nodding off. Sleep dragged at her eyes until she succumbed.

"Ginger? Ginger?" She heard the voice but found it difficult to wake up. A woman sang softly. "Jesus loves me this I know, for the Bible tells me so." Ginger rolled over and smiled up at her mother.

Her mother stroked her hair. "I love you."

Ginger touched her mother's cheek. "I love you, too."

"I wanted to say goodbye before I go."

"Why do you have to go?"

Her mother smiled and kissed her forehead. "Remember? I start my new job today. I'll see you after school."

Ginger hugged her mother one last time before she slipped out of her room, then Ginger drifted back to sleep. A thump startled her, and she jerked awake. *Mother?* She looked around in a fog. Her book had fallen to the floor and her tea was now cold. She reached for the lap blanket.

Dreams about her mother had visited her nights throughout the years. Some of them were treasured memories. But of late this one plagued her more than most. Comforting to start, then every time she woke up, she remembered. The morning in her dream was the last time she saw her mother.

She drew her legs up and wrapped her arms around her knees. Bowing her head, Ginger gave in to the grief of an eleven-year-old child the way she had never been allowed to when her mother died. As an adult, she understood that her father had his own grief to deal with and a business to run. Her counselor had suggested that he probably had no clue how to raise an eleven-year-old daughter without the influence of his wife. Parenting advice was far different back then. What she had heard most days was that they had work to do, and there wasn't time for tears. If it hadn't been for Grandpa's willingness to let her cry, her grief would have been completely bottled inside of her.

Grandpa's cane-thumping as he made his way to the bathroom startled Ginger from her remembered grief. She glanced at the clock hanging on the wall between the front room and the kitchen. One a.m. She was too old to stay up this late and function the next day.

She grabbed the box of tissue then blew her nose, cried some more, and blew her nose again. Tossing the box on the side table, she dipped her head when she saw Grandpa from her peripheral vision. Careful to keep her back turned, she gathered up the tissues and headed to the kitchen trash can.

A few minutes and a couple thumps later, she peeked around the corner, confirming Grandpa no longer haunted her nighttime grief. Back in the kitchen, she grabbed a saucer and dished up a piece of her chocolate pie. Not the best choice at this time of night. Make that morning. Shrugging, she added a dollop of canned whipped cream, grabbed a fork, and sat at the kitchen table. After a few bites, her emotions leveled off and she allowed her mind to meander back to the jewelry box.

Ginger doodled on her ever-handy notepad, brainstorming about the box. With all the uncertainties of what she might find, asking for help on this project felt like jumping into the deep end of the pool with no life jacket after only two swimming lessons. She tapped the end of the pen against her lips. However, if she enlisted some help, this could work. After a few minutes of scribbling, she had a list.

> Bought jewelry box at the flea market – talk to Beth: where did she get it?
> Tag on bottom of jewelry box: When was it made? Brand? Old advertisements?
> Grandpa thinks it belongs to Grandma/convinced she is alive.
> Look in the attic. Journals? Pictures?
> Is Grandpa keeping more from me? In his room?
> Old photo album of Grandpa's.
> Are there any letters?
> Article on missing woman. Anything else in papers? Visit library? Classified ads?
> Ask Grandpa what he remembers.
> Ask book club for ideas.
> Ask Mike about military.
> Ask Grandpa's buddies about the box and Irene.

She tore the page filled with ideas off the pad and hid it in her Bible. Glancing at the clock, she groaned. Today was going to be a long day.

CHAPTER FOURTEEN

"Thanks for coming in early, Harry."

He nodded. Willing to work, but not much for talk at five in the morning. Ginger put the last tray of cinnamon rolls in the oven and headed out to grab a cup of coffee and double check that everything was stocked for the day.

Grandpa and his buddies strolled in around six. Still no Mike.

Over the last several days, Mike had missed their morning coffee conversation, and it seemed as though at church he spent his time visiting with everyone else. Some part of her felt something was amiss between them, but he had missed morning coffee before. They were both busy and at times went a while between conversations.

Within the hour, regulars filled a good share of the tables. As much as they needed a full house, Ginger was grateful for fewer people to wait on. Rachel showed up by noon, and the day passed in a blur of activity. By the time the supper crowd had dwindled to a couple tables, Ginger was ready to stop before she cleaned up. She grabbed a cup of coffee and sat at an empty table. She pulled over another chair and rested her feet on the seat.

Rachel meandered over from the tables she had finished wiping and sat across from Ginger. "We never really talked about family much last summer, but with Walter going through what he's going through..."

"What's on your mind?" Ginger almost regretted letting Rachel know about Grandpa, but it did make things simpler when she didn't have to explain every conniption fit that he had. She poured creamer into her coffee from two tiny creamer cups.

"Do you have any family besides Walter?" Rachel glanced at the military buddies huddled together and scrunched her shoulders. "Someone to help you with him?"

"I wish I did, but I'm an only child. My mom was killed in a car crash when I was eleven, and my dad died of a heart attack while I was still in college."

"I'm sorry." Rachel bit her bottom lip as though she didn't know what to say.

"Thank you."

"Did you ever finish college?"

Ginger shook her head. "Between running the café and taking care of Grandpa, it wasn't feasible."

"What were you studying before you left? Do you ever think about going back?" Rachel lined up the sugar packets on the table.

"Theater. And no, not at this point. With the café, that's not an option."

"You wanted to go into acting?"

"Teach it, actually. What are you going to do with your graphic design degree?"

"I have no clue. There are a lot of possibilities, but I want to make a difference, whatever it is."

"You make a difference right here, and I'm sure you will make a difference whatever you end up doing someday."

"Thanks. So how are you doing with Walter and all the changes?"

She sighed. "Most days I do fine with him, but..."

"It's hard to know what to do in the long term?"

"How did you get so perceptive?"

Rachel chuckled. "My mom and her brother are trying to figure out how to best help my grandpa. He puts up a stink every time they talk about it. My great-grandmother, on the other hand, cooperates like an angel."

"Is she in a facility?"

"So far she's at home. She's strong in mind and spirit, but her health is starting to decline. She recognizes the drain it can be on everyone to worry about her, so they've talked about when her living situation might need to change. My grandpa is cut from a different cloth."

"It's hard when they fight you on changes." Ginger took a sip of her coffee. Her thoughts wandered away from her conversation with Rachel. What kind of secrets did Grandpa hold in his head? It would sure help finding his wife if he would share them with her. "Tell me more about your family."

"My parents moved around a lot while I was growing up. I think there was some conflict about my mom's choice to marry an artist. I didn't get to know my extended family till the last couple years when my parents settled down about an hour away from where my grandmother lives. They're pretty cool." "Where do your parents live?"

"They're in western Nebraska, a little town about an hour away from Renegade where my grandmother lives."

"Take advantage of being that close to them. Grab as many memories as you can." Ginger scooted her chair back. "We better get this place cleaned up."

"Why don't you go on home? I can get the rest and lock up."

"You sure?"

"I am. Now leave before something comes up to keep you here. Tomorrow comes too early." Rachel grabbed her rag and wiped a nearby table.

"Grandpa, time to go home." Ginger maneuvered the extra chair back into place.

Walter cleared his throat. "I don't want to go home yet."

"But I need to go."

Walter slapped the tabletop. "I'm not ready."

Why did it always took an out-of-proportion argument to convince Grandpa to go home? The parent-child switch stressed them both.

Rachel paused from wiping a table. "I can bring him over later so you can have a little time to yourself."

"I'll let you. Thanks."

"Can I walk you home in a bit?" Rachel gave Walter a big smile.

Bo jabbed Grandpa in the ribs with his elbow. "Pretty lady escorting you home. Hmmm?"

"Shut up." Walter glared at his friend.

Bo grinned at the ladies. "He would be honored, Miss Rachel."

Rachel gave them a thumbs-up. "Give me about half an hour." She linked arms with Ginger and ambled through the kitchen with her. "I almost forgot. Walter and his friends were talking about some woman during the war and a kid."

"My grandmother disappeared after Pearl Harbor. But it might be a few old guys carrying on. If you hear anything else, let me know."

"Will do. Go grab some quiet while you have a chance."

As Ginger heated water for tea, she tried to remember the stories her mom had told about Grandpa. Her mother had been so young when Grandpa returned from war that most of her early memories had been vague. And it had been years since Ginger thought about it. She mentally replayed conversations with her mom. Grandpa had served in the military from 1942, right after Pearl Harbor, to 1947, two years after WWII ended. His wife Irene lived with his parents while he was gone. No one ever talked about his wife, although Ginger's mother had held on to some vague memories of her before she disappeared—the typical ones of reading a bedtime story and cooking together.

Patricia was six when her dad returned from the war. She remembered her dad fighting with his parents. Their voices were angry. Patricia had listened at the door. She heard words about her mother being gone and who cared where she went, that his daughter was better off with them and he should forget his wife. He had stormed out of the house and hadn't come back for a few days. To Patricia's knowledge, her mother was never mentioned again.

Had Grandpa met someone else? Maybe during the war? Did he have a family somewhere? She planned to sit Grandpa down and ask him what he knew. He couldn't keep secrets and expect her to figure it out on her own.

Sighing, Ginger reached for the phone to call Betsy. Maybe the ladies in the book club could help her do some research.

CHAPTER FIFTEEN

Another restless night put Ginger on edge. A week and no one had answered the ad for the waitress position.

Pitching in to help Rachel during the lunch rush, Ginger cleared several dirty dishes from one of the tables and headed toward the kitchen. The cry of a child startled her, and she turned slightly. A plate began to slip. She tried to stop it with the pile in her other hand, but instead lost her grip on the entire load. As if in slow motion, the plates crashed to the floor. Her gut clenched as she stared down at the mess. This pace couldn't continue. An urge to run into her office and lock the door almost overwhelmed her. She was a grown woman. If she didn't know better, she would think she was going through puberty again. *Get a grip.*

The bell over the door jingled and she looked up to meet Mike's concerned gaze. The kindness in his eyes at that moment almost undid her. Grabbing a nearby bus tub, she knelt, keeping her eyes averted as she reached for the broken pieces.

Strong hands rested on top of hers. "I got this."

Ginger stilled under the calm of Mike's voice. She took a shuddering breath. "I have to get this cleaned up."

"Let me do this for you."

She wanted to insist she could do it. That she was strong enough. But today she wasn't. She nodded. Avoiding everyone's questioning eyes, she hurried past Rachel, through the kitchen and across the alley to her house. How had Mike's presence become so needed in her life?

At the house, she hurried into her room and crawled under the covers. She was so tired that by the time her head hit the pillow, she was asleep.

Ginger bolted awake to the noise of Grandpa stomping around in the kitchen. The late afternoon sun streamed through the window and she shielded her eyes as she slipped out of bed. She closed her bedroom door and picked up her phone. A text from Rachel put her mind at ease. Betsy would help serve dinner, and Bo and Eugene would bus tables. Ginger went back to bed. She could go back to sleep if Grandpa wasn't making so much noise. A knock prevented her from relaxing.

She flung open the door. "What?"

"Why aren't you trying to find Irene?"

She clenched her fists. "Give me time to change." She closed the door in his face. So much for rest.

Ten minutes later, she joined Grandpa, reminding herself to stay calm.

"What's the plan? When are you getting started?" He thumped his cane.

"I have to run the Jukebox, too."

"Pshaw. That new girl is doing fine."

"Grandpa." This badgering made her mad. "If you would stop talking about Irene for half a minute…"

"What?"

"Then maybe I could actually get something done around here."

"Am I getting in the way?"

"I didn't say that, Grandpa."

"Maybe you should put me in one of those homes. Put me away where I won't bother you."

How did this conversation go there so fast? "That's not what I mean, and you know it."

"Maybe I don't."

Usually able to keep her cool, Ginger felt life pressing in around her. The air grew heavy with accusation and uncertainty. She grabbed her phone and hurried out of the house, heading down the alley toward Center Square Park.

"I can't believe the audacity of that man. The things I do for him." Head down, she moved at a pace that would have put her younger, track-running self to shame. Grandpa drove her crazy. One day up. One day down. She never knew what mood he would be in. In one part of her head she knew Grandpa's change in attitude had more to do with fear than with her, but it still hurt. She missed the Grandpa she grew up with. A bit gruff around the edges, but always Grandpa. Always there for her, loving her and listening.

A shadow caught up with her and then passed, stretching out on the sidewalk in front of her then keeping pace with her. She glanced sideways at Mike.

"Must be important."

"Argh." She warred between wanting him to go away so she could fume and longing to share this burden with him. She picked up her pace, running from the need to need someone.

Mike kept in step with her. "Walter?"

She stopped and faced Mike. "That man drives me crazy. One day all smiles and cheerfulness. The next, he can't stop nagging me about finding his wife. Doesn't he know I have the Jukebox to run? How can I provide for him if we don't have the café? But no, he's more concerned with yesterday than with today." She paced in front of Mike. "I can't afford to let things go at the Jukebox. Especially not now."

"Why not now?"

Ginger ignored his question. "He had better ease up. I don't know how much more of his nagging I can take."

"Want me to talk to him?"

"Why not?" Ginger slowed her pace. "He listens to you better than me. Even though I'm family." Why did Irene matter to Grandpa more than she mattered to him?

"You know he loves you, right?"

"I keep telling myself that."

"And some of this is out of fear?"

"Yes, Pastor." She glanced sideways at him.

"I'm speaking as...someone who cares for you." Mike released a sigh.

"Don't you get all prickly on me, too."

"Sorry."

She left the sidewalk and sat on a nearby park bench. "Me, too."

Mike sat next to her. "Maybe you guys need a break from each other. He could stay with me for a while."

"He suggested I put him in a facility."

"Think he meant it?"

"No clue. Besides, I couldn't afford it."

"Might be good to check into for future reference."

"Maybe."

"Bo's place is nice. I stop by there once a week on a chaplain rotation. It's independent living with the option of assisted. Might be nice for them to be neighbors. In the meantime, I'm serious about having him stay with me a while."

"Hate to see how he would respond to that idea." She shielded her eyes from the sun and looked up at him. "What were you doing out here anyway?"

"I was coming to check on you and saw you storm out of the house."

She winced. "Thanks for being there. I guess I'm not as strong as I think."

"That's not a bad thing, Ginger."

She gazed off into the distance. Needing someone didn't feel like a good thing. "Have you been avoiding me lately?"

He kicked the grass with his toe. "Sorry about that."

"I thought maybe I did something to chase you off. Like getting all stressed out lately."

He shook his head. "You're not going to chase me off that easy. "I needed to figure some things out."

"Did you?"

"I did."

"Something you want to talk about?"

"All in good time. You ready to head back?"

They walked back to the café in comfortable quiet. Ginger bumped her arm to his. He looked over and grinned and bumped her arm. That feeling of things changing between them knocked on the door of her heart again. She closed her eyes and locked the feeling of right now into her memory, never wanting to forget this comfortable feeling of belonging. She sucked in a breath. Was that what pressed Grandpa in his desire to find Irene? The memory of his and Irene's yesterday that he held in his heart?

CHAPTER SIXTEEN

Ginger turned off the engine and stared at Custer's Retirement Home in front of her. The last several days had been difficult at best with Grandpa. He fought her at every turn.

Yesterday he brought up moving into a home for the second time in only a few days. He asked her about the progress on the jewelry box, then blew up when she told him Betsy and Lillian were going to help, and they had a meeting planned to divide up the research.

"It's none of their business," he yelled at her.

"How am I supposed to run the café, look after you, and research some archaic box I have no clue how to start on? I need help." Ginger moved her hands as she talked as though conducting an orchestra.

"If taking care of me is such a hardship, maybe I should move out. Bo says that retirement home he lives at is great."

"Are you serious?"

"You brought it up." Grandpa's glare grew more intense.

Ginger attempted to slow his escalation with a calmer tone. "I said nothing about you moving out."

"It's what you meant."

Still unsure how to deal with the moods that came with Grandpa's new season of life, Ginger threw back her own accusation. "You're putting words in my mouth."

"Am I?"

Ginger couldn't abide his expression of hurt. She looked away and hid her watery eyes. "I can't do this anymore. If it's what you want, I'll check it out."

"Fine." He stomped off to bed without another word.

This morning, he had ignored her and left for the café before she finished breakfast. By the time she arrived, even his buddies were in on the silent treatment. She doubted he was serious, but she needed to check into it in case he was, or he would be all over her. She couldn't win for losing.

She went to the home before lunch while Bo was hanging out at the café. No good would come of news getting back to Grandpa before she was prepared to share.

After entering the retirement home, she walked past the main office, through the community room, and to the recreation area, hoping to see the staff in action before they realized a possible new client was there to impress. She felt as though she was betraying her grandpa by looking for another place for him to live. But this was on him. She needed breathing room.

Straightening her posture, she checked in for an appointment at the front desk.

While waiting, she noticed through a window a commotion in the central courtyard. Ginger slipped outside. Several of the residents were gathered around a golden retriever. Beth, the young lady from the flea market, stood to the side, holding the leash. That must be her dog, Mustard.

An older woman with a rounded back and white hair shuffled up next to Beth. She led the woman closer to Mustard. A gentleman joined them, and they started laughing. The dog barked and went from resident to resident leaning in for a head scratch. Joy was evident on their faces as they reached out to touch Mustard.

Ginger sighed. Would Grandpa be happy here? She didn't want him to feel as though she was getting rid of him. *But I don't know what to do.* She made a mental note to call the doctor and make that appointment for a consultation. She needed to understand what exactly she was looking at with Grandpa.

"May I help you?"

Ginger startled and turned to the woman at her elbow. "I'm looking for a place for my grandpa. I think."

"It's hard on everyone to make that kind of decision. I'm Peggy."

"Ginger." She liked the younger woman's kindness toward her.

"You run the Jukebox Café, don't you?"

Ginger nodded.

"Everyone raves about your cinnamon rolls. One of these days I plan to stop in."

"Please do. Be sure and ask for me."

"Let's walk." Peggy motioned toward the other side of the courtyard.

They found a bench and sat. Ginger stared off into the distance, wishing the moment would go away and Grandpa would never need to be anywhere besides his own home. She wished they never fought, and she had someone to share the load with. She had hoped Grandpa would be like that man she read about who died at a hundred and three, strong in mind even if his body was weaker than in his younger years.

"Tell me what's going on."

"Where do I start? Grandpa served in World War II. He's a buddy of one of your residents, Bo Culver."

Peggy nodded. "Sweet man. Go on."

"Grandpa is ninety-eight but still strong. At least physically." She explained about his possible dementia and finding the jewelry box and his obsession with it. "I've always had a good relationship with him, but with his moods are all over the place. It's hard. I'm struggling financially, and I'm not sure what's going to happen to the Jukebox. My waitresses keep quitting, so I'm pulling double duty in the café. I'm supposed to be working on changing his diet and making sure he exercises, but when am I supposed to do that?" Ginger covered her face and cried. "I'm sorry."

"You don't have to apologize. You have some big changes ahead of you. Some seasons have more tears than others."

"I'm afraid of losing Grandpa. He's always been there for me. What will I do without him?"

"Do you have other family to help you care for him?"

Ginger shook her head.

"Friends? A church family?"

"I go to Hillside Community church."

"Good place. I've visited a couple times. Anyone else?"

"There's Betsy and Mike."

"Are they married?"

"No. Betsy is one of my closest friends. And Mike..." Ginger looked down at her lap. "Mike is one of my closest friends, too. He's the pastor at Hillside."

"Ah...I think perhaps more than a friend?"

"No. How can I even think about that in the middle of these changes with Grandpa?"

Peggy touched Ginger's clasped hands. "The right relationship will help you, not make things worse. Don't rule it out. Either way, you have support from friends. What are you doing to take care of yourself?"

Ginger laughed.

"That's what I thought. Tends to happen when normal living collides with an aging relative. But you can't not take care of yourself."

"I know. It's just...most days I'm fine."

"It's the other days you have to prepare yourself for." Peggy waved to Beth, who headed their direction.

Beth led her dog next to the bench. "How's your grandpa doing?"

Ginger petted the dog. "Cantankerous as ever. And as fiercely loyal and loving as ever. He's obsessed with that jewelry box, and it drives me crazy."

"My grandpa is hard to understand, too." Beth told Mustard to sit.

Peggy stood and handed Ginger her card. "Call me anytime. I'll leave you two to visit. Come by the office before you go, and I'll give you some information about our place as well as a few resources for you, including a support group that meets here weekly. In the meantime..." she nodded at the dog. "Hang out with Mustard. He's good at bringing down stress levels."

Beth sat on the bench next to Ginger. "Tell me about your grandpa. I know he's a WWII veteran."

"He has all the pomp of being an officer." Ginger petted Mustard, who rested his head against her leg.

"Pretty commanding, eh?"

"Sums it up well. He likes things to go his way. Speaking of which, do you have any information about that jewelry box? Do you remember where you acquired it?"

Beth chewed on her bottom lip. "If I recall, I found it at a flea market somewhere east of here. Call me next week. I'll see what I can dig up."

"That would be great." Ginger scratched under Mustard's chin. Grandpa would enjoy being around a dog. For that matter, sitting here with the animal calmed her nerves as well. "Beth, when can Grandpa and I meet up with you and Mustard?"

"Give me a call when you're going to be out. I'm usually able to get away from whatever I'm doing to introduce Mustard to new friends."

CHAPTER SEVENTEEN

"Grandpa? Want any breakfast?" Silence answered. "Must have gone over to the café already." She was glad the last couple days had been more peaceful with Grandpa. She dished up eggs and bacon and poured a cup of coffee. It was nice to eat breakfast in her own home for a change. Rachel said she would take opening shift today to give Ginger a break. Bowing her head, she offered up a prayer then picked up her fork.

The door banged closed. "Yoo-hoo." Betsy bounced into the kitchen and grabbed a mug from the cupboard. "Where's Walter off to?" She poured a cup of coffee then sat down.

"No clue. Want some breakfast to go with your coffee?" Ginger took another bite of her bacon.

"I had breakfast at my place." Betsy stirred in a couple teaspoons of sugar and topped it off with creamer. "Spill it. What's going on? You haven't been yourself lately."

"I'm losing Grandpa and it hurts."

"Ahh, sweetie. Come here." Betsy wrapped her friend in a hug. "You're going non-stop these days, too. You need to slow down. Rest always helps."

"You sound like Peggy at the retirement home. She told me to take care of myself."

"She's right."

"So how am I supposed to slow down?" Conflicting expectations competed for Ginger's attentions most days, and they were all valid needs, but there were only so many hours in a day. No matter what she chose, someone would be disappointed in her. She took a deep breath.

"Cut some things out, girlfriend."

"Like what? I wish I could be more like you, Betsy. You keep up with everything."

"Girl, we're as different as apple pie from chocolate pie. No use trying to be someone you're not." Betsy drank some of her coffee. "Let the women at church do more of the work at the Jordans'. You don't have to be the one doing everything for them."

"But Megan is my friend."

"And she'll understand. It's not like things won't get done."

"You're right. Okay, I'll call a few ladies—"

"*I'll* call a few ladies. You take a nap or a long bath or eat a piece of chocolate pie."

Ginger laughed. Leave it to Betsy to cheer her up.

"Now, let's figure out how to lighten the load on your quest to find Irene."

Ginger pushed her plate away. "You know about the jewelry box and how Grandpa is convinced Irene is still alive. Grandpa turned over a bunch of his and Irene's things—photo album, news clipping, marriage certificate, and other memorabilia to help me find her. I've made a list of what I need to do." She pulled her list out from her Bible and handed it to Betsy.

Betsy took the paper and glanced over it. "I'll call Lillian about researching at the library for anything on that jewelry box she can find. Send that picture to me. Maggie and Millie might be a good source of information, too. They're like walking encyclopedias about anything too far back for you or me to remember. I'll check with them. I'll ask Megan to call Beth about where she bought the box." Betsy set her coffee mug in the sink. "Better go for now. Promised the librarian at the school that I would help with story time. I'll stop by the café later." She waved and hurried out the door.

Ginger glanced out the window at the café across the alley and thought about the inventory she planned to do that day. She felt more like going back to bed than going to work. She set her dishes in the sink. *Better get to it. The inventory won't take care of itself.*

Ginger stopped next to the pots-and-pans sink where Harry was drying off a soup pot. "You know where Grandpa went?"

Harry tossed the towel on the hook. "Said they were heading over to Charlie's."

"Really? He hasn't spent any time at the garage for years."

"Haven't seen him that animated in a long time. Had me fix lunch for the four of them to take along."

Ginger wrinkled her brow. "Four? What is he up to?"

"Whatever it is, it's doing him good." Harry grabbed the pot and headed to the stove.

"I'll sneak over later and see what's up. Where's Rachel?"

He tilted his chin toward the dining hall. "Back at her take-charge style of working. I've been thinking..."

"Yes?"

Harry draped an arm around her shoulders. "Rachel would make a great manager if you ever thought about stepping back from the day to day of this place."

Ginger shook her head. "She's not planning to stay."

"Have you asked her if she would consider it?"

"Think you could work for someone so young?"

"Only someone as good as Rachel."

"I'll think about it."

Rachel joined them in the kitchen. "Ginger, I was thinking, can we take the day-old bread out to the Jordan family? It's still fresh and going to waste."

Harry offered Ginger an I-told-you-so look.

Ginger smiled. "That's a great idea."

Rachel gave Ginger a hug and then started chopping veggies for lunch.

Harry pointed at Rachel with his spatula. "See?"

"I see. Now get back to work." Ginger was afraid that Rachel had no interest in making her home in a town this size. *Lord, is this part of Your plan?* If so, she would have to give Rachel a raise. Ginger needed to look at the books and see how it would work.

Ginger pulled her car to the curb across the street from Charlie's. The large rolling door stood open, but the place was empty. One of Grandpa's friends came from around the corner, followed by Josh. They disappeared inside the garage. Ginger wrinkled her brow. What were they up to?

A few minutes later, her grandpa and his other two buddies came around the corner. Grandpa was covered in grease.

He was working on cars again? After his parents and he moved to Preston Hill, he worked part time in the garage for Charlie's great-grandfather. From what her dad had told her, Grandpa's parents didn't like him being gone from the café so much. But they didn't do more than complain about it. Ginger got out of the car and headed to the garage. Mike walked out and motioned her over. He was covered in grease and she covered her mouth with her hand to hide her laugh.

"That's right. Laugh." He swiped a clump of unruly hair out of his face, leaving another smudge of grease on his face.

This time she couldn't hold in her amusement. He smirked at her then joined in with his own laugh.

The three men and Josh came out of the garage and stopped when they saw her and Mike. Grandpa waved. "I'm fine. You can go home now."

Ginger offered a mock salute and turned to leave.

"I'm teasing. Come on."

She followed them around the corner, relieved at his lighthearted mood. When she saw the project in question, she stopped and gasped. "Where did this come from?" The old single-engine plane took up all the space under a double-wide truck port.

Grandpa grinned. "Isn't she a beaut? It belongs to a friend of Charlie's." He puffed out his chest and wiped his greasy hands on a mechanic's towel. "I'm teaching this kid a thing or two about engines." He inclined his head toward Josh.

Josh nodded at Ginger, then tucked his hands in his pockets and ducked his head, the bill of his cap hiding his eyes.

Grandpa reached over and knocked his cap off. "What did I tell you?"

"Sorry," the kid mumbled.

"Well?" Grandpa glared at Josh.

"Fine." He looked Ginger in the eye. "Good to see you."

Grandpa elbowed him. The kid stuck out a hand.

Ginger smiled and shook it. "When you're done, why don't you come by the café with the guys for a piece of pie?"

His eyes lit up. "You got any of that cherry pie left?"

She laughed. "I'll be sure to save some for you." Waving, she headed back to her car. This new project might be just the thing to keep Grandpa occupied and in a better frame of mind.

The men and Josh made it back to the café during the mid-afternoon lull when Ginger was taking a break from the inventory. Once the men were seated with drinks, she passed out cherry pie to Josh, chocolate deluxe pie to the older men, and strawberry rhubarb pie to Mike.

Mike stopped her before she moved away from the table. "Hey, do you have a bit of time later? Thought we could enjoy a cup of coffee together."

"Sure. Catch me before you leave." She sat back down across the dining hall where she was taking her break and watched the group of men. As they ate, conversation ranged from boisterous laughter to almost secretive quiet. She enjoyed watching the interplay between the generations from where she sat.

A comparison of tattoos ensued between military men and young teenager, each pointing to their own then looking at the others in turn. Josh sat straighter as the men spoke to him with respect and listened intently to what he had to say. Ginger couldn't help but notice how Mike continually drew the boy into the conversation when there was a lull.

The jingling of jewelry announced Betsy's approach from the kitchen. She sat next to Ginger. "Mike's a good man."

"I know."

"If you don't wake up, one of these days someone will snatch him up."

"Betsy."

"You know it's true. How will you feel when that happens?"

The bell over the door jingled. Relieved, Ginger excused herself to greet the new customer. She grabbed a menu. "Welcome to the Jukebox Café."

"Ginger?"

The man looked familiar, but Ginger couldn't place him. "I'm sorry?"

"Barry. Barry Allen from high school."

"This is embarrassing." They had dated for a bit during her junior year, then Barry had left for college and they lost touch. This was the first time Ginger had seen him since he graduated. She didn't recognize him with his beard and mustache.

"The years haven't been as kind to me as they have been to you."

"Uh...what have you been up to?" She shifted on her feet.

Barry grinned. "I'm living in Iowa now. I'm in town visiting my parents and got a hankering for some of your lemon cream pie."

Ginger remembered that being their favorite pie to share at the end of a date. This was awkward. "Window seat or counter?"

His eyes teased. "How about the one next to the jukebox?"

The one they sat in when they shared their pie. What was he up to? "Sure."

"Can you join me? It would be great to have company."

"Ginger?"

She turned at Mike's voice right behind her.

"Can I get a slice of strawberry rhubarb pie to go?"

She lifted her chin toward her new customer. "Let me get him seated then I'll be right over."

She left Barry with a menu at the booth next to the jukebox, then dished Mike's pie into a box and took it to him. Grandpa stopped talking as Ginger approached the table. Did he remember Barry? And had he told Mike? What did it matter? Barry was a stranger to her now.

She set the pie on the table. "Here you go. Did you still want to have some coffee?"

"You're probably busy. I'll see you later."

Mike must have changed his mind about catching up. Or not. Ginger followed his gaze over to Barry as he left with the other men. She was flattered that Barry remembered her and stopped by, but Ginger wouldn't encourage any of his flirtations. With two men in the room willing to pay her attention, her heart only wanted one to look her way. She was more attached to Mike than she dared to admit.

CHAPTER EIGHTEEN

"Got a minute?" Rachel peeked her head into Ginger's office.

Ginger stopped her work. "What's up?"

Rachel came in and sat on the chair situated between the front of the desk and the wall. "I've got to show you something." She pulled out her phone.

Ginger watched the video Rachel indicated. In fast speed, the video showed a young man lettering on a storefront window. Over the course of a sped-up minute, the storefront went from dull to eye-catching.

"What do you think? It would freshen things up and draw people in."

"It's a great idea, Rachel. But I can't afford to hire anyone."

"Sorry. I always get ahead of myself. I do lettering." Rachel held up her hand. "And I won't take any money for it. I can use it in a portfolio, and you can recommend me to people. All you would have to pay for is the paint, and that shouldn't cost much."

"Well…"

"I can do it in my time off from waitressing."

"You sure?" Ginger liked Rachel's enthusiasm. She hoped it was contagious.

Rachel nodded. "Absolutely."

"Who am I to stand in the way of progress? Make your list and we'll go shopping for supplies as soon as we get a chance." Watching Rachel bubble her way out of the office, Ginger grinned. Rachel brought joy to her soul. Between Grandpa's new project and Rachel taking a hand in the café, maybe life would smooth out a bit.

Ginger closed her computer and headed out to the kitchen. An hour before the noon rush. "Harry, how's the prep coming?"

"All sunshine and roses."

"Got a date tonight?"

"How did you know?"

"How long have we known each other?" Ginger laughed. "Who is it tonight?"

"Don't think you're getting it out of me this time. If it lasts past three dates, I'll let you know."

"Fair enough." Ginger went to the break room. Dish washer and chef's assistant accounted for. Out in the dining hall, Rachel whizzed through prep. Ginger checked the stack of menus next to the cash register before grabbing a wet rag and wiping off each one.

"I don't care what you think. You need to tell her." Bo's voice reached Ginger from the dining hall to the office where she sat working on ordering supplies. The voices faded as Ginger imagined Grandpa shushing everyone, aware that she could hear them. She returned to the order, sure that he planned to leave her out of the loop of what he was up to once again.

A few minutes later, a giggling Rachel stood at her desk.

"You'll never guess what he's up to."

"I give."

"He's planning to take a DNA test to help find his wife." Rachel shifted from foot to foot.

"It won't do him any good to have his DNA tested. He's not related to Irene."

"But you are. Have *your* DNA tested. That's a great idea."

Ginger had to agree that Rachel had a point, but it would depend on Irene having done the test. What was the likelihood? "I wouldn't have any idea where to start."

"My parents had some DNA testing done a while back. I could ask them what company they used."

"That would be great. But—"

Rachel put a hand on Ginger's arm. "Don't you think it's worth a shot?"

Ginger held up her hands. "Fine. I'll do it."

"Great. I'll call my parents tonight. Now back to work." Rachel hurried out of the kitchen.

Ginger focused on her computer. "What am I getting into? Do I really want to do this?" She muttered as she typed. "I wish he wouldn't go off on his own and not tell me what he's up to. Might save me some time."

Someone cleared his throat, and she glanced up. "What?"

"Might want to close the door." Harry stood in the doorway and watched her.

"How much did you hear?"

"All of it."

Ginger huffed. "At least Grandpa didn't hear what—"

"He just walked past your door."

Tonight would be interesting. "Thanks, Harry. Close the door on your way out, please."

Ginger closed the front door and threw the keys onto the entry table. The mirror hanging to the side reflected an overextended, almost at the end of her rope granddaughter. If only she had had more family to help carry the load. So why wasn't she more gung-ho for this search? She kicked off her shoes and sat on the couch. Because she didn't want to be disappointed. Head against the cushions, she closed her eyes and let out a heavy sigh. Her body relaxed. A vacation would be nice.

"Ginger?"

She jerked awake at the tap on her leg. "Grandpa?" She glanced at the clock. Had she really been asleep for two hours? No wonder she felt stiff.

"You okay?"

"Yeah." She stretched her neck from side to side. "I needed to take the load off for a minute."

Grandpa sat on the couch next to her. The robe wrapped tightly around him and the slippers on his feet indicated that he had not been waiting up for her but discovered her when he got up for one of his nightly treks to the bathroom.

"You work too hard."

She raised her eyebrow. "It's not like I can take a vacation."

Grandpa's slumped. "I'm sorry."

"For what?" This wasn't like Grandpa.

"I never say thank you, but you do so much for me." He sniffled. "If I ever lost you…"

She reached an arm around her grandpa. "I'm not going anywhere."

"Bo's friend saw you at the retirement home."

"You told me to look into it."

"I didn't mean it. I was mad. Please don't send me away."

"Sometimes I worry what would happen to you if something happened to me."

He nodded. "You already have a lot on your plate. You can forget about the jewelry box. I don't think…"

Something inside Ginger broke at her grandfather giving up for her sake. Tears stung the inside of her eyelids. "I'm not giving up. Besides, a bit of a mystery might be fun."

He glanced at her and shook his head. "I don't want this to get all over town, young lady."

She raised both eyebrows. "Really?"

"Fine. You do it your way. I don't like it, but I'll cooperate. I promise."

"Let's start by talking about this DNA test."

"That was Josh's idea. He sent for the test and took care of everything." Grandpa laughed. "I thought they were going to take all the spit I had in me."

"You realize that sending in your DNA won't help since you're not related to Irene, don't you?"

Grandpa shook his head. "I thought...I don't know. It sounded like a good idea. I wanted to help."

Ginger smoothed out her jeans. "I'll send in my DNA. Since I'm her granddaughter—"

Grandpa slapped his leg. "That will work." His grin lit up his face.

"But Grandpa, in the future, tell me what you're up to. We'll find her more quickly if we work together."

He nodded and looked down at his lap.

"And I'm not sending you away. We're going to be okay."

CHAPTER NINETEEN

The musty, old-book scent of the library took Ginger back to when she had crammed in research for papers during high school. She lay the old news clippings from Grandpa on the table. Several headlines announced news about Pearl Harbor and men registering for the draft. Another headline spread fear about the Japanese in America. She thumbed through the pile. Article after article about the internment camps.

Turning to her laptop, she typed in the search engine "Japanese Internment in Nebraska." She clicked on the first link and read an article that said the internment was for Japanese Americans on the west coast. But there was fear of the Japanese throughout the country, leading to racism in many places.

Ginger tapped the end of her pen against her lips. Irene's maiden name was American. Could Irene be of Japanese descent? Ginger certainly didn't have any looks that would indicate that in her genealogy, but Irene was two generations back. If she was of Japanese descent, might she have been interned? That would explain how she went missing.

Ginger jotted down a note to ask Grandpa about this angle. Her mind wandered to her grandmother's perspective. If Irene had been interned, did she look for Grandpa when she got out? How would she have gone about it? Ginger doodled random ideas around the edge of the paper.

Place an ad? Check if they did that back then.

Go back to where Grandpa and Irene lived. Get address from Grandpa.

Would Irene have hired a private investigator? She had no clue how to check on that one. She scratched it out.

Ginger glanced at the clock hanging on the wall. Maybe she could get Grandpa to go on a walk with her. She sent Rachel a quick text to let her know she might be a bit late getting back to the Jukebox and an S.O.S. to Betsy to help Rachel until she got there. The librarian directed her to a book on the Japanese internments and, ten minutes later, she was headed back home. Hopefully Grandpa would be in a talkative mood.

Ginger slid a hand through the crook of grandpa's elbow. The warm glow of the setting sun lit their way as they strolled through town. They used to walk together every evening. But those times had slowly dwindled when he got grumpy anytime she suggested it.

For a few moments, it was pleasant to imagine things as they used to be. Grandpa strong and in charge. Ginger leaning on his strength. She sniffled. There was no going back.

"What is it?" Grandpa put his left hand on top of hers.

"I miss this. You and me."

"Me too."

They strolled in silence to the park in the center of town. He stopped in front of the bench under the gazebo. "Mind if an old man takes a breather?"

"Not at all. I'd enjoy stopping for a bit." The evening breeze brought the scent of magnolias from several nearby trees. "Mom loved the scent of magnolias. Too bad they didn't have these planted while she was alive."

"She would love smelling them so close to home."

Ginger shook off the melancholy. "How are things going with Josh?"

"He misses his mom. And her cherry pie."

That was why Josh always asked for the cherry pie. "Has he shared what happened?"

"His parents were in a car crash when he was ten. No family, so he and his younger brother got stuck in foster care." Grandpa shook his head. "They couldn't place them together, and Josh got pretty angry about it, started acting out. He's been bouncing around for several years now."

"I hope he's able to stay with the Jordans."

"They're trying to track down his brother and take him in, too."

"Does he like it here?"

Grandpa shrugged. "This is the first family willing to take both of them. He doesn't want to mess that up."

"At least there's that."

They sat in comfortable quiet for a few minutes. Ginger hated bringing up the search for Irene in case it broke this mood they found themselves in, but this was the most likely time for him to be willing to talk. "Grandpa?"

He patted her hand. "Yes?"

"Can I ask you about Irene?"

He remained silent for so long, Ginger though maybe he was clamping down on sharing any information.

"Go ahead." His voice wavered.

"In all those things you gave me to search through, there were quite a few articles about the Japanese internments."

"For a while, I was afraid that was what happened."

"But her maiden name is Hutton."

"Her mother's parents were first generation Japanese immigrants. Irene was third generation."

"Didn't your parents know what happened?"

He stiffened.

She would much rather have a few more minutes of companionship with Grandpa than know the answer to every question swimming in her mind. "We don't have to talk about—"

"You need to know." He paused. "When I came back from the war, Irene was gone. She left our daughter—your mother, Patricia—with my parents. That much you know. What you don't know is that my parents were never happy about my marriage to Irene. Neither were her parents. We eloped when I was eighteen and she was seventeen. We had Patricia within a year." Grandpa's voice trailed off. The look on his face suggested to Ginger that he was thinking about happier days. He shook his head. "But they loved Patricia."

"They told me Irene went to stay with her parents and that they had a plan to keep her safe during the rampant fear of the Japanese in our country. My parents claimed that was all they knew. I went to see my in-laws, but they had sold their house by then. I couldn't find where they moved to. I checked into the possibility of her having been sent to an internment camp but found nothing. I had no idea where else to look and I quit. What if she had been looking for me? By that time, my parents were already living in Preston Hill, and she wouldn't have known where I was. If I hadn't given up, we might have found each other. Giving up is my greatest regret."

"I'm going to do my best to find her."

"I know you will. Should we head back home?"

"This is nice. I hate to go back yet."

"Your grandpa is about done." He slapped his leg and pointed to the center of the park where Mustard was leaping into the air to catch a Frisbee. "Don't that beat all? I used to play catch with my dog when I was a kid, but never Frisbee."

Beth waved and jogged toward them with Mustard next to her.

"I didn't know you had a dog, Grandpa."

"Had to get rid of him during the depression."

"Did you ever get another one?"

"Nope."

Ginger couldn't read Grandpa's mood with that quick response.

"Hey Ginger. Walter." Beth nodded at Grandpa.

"Where do I know you from? You seem to know us." Grandpa narrowed his eyes at her.

Beth laughed. "The flea market."

He smiled and reached over to pet Mustard. "And this is?"

"Mustard."

Mustard moved close to Grandpa and pressed his face against Grandpa's knee. He laughed and scratched behind Mustard's ear. "He's a good dog."

"I got him at the humane society."

Beth and Ginger visited a bit while Grandpa enjoyed Mustard's company. After a few minutes, he stood. "I need to head home, Ginger." He gave one last scratch behind Mustard's ear.

Ginger thanked Beth for stopping by with Mustard then strolled with Grandpa down the sidewalk.

"Might be nice to have a dog again."

Ginger held the words back that tried to flood out, not wanting to push him away from the idea. "Might be."

"Maybe we could visit the humane society. Just to see what they have."

"If you want to."

He climbed the steps to the porch. "I think that was a set up."

"What?"

"Running into Mustard and Beth at the park."

"What if it was?" Ginger held her breath.

"We'll have to see." Eyes twinkling, he grinned at Ginger. "Might get a dog anyway. Might not."

Thankful that this was one of Grandpa's good days, Ginger followed him into the house.

CHAPTER TWENTY

Ginger flipped pancakes with the spatula in one hand while swiping to end a call on her phone with the other. "No more calls this morning." That was the third one. "Drats." The pancakes were almost ready for the compost pile.

She tossed the partially burnt pancakes in the trash then ladled another batch onto the griddle before pulling the bacon out of the oven. Betsy's suggestion that she bake the bacon had proved useful. Not nearly as time consuming as cooking it in a pan. "Grandpa, food's ready."

"I'm right here."

Ginger jumped at the sound of Grandpa's deep voice at her side. The pancake she had balanced on the spatula slid off onto the floor, and she blew out a huff of air. If they got a dog, it wouldn't go starving with all the food she ended up tossing for one reason or another.

Grandpa picked up the pancake and tossed it in the trash. "No harm."

"Can you grab the orange juice?" She slid the other pancakes onto a platter.

He retrieved the juice from the fridge and poured two glasses. After setting them on the table, he came back over to the oven and reached for a piece of bacon.

She swatted his hand away. "Don't go eating my share."

He grinned and picked up the platter. "I'll set this on the table."

The man liked his meat. Good thing he still had his teeth. "Right behind you." She took the platter of pancakes into the dining room, and then returned to the kitchen for the butter and syrup.

"Better eat before the food gets cold." Grandpa clasped his hands in front of him.

"Yes, sir." Ginger bowed her head. Grandpa said a prayer before dishing out a generous serving for each of them. "What are you up to today?"

"Me and the guys are going over to Charlie's to work on that plane."

Ginger picked up her fork. "If you want a ride..."

He pointed to his cane. "The exercise is good for us."

She smiled. Stubborn no matter what he was doing. But he was right. The exercise was good. She could only imagine what kind of fuss he would put up if she ever needed to move him to a home of some sort. This had been his home for so long. Lifting a silent prayer asking for health for them both, she watched him drown his pancakes in maple syrup while she stabbed a bit of bacon and layered it with her own pancake covered in maple syrup. She reprimanded herself. Cutting down on sugar was one of the dietary changes she needed to make. Next shopping trip, she would stock up on everything they needed.

"What do you think of Rachel?"

He chewed his food. "Nice girl."

"As a waitress." She scooted her pancake around in the syrup lake on her plate. "I could use more permanent help around the place."

"Thought she was leaving again at the end of summer."

"She seems to like it here. Maybe she'll change her mind."

"For a waitressing job? Thought she wanted to go places and do things."

"Do you think she would make a good manager?"

He paused. "You ready to turn the place over?"

"Thinking about it."

He patted her arm. "You do what you need to take care of yourself."

He looked down at his plate. "You're all I have left."

Straightening her posture, she took a deep breath. He was right. She had to take care of them both. "Don't you worry. We'll be okay."

Ginger's car slid in the gravel as she took the turn for the Jordan farm.

Rachel grabbed the door handle. "Wild driver."

Ginger threw a sideways glance at her passenger. "Like you could do better."

"Probably not." Rachel giggled.

Close to the house, Megan and two young children followed something on the ground. They noticed Ginger park the car and came over. Greg came out of the barn with an angry looking Josh trailing him. Their voices carried over the distance.

"I don't have time to take you to town."

"But I finished my work."

Greg paused. "I know you did. And I'm proud of you. You've had a great attitude." He raked a hand through his hair. "Maybe this afternoon. Okay? I'm a lot slower now with this arm still in a sling."

"Whatever." The kid kicked the gravel then stomped off toward the house.

Greg joined his wife.

"Hi! We brought you some more bread and stuff." Rachel handed Ginger a box full of bread, then grabbed another one of muffins and pastries donated from the bakery in town.

Greg took the box from Ginger and held it in one arm. "You don't have to do this."

"But we appreciate it. Really." Megan's broad smile showed her dimples."Did you hear? Greg gets to return to work next week."

"That's great." From the restlessness she sensed in Greg, Ginger guessed that it was past time.

"I'll take these to the house." Rachel looked at the two younger kids standing behind Megan. "I bet if you worked together, you could carry that box your dad has."

They nodded eagerly and each one held on to a side of the box and carried it between them. "Look, Rachel." They managed to lift the box and balance on their heads. They giggled as they went through the door Rachel held open.

Megan sighed. "Rachel has a way with them. Wish they listened to me that well."

"Sometimes kids listen better to others than to their parents."

Megan nodded. "I should know that by now. But it doesn't get any easier."

"It's great, what you do. Opening your home. It's a wonderful place to raise kids."

"I wish everything wasn't falling apart. Speaking of which, I better get back to work. Thanks again for bringing the bread by. Every little bit helps." Greg stuck his cap on his head and headed toward the barn.

The door to the house slammed. The two youngsters came running out. Rachel stood on the stoop talking to Josh.

Ginger angled her chin toward the young man. "How's he doing?"

"He's so used to things not going his way, he fights us on almost everything. Working with your grandpa on that plane has made a difference, though. The men don't let him off when he's disrespectful. Some of that follows him home. At least through dinner."

Ginger laughed. "Grandpa has that effect on people."

Rachel jogged over to where they stood. "You want us to give Josh a ride to Charlie's?"

"That would be great." Megan waved Josh over. "When should we pick him up?"

"If you don't mind him having supper with the men, you can pick him up at the café after that." Rachel glanced at Ginger, who nodded in confirmation.

Josh bumped against Rachel. "Thanks."

Ginger watched Josh join the men inside the garage. Bo handed him a can of soda. The kid nodded as the older man talked. Ginger put the car in gear. "I think Josh is good for the men."

"I don't think their special project hurts either." Rachel grinned.

"Did you see them yesterday when they came into the café?"

"I know, right? Covered in grease but happy as a litter of puppies let out to play."

Ginger laughed. "I like having you around, girl."

"I like being here."

Ginger glanced over at Rachel's soft answer. "What's up?"

"I still don't know what I want to do when summer is up."

"You're welcome to stay here as long as you want." She needed to ask Rachel about the manager position before she found something else.

CHAPTER TWENTY-ONE

Ginger stared at the church wall as she drove down the street toward the building. More graffiti? Obviously the same person was at work. The style was unmistakable. Whoever painted this had talent, but they were using it in the wrong way. She cringed at the hate scrawled across the brick. The images on the church wall were more disturbing than those found on the wall of the café.

Hopefully Mike had taken pictures, because there seemed to be a story in this one. The left side was colorful and light. Moving toward the right, the colors changed to dark, the images and words reflecting the same mood. An image in the shadowed area reminded her of a painting she'd studied in art appreciation during college—*The Scream* by somebody Munch. But more modern and more detailed. Whoever did this seemed to be expressing a lot of pain.

Mike waved and set down his paint roller as she pulled into the parking lot. He joined her next to the car. "Like the new image?"

"You wear it well." She nodded at his shirt covered in dark gray paint.

He held out his arms. "Trying it on for size. Should I wear this on Sunday?"

"Maybe not."

"That's what I was afraid of." He led the way back toward the building.

"Why is someone targeting Preston Hill?" Ginger focused on the image of the screaming woman.

"Who knows?"

"Do you think they'll catch the culprit?"

He shrugged. "The sheriff said that so far there are no solid leads. A lot of supposition."

"Josh again?"

"Not so much at church anymore. But several folks around town are pointing fingers. Once rumors and accusations start, they're hard to tame. Sam stepped up to bat for him, though. There were also a couple accusations aimed at residents of Sunrise. But enough about this vandalism. Did you need something?"

"Let's work while we talk. Got an extra roller?"

"That would be great. Several of the youth are stopping by after school to lend a hand." He retrieved another roller and set up a paint tray. "Paint over everything. Work on the lower portion then I'll get extensions for the poles to reach the top portion later."

She dipped her roller in the paint then began at the farthest right. "It's about Irene."

He stood, shielded his eyes, and looked at her, his brows furrowed. "And?"

Maybe she shouldn't ask for his help. "I can ask Bo or Eugene."

Mike set his roller down. "You can talk to me about anything. I promise I won't bite."

"Or avoid me for several days?"

"Ah. That's it." He picked his roller back up. "That wasn't about anything you said about your grandfather. But I promise I won't avoid you."

She really did want his perspective. "I found out that Irene's grandparents were Japanese. Grandpa thought she ended up in one of the internment camps. He looked into it but didn't find anything. His parents told him she went to live with her parents, but they moved and he couldn't find out where. And by the time he got back from the war, his parents were already in Preston Hill. She wouldn't have known where to find him. But what if she looked for him? Here's what I wanted to get your help on. Could she have found out anything through the military?"

Mike dipped his roller in the paint. "Not sure. That's an interesting angle. I have a friend I can put you in touch with who should be able to answer your questions."

"I appreciate that."

"For you, anything."

She rolled her brush in the tray of paint. "I hope…" She held back her doubts about her grandmother. She didn't want to lose this connection with Mike.

"I understand your fears about what you'll find. I know you don't want Walter to get hurt, but trust what he knows about his wife. Have you considered other ways Irene might have tried to find him? Maybe she left a trail."

"Grandpa said he put an ad in the classifieds. Maybe Irene did the same. I'm going to ask Lillian to help me on that one. She's great at the research."

They worked in silence for a while. From the corner of her eye, she could see Mike turn her way every so often. "Got something on your mind?"

"Not much. I met someone you know at church last Sunday."

Ginger searched her mind for someone new as she rolled the paint. "I give. Who?"

"A Barry Allen."

Interesting. She hadn't noticed him at church. "Is he still in town?" She avoided looking at Mike and kept rolling paint over the same place on the wall.

"Yep. And he couldn't stop talking about you. Said he never did get you out of his head after you guys dated, and when he saw you after all these years, he was as smitten as before. My paraphrase, of course.

He asked if you were dating anyone now."

"He lives in Iowa."

"Said he was thinking about moving back closer to take care of his parents."

"And what did you tell him?" Was Mike slightly jealous or teasing her?

He held up his hands. "I may be the pastor, and I was nice, but I'm not going to help the guy out. Might ruin my chances."

If anyone could win her heart, it wouldn't be Barry Allen. She dipped her roller in the paint.

"Guess I made the right call." Mike inspected their progress and looked pleased. "Maybe, come Sunday, I won't have an entire congregation yelling at me."

"They wouldn't be yelling, and you know it. They would show up in their work clothes." She flicked a bit of paint at him.

"You have no idea what you started." He flicked a bit of paint at her.

She set her paint roller down. "I give."

"You don't get out of it that easy."

"I have to go to work."

"Should have thought of that first."

She backed toward her car. Looking down at her clothes, she groaned. She couldn't get in her car with wet paint on herself.

Mike laughed. "You should see yourself."

"That's right. Laugh at my expense." She planted her fists on her hips.

"Truce?"

She watched him from the corner of her eye to be sure he wasn't up to some trickery before she headed back to her side of the wall.

Mike returned to painting. "We really need to stop meeting like this."

The truth behind his statement gave her pause. Lately they had been doing more together and finding each other in playful moments more often. Things between them were changing. She stretched her neck.

"Getting tight?" Mike set his brush down. Pushing her hair out of the way, he began rubbing her neck.

After her current train of thought, his touch added to her confusion. She tried to enjoy the release of tension, but her thoughts raced toward the what-ifs, creating more tightness in her neck.

"Yoo-hoo. Mike? Anyone here?" Betsy's voice grew louder.

Mike dropped his hands. "That help?"

"Thanks."

He went back to painting as Betsy rounded the corner from the front of the building. She stopped and peered up at the partial mural. "Another one? Need some help?"

Mike pointed his roller brush toward Betsy. "In that?"

Betsy looked down at her colorful expression of herself. Bright yellow tights with a Monet inspired tunic. "I'm a neat painter."

"Or you could go change." Ginger laughed.

"I thought you liked me the way I am."

"And I don't want to hear you complain about ruining your outfit." Ginger rolled her eyes.

Did you stop by for something, Betsy?" Mike interjected his question between the bantering.

"Give me that brush." Betsy marched over to the pile of supplies and grabbed an extra one. "I'm already wearing a painting. You won't be able to tell if I get any of this on it."

Mike stopped arguing and set her up with a paint tray.

CHAPTER TWENTY-TWO

Ginger closed the café for a day and allowed Rachel to give full attention to her window project. The early morning sun warmed Ginger's back as she watched Rachel at work. A crowd gathered on the sidewalk as Rachel worked her lettering magic on the café window. She had a way with the brush. And the people. She engaged each person watching with a smile, a word, or an acknowledgment of some sort.

Ginger's attention wandered the crowd. Some were regular patrons while others had never stepped foot inside her café. Rachel's assertion was on the nose. This would be good for business. To her left, someone from the local news station filmed Rachel's process. Several in the crowd held up their phones, recording for their own personal purposes. Didn't take much to make the news in Preston Hill.

Time for a new lunch special. Her mind raced through what they had on hand. Her mouth watered. With Harry working his magic, she had an idea.

Ginger skirted the crowd and reached for the door, then stopped when a young man placed himself in her path.

"Are you the manager?" He held out his hand. "I'm Craig. A travel blogger. Do you have a minute for a few questions? I think city art in the small town is great and would love to write about this for my readers."

Trying to drum up a reason to escape, Ginger made eye contact with Rachel through the glass. She shook her head and went back to her work, ignoring Ginger's silent plea. *Hmm.* An idea sparked in

Ginger's mind. Time to play a bit of matchmaking. She chuckled and shook his hand. "Nice to meet you. I'm Ginger, owner, manager, sometimes waitress and cook. Come on in. I'm getting ready to work on a new item for the menu. You can visit with Rachel, the artist, then do some taste testing for me."

"That would be great. Thank you."

After sharing her new menu item idea with Harry, who was there working on a catering order, Ginger returned to the dining room where Rachel answered Craig's questions as she brought the window to life.

"It looks great, Rachel. Even backwards."

"How long have you owned the place, Ginger?" Craig sat with a laptop, ready to tap away on the keys.

"Been in my family since shortly after World War II ended."

"I'm sure this place is full of stories. Any you would like to share?"

"Grandpa is the storyteller. If he weren't off working on a project with his friends, I'm sure he would share a story or two. We've had some interesting guests over the years."

Craig grinned. "If he shows up, I'll ask." He looked down at his screen. "How did the place get the name the Jukebox Café?"

"That was well before I was even an idea in my parents' minds." Ginger laughed. "From what I understand, this was a dance hall before my family turned it into what it is today."

Rachel turned from the window and glanced at Ginger. "Did your grandpa ever tell you that he met several famous actors while serving in the war? According to him, more than one of them stopped by over the years to have dinner."

"No way. That old rascal. Never mentioned a thing."

"Did he say who?" Craig waited with an eager look on his face.

Rachel shook her head. "I wouldn't tell you if he had told me. Which he didn't. He wouldn't take advantage of a friendship to attract more business."

"A man of integrity. Seems like those are few and far between these days." Craig tapped on his keyboard then looked up. "May I take a few pictures of your work?"

Rachel shrugged. "Doesn't matter to me. Get permissions from kids' parents if they're in the shot you use." She indicated the crowd on the sidewalk.

"I brought permission waivers." Craig held up a handful of papers.

Rachel waved at several kids with their noses pressed against the window. She went outside and squatted next to the kids. "I need some help with a few handprints. Any volunteers?"

Kids ran to parents. Parents nodded, and the café welcomed about half a dozen eager kids ready to get their hands dirty. Parents followed them inside. Rachel set out several paper plates full of a variety of paint colors and indicated where she wanted the handprints, then turned them loose. Craig snapped pictures of the kids playing at work.

Within minutes, it became apparent that springtime had come to the Jukebox Café. Underneath the new lettering splashed across the front window, handprint flowers and butterflies danced.

Ginger clapped. "That's beautiful."

"My readers will enjoy this." Craig closed his laptop.

Rachel grinned. "Thanks." She helped the kids wipe the bulk of the paint off their hands then sent them to the bathroom to wash off the rest.

Harry stuck his head out the kitchen door. "Food's ready to dish up."

"Thanks. We'll be there in a few minutes." Ginger opened the door of the café. "We're done for a while, folks. Thanks for stopping by." Inside, she invited the parents of the children who helped on the window to stay and have lunch. "I have a new menu item that needs testing, otherwise, we have sandwiches, chips, and fruit. Sit wherever you like and let us know which option you want then go ahead and grab your drinks." Ginger watched as they followed her instructions. With the Jukebox budget being so tight, she wasn't sure if she could really afford to feed them for free, but it didn't sit well with her not to. One way or the other, she would make it work.

The choice between the new item and sandwiches split fairly evenly between parents and kids. No surprise there. Craig opted to try the new item. Rachel and Ginger hurried back to the kitchen to help assemble Ginger's brainstorm menu item. While parents and kids visited, Craig got signed permission to use their kids' images online.

"I never would have thought of this combination." Rachel spooned Pico de Gallo on top of tortilla chips laden with grilled salmon, mango chunks, bacon, and melted cream cheese.

"Yeah, don't know where it came from. Kind of the everything-but-the-kitchen-sink-that   -I-can-find-in-the-cupboard   method   of designing a recipe."

Rachel laughed. "That's a mouthful."

"Believe me, I'm not going to put that on the menu. Can you imagine taking that order?" Ginger joined her laughter with Rachel's as she added a few slices of jalapeños to each plate of nachos. "It needs a name."

Rachel stared up at the ceiling a moment as though in thought, then held up a finger. "I've got it. Mango Salmon Nachos Supreme?"

"And so, our newest menu item has a name."

"Really? You like it?"

"You have great ideas." Ginger finished dishing up another serving of Mango Salmon Nachos Supreme.

"I'm glad I can help."

"Now, we need to sample this." Ginger piled a small plate with the nachos then she took a bite of a chip with a bit of each topping piled on. "This is good." She picked up a chip for another bite.

Rachel took a bite and agreed, then poked at the nacho toppings with a chip.

"What is it?" Ginger added another spoon of Pico de Gallo to her concoction.

"Working on this project got me to thinking. I wish I knew what to do after this summer. I know I sound end-of-the-world-ish, but all my friends know. They think I need a life plan. Half the people I know are vastly disappointed that I haven't gone on to get a bachelor's degree or started working at some animation studio. But I'm only twenty-two. My parents would like me to find a direction too, but they're artists, so they get it even though the rest of my family doesn't. How am I supposed to know what I want to do for the rest of my life?"

The first bit of hope that Rachel might consider staying took root in Ginger's heart. She lifted a prayer and took a deep breath. "Have you ever—"

A loud crash and a cry of dismay from the front of the café pulled Ginger away from the food prep. In the dining hall, she stopped at the sight of brown liquid running across one of the tables and onto the floor. Two kids sat glaring at each other. A woman stood behind them. She looked up with a grimace on her face. "Sorry. I'll help clean up."

Ginger eased into her role of hostess. "Spills happen. Kids, can we move you to another spot while we clean up? Mom, there are rags and a bucket of soapy water under the counter where the coffee pot is. Can you grab that?" She directed the kids to step over the sticky soda and sit at the far end of the table, then placed a gray tub under the edge of the table and scooted the wet napkins, silverware, and placemats along with a fair amount of the liquid into it. The mom wiped the table and chairs down, and Rachel took care of mopping the floor.

"No worse for the wear." Ginger took the rag from the mom.

"Thanks for being understanding. And thanks for lunch. I wasn't sure what I was going to feed them today."

"It's my pleasure. I'm Ginger, by the way."

"I'm Bridgette." She tilted her head toward her kids. "Better get back to them."

Ginger felt a nudge in her spirit. Maybe not knowing what to feed her kids had more to do with supply than imagination. "Uh...quick question. Would you be interested in a job? I need to hire another waitress."

"A job?" Bridgette's eyes grew wide.

"I was planning on placing an ad this week, but I thought..."

"Yes. Absolutely yes. When can I start?"

"Let's talk after lunch."

"I'll be here." Bridgette joined her kids, who had already demolished the food on their plates. Ginger waved Rachel over. "Think they could use another sandwich."

"I'm on it. What about you?"

"What about you?"

Rachel laughed. "Eat later?"

Ginger nodded and then checked that everyone had what they needed.

Ginger was pleased to discover that Bridgette had plenty of waitressing experience and could start the next day. They worked out a schedule that would allow her as a single mom to be there for her kids when they needed her. Fortunately, Sunrise, where they were staying for now, had a daycare center she could use during the summer while she saved up money. After that, the kids would be in school.

Ginger wiped off tables while Rachel and Craig chatted about his upcoming blog post. Ginger figured this wasn't the last time they would see Craig. Not by a long shot. Happy for Rachel, she finished cleaning up after their impromptu guests.

An hour later, the dining hall empty, tables cleared, Ginger and Rachel sat down to their own plate of nachos.

"This is really good." Rachel took a second tortilla chip and scooped up a bite of salmon and mango to go with it.

"Harry did a great job. He didn't have the original ingredients I suggested, but I think this is perfect."

"The Jukebox needs a new menu." Rachel picked up her glass of soda. "Now that we have a new house special."

"I suppose you already have a design in mind?"

Rachel's eyes twinkled. "Yep."

"Who am I to stand in the way of progress?" Another expense she needed to find a way to pay for. Ginger took a deep breath. One way or the other, it would all balance out.

"Hello." The door from the kitchen swooshed close as Megan came into the dining hall. "Got a minute, Ginger?"

"I'm going to finish my lunch while we talk. Want some?" She pointed at their plates of nachos.

Megan scrunched her face. "No thanks. Don't like fish. Besides, I ate right before I came over."

"If you're sure." Rachel took another bite of her nachos.

"Absolutely." Megan sat at the table. "I followed up with Beth from the flea market today."

"Where did she find the box?" Ginger pushed her plate to the center of the table.

"Mountain Home Flea Market."

"That's the same town my grandpa and his parents lived in before they moved here right after the war."

"That sounds like a promising lead." Rachel stacked her plate with Ginger's. "Maybe good enough for a day trip?"

"I would have to close the café again for a day. Unless..." Ginger turned to Rachel. "...you could run the restaurant for a day."

Rachel shook her head. "No way."

"Yes way." Ginger grinned. And she could find out if Rachel was interested in being a manager.

"Knock, knock." Lillian poked her head into the dining hall from the kitchen.

"Come join the party." Ginger got up and poured a cup of coffee for herself and Megan. "Want some?" She poured the rest of the pot into a carafe and grabbed a mug for Lillian. "Forgot the cream." She went back to the kitchen and grabbed a container of half and half, Betsy's preferred addition to her coffee. Their friend would be joining them soon.

Lillian filled her mug halfway with coffee then the rest of the way with creamer and a drizzle of honey. Stirring the concoction, she sighed.

Ginger raised an eyebrow. "A bit of coffee with your creamer?"

"What can I say? I have refined tastes." She held it with her pinky extended and took a sip, an aristocratic tilt to her eyebrow.

Ginger, Megan, and Rachel laughed at their friend's theatrics.

"Do you want to know what I found out?" Lillian wrapped her hands around her mug.

"Do tell." Ginger started to get up. "You can stay. Might as well get all the scoop."

Rachel smiled. "I'd like that." She sat back down.

Lillian leaned forward. "I checked the information on the tag. A small business located near Mountain Home handmade these boxes shortly before the war. They went out of business before the war was over. You'll probably need to visit the town to dig up any more information. I was thinking town hall. Or maybe family of the owners still live there."

"We were just planning a trip to Mountain Home anyway. Megan found out that's where the flea market is located where Beth purchased the box. I can make both stops on the same trip." Ginger's mouth lifted in a grin.

"One more piece of the puzzle."

Ginger took a sip of her coffee then pulled her list out of her pocket and marked off Lillian's task and Megan's task.

"Looks like after that, the rest is up to me. Rachel, want to help dig around in my attic?"

"Absolutely." The young woman nodded.

"Hey, girlfriends. Getting started without me?" Betsy sauntered up to the table and ran her finger down the list. "Gotta get Walter out of the house for a while, so you can go snooping in his room?"

"Good thing he's been spending so much time working on that plane." Lillian poured more cream into her mug.

Betsy made a face at Lillian. "Let me show you how it's done." She grabbed a mug, poured more sugar in the bottom than any grown woman ought to put in her coffee, then filled it to the top with black brew. "Glad I wasn't born in the South. I hate tea. I would surely be the odd one out with my sweet java. Oh, now there's an idea. Betsy's Sweet Java Shop." She splayed her hand out in front of her as though she were painting an image in the air.

Ginger rolled her eyes. Ever since Betsy's husband had died, she'd been living on what he had left in his bank account and investments, which apparently had been quite substantial. But Betsy was determined to come up with an idea to give her life purpose. A new one rolled off her about every week or so. One of these days, one might stick.

"Well? Think I could make a go of it in Preston Hill?"

Ginger laughed. "Girlfriend, when you finally stick with an idea, I have no doubt you'll make a go of it."

CHAPTER TWENTY-THREE

Ginger slipped out of the house as pink tinged the horizon, promising a beautiful spring day. She looked forward to escaping the café while she explored Mountain Home, two hours away near the Nebraska-Colorado border. She also hoped that, as Rachel ran the café for a day, she would discover that she had what it took. Ginger inhaled a breath of spring air. This was going to be a good day.

Tossing her purse onto the seat beside her, she climbed in and turned the key. Nothing. She got out and slammed the car door. Today of all days.

"What's got you all riled up?" Grandpa stood at the edge of the drive, watching her frustrations in action.

"The car won't start, and I was planning on going on an Irene research trip." She swept her hand toward the car. "Care to take a look?"

"Could be the battery. Or the alternator. Either one takes time. Why don't you call that Betsy girl to give you a ride?"

"She has plans with George."

"What about Megan?"

"Don't you think I've been through the list, Grandpa?"

The back door to the café bumped against the wall as Mike came outside. "Walter, you ready for that chess game?"

Grandpa looked back and forth between Ginger and Mike. "Nah. Think I'll go for a walk. Maybe Ginger will play chess with you. Ha."

"What was that about?" Mike rested against the hood of the car.

"Who knows?"

"You're a bit testy."

Ginger opened the car and reached in for her purse. "I was planning on taking a day trip to do some research for Grandpa's quest, only my car won't start. Grandpa said it's either the battery or the alternator. But he's not going to take the time to figure it out. None of my friends are open to drive me today, so I guess I'll stick around and work." She slammed the car door shut. "I don't even know why I'm getting so upset."

"Sometimes little things wear us down without us realizing it. You've had a lot going on with Walter. Maybe you needed a day away."

She slung her purse over her shoulder. "It's not happening now."

"If you don't mind my company, I could take you."

"I don't want you using up your day off to take me on a road trip."

"I hadn't made any plans other than to start the day with Walter. And he let me off the hook."

Ginger's frustrations slipped away. "If you're sure."

"We'll have to go get my SUV."

"Lead the way."

Mike pulled out of town headed west. Avoiding the state highway, they followed a route that wound its way toward Mountain Home. They watched the passing scenery and settled into a comfortable silence. Ginger rolled her window down and listened to the serenade of the birds. This was going to be better than doing all the driving herself. A deep sigh escaped as she relaxed for the first time in ages. Today would feed her soul regardless of what she found.

Thoughts of Grandpa and what the future held swirled in her mind. Thinking about it right now couldn't change anything. But enjoying the day would be taking care of herself. She set all the unknowns aside and gazed out the side window.

The light of the rising sun reflected off her side view mirror. The colors of the sky were changing dramatically from moment to moment as full light lit her view. From shadows to brilliance, the display of the sunrise thrilled her heart. She rarely had time to watch one of her favorite things anymore. By this time of day, she was typically full scale into her work at the café.

Mike slowed as they passed several deer on the side of the road. They crested a hill and she gasped at the view in front of them. Able to see for miles, she watched as sunlight danced from behind them and overtook the shadows in front of them.

"This is beautiful." Mike looked to his right and left.

Ginger nodded. "Ever been this way?"

Mike shook her head. "I've been missing out."

"You aren't the only one." Ginger glanced at her traveling partner. "How is Josh doing working on the plane?"

"He's a natural with the mechanical stuff. He really likes working with Walter. He's good for Josh."

"It's a two-way street. Grandpa has a spring in his step since they started working together on the plane." Ginger pulled a pack of gum out of her purse and offered a piece to Mike before grabbing a piece for herself.

"Greg said Walter's working with Josh has been a blessing. They haven't met many people willing to engage with him. Greg says it's his sullen attitude. But I can't blame him. He's lost a lot in his lifetime." Mike checked his rearview as someone came up on his bumper then passed them.

"Yeah, I can't imagine after the sudden death of parents being thrown in with strangers and then to be separated from your brother and not be able to reconnect with him." Ginger understood the pain of losing a parent. But both at the same time?

"I'm glad the Jordans were able to offer him a stable, loving home.

And that they're considering taking in his brother, too."

"If they can locate him. Seems he ran away from his last home."

"They'll find him. How's Walter doing? He's called off the last couple chess games I set up with him."

"He has good days and bad. I see him drawing back from things that frustrate him." She sighed. Her mind drifted to his insistence on finding Irene. "Tell me something."

"Go ahead."

"Is it really good to encourage Grandpa's obsession with the past?"

"You really want my thoughts? I don't want to start World War III."

"I'll try to keep the hostility down."

Mike thumbed the wheel as though in thought. "Walter's insistence on finding Irene is based on love, not on fear like some people base their choices on."

She stiffened as though he had painted a bullseye on her forehead. She knew she held back out of fear. Remembering her promise, she measured her words. "But still, he seems as stuck as someone who is fearful."

He thumbed the steering wheel as though in thought. "There's a difference. When we hold on to something out of love, it gives us hope and moves us forward. But when, out of fear, we hold on to regrets, hurts, and the pain of loss, it holds us back and shackles us to all our yesterdays."

Ginger mulled that over a bit, trying not to overreact. There was uncomfortable truth to what he said. A truth she didn't want to face right now. "Grandpa's been talking about getting a dog ever since we ran into Beth and Mustard at the park. I'm not sure that I'm up to having one more thing to take care of." Ginger had never had a dog. The idea of one more body in the house to maneuver around made her feel crowded, but if a dog helped Grandpa, she wouldn't argue.

"A lot of older people find having a dog to be helpful. Holler if you need help."

They rode in silence for a few miles before Mike glanced down at the fuel gauge. "I knew I should have filled up before we left Preston Hill." He pulled off the main road into a small town about the size of a gnat on a map and stopped at the local gas station, which didn't look open yet. "There's a diner down the street. We could grab a cup of coffee while we wait."

Ginger laughed. "I was so happy to be free from the café for a day I completely forgot my caffeine infusion this morning. I was starting to feel the need."

Mike parked in front of the diner. They got out and strolled around the building a couple times to stretch their legs before going inside.

The bell above the door jingled a welcome. A short chat with the waitress and a phone call opened the gas station within minutes. Small-town charm at its best. Coffee to go and a full tank saw them on their way with only an hour left to their stopping point. Excitement jittered inside Ginger. Perhaps today she would discover a vital clue to the whereabouts of Grandpa's wife to help him find closure. She hoped, for his sake, that Irene was still alive and waited for him.

"Can I run something past you? It's about the café." Ginger turned in her seat slightly so she could see Mike.

"Shoot."

"I'm thinking about asking Rachel to be the manager at the Jukebox."

"She would be good. Do you have concerns?"

"I'm not sure that I can afford to."

"I can't speak to the financial part of whether you can afford to pay her more without looking at your financials, but it makes sense. What do you see as the benefits of hiring her as your manager?"

"Grandpa is taking up more of my time now, and she's good at what she does. She has great ideas for improving things and she's willing to jump in and do what's needed."

"Sounds like she's already a benefit to the café. Can you afford not to promote her to manager?"

"I've never thought about it from that angle. I guess I have more to consider. I wish we could find another waitress who would stay. Bridgette started a couple days ago, but that means both are working every day, and we all need a break."

"Have you thought about closing during the lulls?"

"Not on a regular basis. But that might work. Thanks."

They settled into a comfortable silence as they covered the last portion of the drive. A couple miles outside of town Mike pointed at a sign advertising the flea market. "Explain to me what we're looking for in Mountain Home."

"Irene and Grandpa lived there when they first got married. His parents lived in town as well. But what I want to research today is this jewelry box that we found. Beth, the gal who runs the local flea market outside of Preston Hill, purchased it from the Mountain Home Flea Market. When we called, we couldn't get any answers. We're going to see if the company that made them is still around as well as talk to the manager of the market. Maybe they can point us to the vendor and the vendor will know something about the box." Ginger pulled up the picture of the tag on the bottom of the jewelry box. "I figured we could stop by the market and town hall."

"Which stop first?" Mike looked over at her.

Ginger checked the website for the flea market on her phone. "The flea market opens at Ten. Town Hall opens at nine."

"Town Hall it is."

The musty smell of historic buildings layered with the dust of new construction tickled Ginger's nose. Navigating around work in progress, she and Mike followed the signs to the county records office.

"May I help you?" The woman's name tag read "Stacy."

Her nasal tone didn't fit with the woman's professional appearance. Ginger smothered a chuckle. "We're looking for any information you might have on The Hidden Treasure Company."

"It was such a shame what happened to that man. I heard all about it from my grandparents. They would have none of it."

Ginger wrinkled her brow. "What happened?"

"The Japanese internment after Pearl Harbor." The woman tapped her pen on the desk. "Why do you need the information?" Suspicion spanned her facial features.

"My grandfather bought a jewelry box made by The Hidden Treasure Company for my grandmother around 1939."

"And...?"

"When my grandfather came back from the war, his wife was gone. The box is the only clue as to her whereabouts."

"You're just now looking into it?"

"My grandpa only recently let me in on his quandary." Frustrated with the woman's attitude, Ginger tried to keep her voice calm.

Mike spoke up. "If you can't help us, could you point us to someone who can?"

The woman grimaced for a moment, as though deep in thought, then her face relaxed. "How long are you in town?"

"Till this afternoon."

"Leave your phone number and give me a couple hours. I'll call you."

Ginger wrote her number down and handed it to the woman. "This is important."

"I can tell."

Ginger doubted anything would come of this lead. At least she could tell Grandpa she'd tried.

Heading out the door with Mike, she felt the weight of this project.

Lord, lead me to answers. Grandpa has grieved enough over the unknown.

As they pulled up in front of the Mountain Home Flea Market, Ginger was surprised at the hum of activity around the place. "I envisioned something more along the lines of what we have back home. But this is going to be like looking for a needle in a haystack."

"Maybe the office can help us." Mike got out of the truck and headed toward the entrance.

Ginger followed him to the office. The man sitting at the desk motioned them in. "We have enough vendors for the month, but we have a stall opening up for June. How much space do you need?"

"We're not vendors," Mike answered before Ginger could open her mouth.

The man set his pen down and rose from his chair. "What can I do for you?"

"We're hoping to find out which vendor an item was purchased from. I can show you a picture." Ginger pulled out her phone.

"My receptionist isn't in. She keeps all the records. I would be lost trying to help you figure it out."

Ginger relaxed her posture. "I should have known this would be another dead end."

"Maybe you would remember something if you looked at the item." Mike took Ginger's phone and handed it to the man.

The manager examined the picture. "Yeah. As a matter of fact. Only because the guy had a couple boxes like that, and I bought one of them for my wife. Hold on, I'll get you his contact info. His name's Pete. He travels around the country every summer visiting other flea markets. May have already pulled out of town for this year. Usually back late summer."

Ginger groaned.

Mike placed a hand on Ginger's back. "Don't give up hope yet."

"You're right. It's so frustrating."

"Here you go." He handed them a piece of paper. "If you follow the highway out of town toward the east, it should be about ten miles out. Turn north at the forked tree, then he's about a quarter mile down the road on the right."

Ginger took the address and thanked him. Two possible leads. Better than what they came with.

Pointing the car east, they headed out of town. When they arrived at Pete's cabin, the place looked all locked up and knocking brought no one to the door. A quick walk around the house proved that at the very least no one was home for the moment, if not completely gone for the season.

Mike scribbled a note and left it on the door. "Maybe he's at the store."

"You're right. I should be more optimistic."

"I didn't say a thing."

"You didn't have to. Come on. Might as well stop at the diner for some lunch before we head back to Town Hall."

Stacy looked up as Ginger and Megan entered the outer office of the county records department. "I was going to call you."

"Do you have information for me?"

"No. And yes. Or at least a maybe. Pull up a chair. I'm going to take my lunch break while we visit." She grabbed an insulated bag and joined them in the waiting area. "The Hidden Treasure Company closed up shop when the Japanese internments happened—the owner being of Japanese descent. Chances are your grandpa purchased one of the last of the jewelry boxes they made."

"Where does that leave me?"

Stacy held up a finger as she finished chewing a bite of her sandwich. "The great-grandson of the original owner still lives in town."

"Is he open to us asking a few questions?"

"He's gone till August."

"Name doesn't happen to be Pete, does it?"

"Guess you've been to the flea market."

"And to his house."

"I talked to him by phone. He asked for your email address and the name of the person who originally purchased the box. Said he would do some digging and get you back to you."

"That would be wonderful." Ginger jotted down her email and handed it to Stacy. "You wouldn't know of any families by the name of Gipson who used to live here, would you?"

"My grandparents used to talk about some Gipsons a long time ago. Said they had the cutest granddaughter." Sandy threw her sandwich wrappings in the trash can.

"If it's the same family, that would have been my mother. Do you think they would mind answering a few questions?"

"I'm sure they would answer your questions and more if they were still alive. I'm sorry. I seem to have only dead ends to offer you."

Ginger rose and gathered her things. "It was all a long shot. You did what you could. Thank you."

CHAPTER TWENTY-FOUR

The ringtone for Grandpa filled the SUV about half an hour away from home.

"Hope he hasn't gotten into mischief." Ginger grabbed the phone out of the console between the seats and clicked on speaker phone. "What's up?"

"Hello to you, too."

"Grandpa."

"Fine. How did your trip go?"

"Grandpa, what do you need?" He didn't usually beat around the bush.

"What? You think I'm forgetful? Want to put me in that home now?"

"Grandpa."

"It's Rachel."

"What about Rachel?" Ginger shook her head at Mike's inquiring look.

"She's bossy. I don't like her."

Ginger, hard pressed to hold back a laugh, met Mike's glance. By all appearances, he was having the same difficulty.

"I want you to fire her." The ire in his voice rose with each syllable.

"No."

"Ginger."

"I'm not going to have this conversation now. I'll be home soon."

"I hope so, 'cause we're in a standoff."

Ginger glanced at the clock. "I'll see you in twenty-five." She disconnected the call.

"Sounds ominous. What do you think is going on?"

"Not sure. Sounds like they're both riled. If he makes Rachel leave, I think I'll sell the café."

"Would you really do that? It's been in your family for so long." Mike turned on his blinker and changed lanes.

"If I can't get help to run it, then what else can I do?" Ginger settled into an uneasy silence, aware of the glances Mike threw her way. What could have gotten Rachel so riled it landed her in a standoff with Grandpa?

"You want me to come in with you when we get there?"

"Thanks, but I better handle this myself."

"It's about time you got here." Grandpa accused Ginger from where he sat with his buddies. Rachel sat at the counter, irritation in her eyes.

"Am I going to have to separate you two?" Ginger put her fists on her hips.

"It's me or her."

Ginger looked at Rachel. "What about you?"

She motioned at Grandpa. "Something has to change."

"Why you little whippersnapper. You come in here and try and change everything. I tell you there are certain things we have always done, and I am not going to change for the likes of you."

"I'm not trying to change everything."

"If I give you half a chance—"

"Grandpa." Ginger stared at the man she had spent her whole life with and thought she knew better than this. "What is so important there can't be a bit of bending?"

"Just...stuff." Grandpa glared at Rachel.

"Rachel?"

"I'm trying to get everything right while you're gone...show you I can do this."

"Well, you messed up." Grandpa thumped his cane.

"Please. One of you tell me exactly what happened." Ginger waited, looking back and forth between the two.

Rachel let out a deep sigh. "I asked him and the boys to hang out somewhere else so I could clean up. But he's been in a bad mood all day."

Ginger took a deep breath. "Grandpa, would it have been so hard to hang out at the house?"

"Are you taking her side?"

"Maybe I am. I need help. If that means a few changes, would that be so bad?"

"You're choosing her?"

Ginger groaned. "Grandpa. Quit. Being. So. Stubborn."

He narrowed his eyes at Ginger but kept his mouth shut.

Ginger turned to Rachel. "I want to offer you the job of manager."

Grandpa huffed behind her back. Rachel opened her mouth then shut it.

"What would it take to convince you to consider it?"

Rachel motioned toward Grandpa. "This would have to be figured out."

"Figure me out of the picture, you mean."

"Grandpa. I'm tired. I can't keep going at this pace. I'm afraid things will change one way or another, whether either of us wants them to or not. Don't you get it? I am not choosing her. I am choosing us."

Grandpa hesitated a moment before he dropped his arms to his sides. "I'm sorry."

"Rachel?" Ginger looked in the young woman's direction.

"I really like it here. But...I'm not sure."

"I know we need to work out details. Think about it?"

"I can do that." Rachel grabbed her purse. "Everything is taken care of for the night except for them." Rachel lifted her chin toward Grandpa and his friends. "The new waitress, Bridgette, did great. I'll see you tomorrow."

After she had gone, Ginger locked the front door behind her. Turning back to Grandpa and his buddies, she sighed. She was done fighting for the night. "Lock up when you're done. I'm headed to the house."

CHAPTER TWENTY-FIVE

"What are you taking so long for?" Grandpa stood outside the car waiting for Ginger to get out.

"You sure are anxious to get a new dog."

"Maybe. Maybe not." He marched ahead of her to the entrance of the humane society. The trip into the city had been pleasant. He had chatted about Josh and the airplane repair the whole way. But in the minutes since they'd arrived, his tension level had risen.

Ginger hoped adding a dog to their family would decrease stress, not increase it. The process of finding a dog had certainly increased it.

Picking up her pace, she joined him as he strolled around the kennels. He stopped to look at a couple different dogs but would shrug and move on. A few enclosures before the last one, Grandpa froze in front of the dog inside.

A golden retriever sat on its haunches staring through the wire gate at Grandpa. It put its paw out and touched the wire.

"Well, I'll be." He looked over at his granddaughter. "Looks like my old dog I had as a kid." He poked a finger through the wire and scratched the side of the dog's head.

Ginger glanced at the page of information about the dog hanging nearby. A two-year-old, purebred golden retriever. "Want me to ask someone about us visiting with...Rabbit?"

Grandpa laughed. "Who names a dog Rabbit?"

"Must be a story in there somewhere. I'll go find someone to help us."

"I'll wait right here, and if anyone else looks interested, I'll tell them we're taking him home." Grandpa took up his post standing guard.

She raised an eyebrow.

"Don't look at me that way. This is the one I want."

A few minutes later, the form filled out, she and Grandpa were directed to one of the visiting rooms and Rabbit joined them. He went straight to Grandpa and put his paw up on Grandpa's knee. He stroked the dog's head, and the tension that had been palpable only moments ago faded.

After a nice visit with Rabbit, Ginger and Grandpa loaded him up along with all the supplies they could get at the humane society for the dog's upkeep. The rest they would have to buy at a pet store.

Ginger riffled through the piles of papers Grandpa had given her about Irene. She knew there was a marriage license in there somewhere. Lillian had suggested they look Irene up using her maiden name. They were supposed to meet at the library this afternoon. It was worth a try.

"Here it is." She pulled it out from between the other papers and found a plastic sleeve to put it in. Once she made a copy at the library, she could leave the original at home.

Ginger walked to the library to enjoy the fresh air. She was inside way too much. Passing through Center Square Park, she waved at Grandpa. He had Rabbit off the leash and was tossing a ball for him. Ginger had worried the dog would tangle him up with the leash but wasn't sure off the leash was any better. She chose to ignore the situation. Grandpa was a grown man. At least he was getting that exercise the doctor had recommended.

Visiting the library took her back to the weekly trips with her mom to check out books. She enjoyed the older libraries that came with so many memories brought to life with a mere sniff.

She stopped at the front desk and made a copy of Grandpa's marriage license and then took the roundabout way to the reading room where Lillian had said to meet her. Mike sat at one of the tables with his Bible and notes spread out across it. He looked up as she drew closer.

"Aren't you a sight for sore eyes." He stood and stretched, reaching his arms up over his head.

"What brings you to the library?"

"Studying for the sermon on Sunday and needed a change of scenery. I like running into people. There are days it's too quiet at the church building. What are you up to?"

She held up the marriage license. "More research."

"Hope it goes well. What happened with Rachel and Grandpa?"

"Rachel needed to clean up, and Grandpa didn't want to move. They're ignoring each other."

"Better than fighting."

"I suppose." Ginger blew out a pent-up breath.

"What's wrong?" He motioned to the chair across from him. "Want to sit?"

She shook her head. "Sometimes I imagine what it would be like without the Jukebox."

"That bad?"

"With Rachel not sure whether she wants to take the manager position, I feel the pressure of keeping everything together on my own. I feel like that scene in *Spiderman* where he's trying to hold the two halves of that ferry together with his web."

"You do have friends." Mike smiled. "Anything I can do?"

"What you're already doing. Keep playing chess with Grandpa. Keep an eye on him. Be his friend. Sometimes I worry about him being out and about. What if something happened to him?"

"He's got a new dog now, right?"

"Rabbit."

Mike busted out with a chuckle then covered his mouth when a couple people looked his way. "Where did he get a name like that?"

"He came with it. Somehow it fits." Ginger waved at Lillian. "There's my research assistant. See you later."

Lillian looked over the marriage license. "Her maiden name is Hutton and her middle name is Grace." She typed in a web address, then waited while the blue circle swirled. "We're going to the website for the county public records for where she and Walter were married. Fortunately for you, I have a friend who does a lot of genealogy research. She's letting me use her account for this. Some stuff is free, some you need an account for."

Once the website came up, she navigated to the right page and typed several combinations of Irene's first, middle, maiden, and married names. Nothing of interest came up. "Drats."

Ginger started to get up then sat back down. "One other thought. What if Irene put an ad in a paper to try and find Grandpa?"

"That's a good angle." Lillian began typing and clicking. After about half an hour, she sat back in her chair. "I can't find anything. It looks like there were a couple small papers. They've closed shop since then. Sorry."

Ginger shrugged. "It was just an idea. I appreciate your looking into it." She hugged Lillian before heading back the way she came. Mike was already gone. Disappointed, she quickened her step. She needed to get back to the café before the rush. Bridgette was scheduled with Rachel, but Ginger was still a bit gun shy about waitresses who might choose to quit.

CHAPTER TWENTY-SIX

Ginger opened the shades in the living room and looked across the alley at the café. Could she really sell it? She'd told Mike on the trip back from Mountain Home that she might be driven to by Grandpa. She returned to her kitchen and poured a cup of coffee. Hopefully Grandpa would come to understand that Rachel wasn't out to get him. Riffling through the stack of mail on the kitchen table, she paused on the envelope from the bank. The mortgage was due next week. Time to crunch the numbers once again. *Lord, I know You provide what we need, but I'm...I'm tired of feeling like I'm at the edge of a cliff with finances all the time. Help me to trust You.*

Sighing, she pulled a carton of eggs from the fridge. "Grandpa?"

Silence replied.

Concerned, Ginger hurried down the hall and knocked on his door. After a brief wait, she cracked the door. Bed was made. Everything shipshape except for a box sitting on the foot of his bed, opened with its contents jumbled, some items spilled over the side as if Grandpa had been searching for something. Not the norm for Grandpa to leave things in disarray. Curious, she entered his domain.

Listening for the front door to open, she looked over the scattered items. A brooch, a lock of hair in an envelope, and several other odds and ends. Some of Irene's things he had kept for himself. Simple things to remind him of the love they had shared. Ginger picked up a small stack of letters tied with a ribbon and laid to the side. No return address, but the handwriting appeared feminine.

Careful not to untie the ribbon, she pulled one letter out from the stack. Did she dare read it? Grandpa would have a fit, but it might contain clues.

Deciding to take a chance, she glanced out the window to ensure a surprise arrival wasn't imminent, and then settled into the wingback chair nestled into the corner of his room. She slipped the paper from its envelope and unfolded another place and time. The script looked rushed. The message short.

> *My Dearest Walter,*
>
> *I don't want to leave, but my parents insist it isn't safe to stay. They won't tell me where we're going, but somewhere we can live without fear of being taken from our homes.*
>
> *I love you so much and always will. There will never be anyone else for me. Like we said in our vows, God brought us together and no one can tear us apart.*
>
> *I don't know what the next few days, months or years will hold. How long can this war last? I pray it will end tomorrow. But I will make it back to you. No matter what it takes. I promise. Please don't give up on me no matter how long it takes.*
>
> *Take care of Patricia. Never let her forget how much I love her. Your parents were at least willing to watch out for her.*
>
> *Forever loving,*
> *Always loved,*
> *Your beloved Irene*

Ginger swiped a tear running down her face. The loss Grandpa must feel. To come back from the war to find your wife gone. The wife you loved beyond life itself. She wished she could have met her grandmother. She considered the fear the Japanese faced. The fear that drove America to take people from their homes and intern them in camps because of their descent. It was an awful time in their country. Grandpa had looked for Irene in those camps but hadn't found anything. She needed to ask Grandpa if he had looked in locations more accepting to those of Japanese descent.

She returned the letter to the envelope and slipped it back into its ribboned home, and then pulled out another one. Drifting back into the past, she opened the next letter.

My dearest husband,

I love you beyond life itself. If it weren't for the hope I have of returning to your arms, to our daughter, and to our home, I would hide in a room and give up.

My parents refuse to bring me back. Their reasons make no sense, so I will not go into them now. But I have a plan. I am working and, with each paycheck, I put away every penny I can afford to. When I have enough, I will come to you.

Don't give up on me. I am counting the days until I can be with you again. You are never far from my thoughts.

Forever loving,
Always loved,
Your beloved Irene

Ginger stared at the page in front of her. Why didn't Irene tell Walter where she was? It didn't make sense. She exchanged the second letter for the last one in the stack.

My loving Walter,

How can I explain to you everything that is keeping me from you? I write in secret, hoping my parents won't discover the letters. I weep every night over the emptiness in my arms. Soon my love. I promise. Soon.

Forever loving,

Always loved,

Your beloved Irene

So many promises, then nothing. What happened?

She tucked the last letter with the others, then returned them to the box and exited the room. More determined than ever to find answers for Grandpa, she put away the eggs before leaving the house.

The smell of bacon in the café kitchen reminded her that she should have eaten at home. "Good morning, Harry."

He nodded her way as he filled up another plate with eggs, hash browns, and bacon and slid it onto the pass-through window. "Had breakfast yet?"

"I was distracted."

"Got something new in mind. Want a give it a go?"

"I'm game. Gotta check on the dining hall first." She pushed through the swinging doors. Grandpa and his crew were gone. She supposed they were working on the plane. Mike was heading out the door. Bridgette served a table on one side of the dining hall, and Rachel served on the other side. Tables were full and the place hummed with the sounds of pleased customers. She made eye-contact with Rachel, who gave her a thumbs up. Satisfied, Ginger headed back to the office to work on the books.

"Don't forget your food." Harry held out a plate of delicious smells.

"What do you call this?"

"No, you don't. No hints."

"Fine." Ginger accepted the offered food and set it on the counter. A steak wrapped in bacon sat on one third of the plate. A pile of glazed brussel sprouts mixed with bits of bacon sat next to the steak. Baby potatoes topped with onion rings rounded out the plate. The fragrance of blended spices invited her to eat. Grabbing a knife and fork, she took a bite of steak. Her eyes widened with pleasure. The brussel sprouts had a sweetness about them with a hint of tart and the potatoes were perfectly tender. "Wow. It's all delicious."

Harry beamed with pride.

"Is this deer? What is that seasoning did you use?"

"I'll give you the deer part, but not a chance on the seasoning."

Ginger rolled her eyes. "It's my restaurant."

"It's my recipe. Trust me."

Ginger chuckled. They went around about this every time he came up with a new dish. "Have it your way. At least give me a name."

He turned back to his duties. "Harry's Special Number Sixteen."

"Ha. Ha." She waved and headed to her office. She sat down in her chair and savored a few bites of Harry's special, then pushed it aside and started to work on the financials.

A few hours later, Ginger pushed back from the computer, stretched, and glanced at the clock. "That's enough for today." She startled when someone knocked on the door.

"Does that mean you'll join me for lunch?" Mike leaned against the doorframe. "Missed visiting over morning coffee."

Ginger glanced at the now-cold dish sitting on the edge of the desk. Her stomach growled. "I guess that's a yes. Let's tell Harry what we want then grab a table."

"Actually..." He held up a grocery bag. "I was hoping you would go on a picnic with me."

"I should probably stick around in case they need me."

"Sunshine. Gentle breeze. Seventy-five degrees. Perfect weather for a picnic."

"You're making this hard, aren't you?"

"I hope."

"Let me check with Rachel first. Make sure she's good with it."

"I took the liberty. She's fine. She said to get you out of here."

"She did, did she?"

"I'll be waiting in the car."

"But—"

Mike turned on his heel and headed toward the back door of the kitchen.

Ginger closed her eyes and took a deep breath. She really could use some fresh air. She grabbed her purse then paused. It might send the wrong idea, though. She set her purse down.

"Go on the picnic." Rachel stood in the doorway. "Didn't you say you needed a break?"

"But I can't just leave."

"You want a break, but only when it comes the way you think it should?"

Was that what she was doing? Turning away the very thing she asked for?

"Don't worry. I have it covered." Rachel gave Ginger a hug. "Now scoot."

"Fine. I'll see you later." Ginger paused halfway to the back door and glanced back. "Thank you."

"Go. Have some fun."

Ginger hurried out and climbed into the cab of the truck with Mike. "Where we headed?"

"Got the perfect spot. Sit back and enjoy the ride."

Ginger rolled down the window. It was nice letting someone else do the driving and the thinking for a bit. And she knew Rachel would take good care of the café.

"How have things been going at the Jukebox?"

Ginger looked over at Mike. "Besides Rachel and Grandpa going after it toe to toe?"

"Have they worked it out yet?"

"Nope." Ginger pressed her lips together.

"Sounds like things might be a bit overwhelming this week."

"To some degree. I mean, I'm getting things done, but..." Ginger lowered her intensity before she sounded like a whiner. "I don't know."

"What's your biggest concern?"

She shrugged. "It's the same thing, and it never ends. I'm worried about Grandpa and all of the what-ifs coming in the next several years."

"You're spending a lot of energy on things that may or may not materialize."

She sighed. "You're right. I need to get my mind off of the negative. There are still things to be thankful for."

"Is there anything I can do to help?"

"This helps. Getting me away from the stress."

About half an hour north of Preston Hill, Mike turned down a gravel road. "Not much farther. Hey, how's Rabbit?"

"Every time I say his name, I laugh. Grandpa seems more content, and he takes Rabbit with him everywhere. I guess I can put up with a strange name." She focused on a sign they passed. "Where are we? I haven't even been paying attention."

Mike grinned. "You'll see." He followed a bend in the road and a view of the river stretched out in front of them.

"Is this Maggie and Millie's land?"

Mike nodded. "I fish out here from time to time and found a spot along the bank perfect for a picnic." He pulled to a stop along the side of the road.

"It's lovely. It's been ages since I've been out this way."

"Up for a walk?"

"You bet." She opened the door and hopped out. He came around the side with the paper bag in one hand and a blanket thrown over his shoulder. "Let's go." He held out his hand.

Ginger hesitated. She knew in her soul that taking his hand would accelerate the changes between her and Mike. She knelt and tied her shoes. She felt rather than saw the moment he dropped his offer. A feeling of loss grabbed her heart.

"Ready." She followed him down a well-worn path.

Closer to the river past a grove of trees, he handed her the basket and blanket while he scrambled up some rocks and stood above her. "The rock plateaus up here and there's an incredible view down to the river. Perfect place to spread out the blanket. He reached down and took the food and blanket from her. After setting them aside, he watched her try to navigate the terrain and find a good hand hold to pull herself up. "You got this?"

She shaded her eyes and looked up at him. "Funny. You going to help me or have a picnic by yourself?"

He lay down, and reached over the edge. "Grab hold."

With no alternative than to take his hand this time, she attempted to ignore the feel of her hand in his. She held tight and began to scramble up to the ledge. Distracted, she slipped, and he tightened his grip. After what seemed like an eternity, with lots of hanging on and scrambling, she pulled herself onto the ledge. "I think you enjoyed that."

He laughed. Tugging her by the hand, he led her to the other side of the rock where no trees blocked their view. "Isn't it beautiful?"

She gasped at the view of the water running past. Not a large river, it still awed her with its ability to cut through the land. "Thank you for bringing me here." She looked up into his eyes. The sensation of their hands together surprised her with its rightness.

"Ginger…"

She stepped back, and he allowed her hand to drop. "Mike…"

Disappointment filled his eyes. "Let's enjoy the day."

"Let's eat." Grabbing the blanket, she spread it near the edge of their table. They dangled their feet over the edge as Mike divided the Reuben sandwiches and fruit he had brought. Comfortable silence cocooned them as they ate and enjoyed the view.

"This is what I needed. Thank you."

Mike drew his legs up onto the rock and wrapped his arms loosely around his knees. Ginger studied him out of the corner of her eye. He looked as if he had something to say.

He got up and dusted off his pants and headed toward the left where the rock sloped down toward the river. "Come on." He waited for her to catch up then headed closer to the water. He picked up some rocks and started skipping them across the river.

Ginger picked up her own handful. Her first rock skipped five times. "Beat that."

He laughed. "I'll have to find the perfect rock." He searched the ground, then finally picked up a couple flat ones. He went back to the edge of the water, took aim, and let his rock fly. "Six skips. Beat that."

Back and forth they challenged each other till Ginger's face muscles grew tired from laughing and her arm grew weary from throwing. "I give. You win." She held up her hand for a high five.

He slapped her hand, then held on. His tone turned serious. "I need to talk."

Ginger swallowed. "About?"

"Let's go sit." He let go of her hand and led the way back to their rock table.

She sat beside him and waited.

"You remember when I had to figure a few things out?"

She nodded. Those were a couple lonely days.

He looked out over the river, then back to her. "I needed to think about us."

"Oh."

"Even though it was only a couple days that I sort of avoided you, I missed our talks. I missed your laughter. I missed your smile. I even missed how you get frustrated sometimes." He grinned. "I know that doesn't make sense, but I missed everything about you."

She looked down at her lap. "I missed you, too."

He reached over and lifted her chin. "Can there be an us?"

"How do I invest in us when I'm so depleted with the rest of life?" She recalled Peggy's words at the retirement home, that the right relationship would be a good thing. She wasn't sure she believed that.

"We've been investing in our friendship all these years. Has that felt like a burden?"

"Of course not." She found strength in his friendship.

"All I'm asking is that you open your heart for there to be more than friendship between us."

"I don't want to lose your friendship, Mike."

He smiled. "You won't."

"How can you be sure? I mean, if things go sideways between us...lesser things have ruined friendships."

Mike rested his arms on top of his knees. "Do you remember that Christmas Eve when I asked you out on that first date?"

"How could I forget?"

"That night I decided that I would wait as long as it took to win your heart."

She tilted her head. "You never told me that."

"How would that have gone over?"

"True. So, what about all those dates you went on?"

He laughed. "You think I would have had any peace from the ladies at church if I hadn't gone out with their choices? Besides, for a while,

I got to thinking maybe I was wrong, so I went on a few dates. Found out I wasn't wrong. Ginger, I can't ignore this anymore."

"What if I disappoint you or you don't like the me you get to know once I let my guard down?"

Mike ran a hand through his hair. "I know that, with everything going on in your life right now, on one level this doesn't even make sense. I know there will be moments when we'll both mess up. I can't promise I won't ever be hurt, offended, or disappointed. I can't promise I won't ever hurt, offend, or disappoint you. But I can promise to work it through. I'm not going to run away." He took her hands in his. "Give us a chance?"

"I think...I think I can work on being open. Nothing formal?"

He shook his head. "Let's take it as it comes for now."

"I don't want everyone to be in our business about this."

"Send them my way if they give you trouble." He held up his fists as though ready for a fight.

She laughed. "I'm not sure I'm ready, but...I'll do my best to stay open to the possibility of us."

"Thank you." He kissed the knuckles on her hand then tucked a strand of hair behind her ear. "You're beautiful when you blush."

What was she getting into?

CHAPTER TWENTY-SEVEN

The next day, Ginger met Betsy in the library before their book club meeting. "Did you find out anything from Maggie and Millie?"

"Good news, bad news."

Ginger pulled up a chair. "Out with it."

"I showed them a picture of the jewelry box. Seems they were all the rage shortly before World War II. However, lots of people bought them."

Ginger steepled her fingers under her chin. "So that box could have been anybody's."

"Was there anything about the box that made Grandpa think it was hers?"

"When I asked him, he kept saying it was hers."

Lillian breezed into the room. "Sorry I'm late. Some guy bumped into me while I was walking the dogs, and I lost my grip on the leashes. They scattered." She took a breath. "Took forever to round them up. What did I miss? Anyone read the book?"

"Not me." Betsy shook her head.

"I started it but fell asleep." Ginger tapped her finger on the table and took a deep breath. No time like the present to start cutting things. "Could we...stop trying to make it into a book club? Someday I would like to read books together, but right now, it feels like another expectation. I'm sorry, Betsy. I know you've been wanting to do this for a while." She waited for their verdict.

Betsy smiled. "You are more important than any old book club. Besides, detective work hasn't left much time for reading. Kind of fun helping you."

The three friends put their heads together to plan the next steps to find Walter's wife. Ginger hoped that letting go of the committees she was a part of at church would go this easy.

Ginger paused when she entered the dining hall. Rachel and Grandpa stood talking near the drinks counter. Glancing her way, Rachel and Walter paused. Walter nodded at Rachel and joined his crew and Josh at their table. Rachel joined Ginger next to the counter.

"Looks like you guys have made peace."

Rachel grinned. "The guys agreed to help clean up and close down at the end of the day, and I agreed they could stay as late as they wanted as long as they were out by ten-thirty."

"What else have you got up your sleeve?"

"Why do you ask?"

Ginger shrugged. Given the chuckle Rachel and Walter shared when they glanced each other's way, something was definitely going on. But if it kept the peace, she would go with that. "Does this mean you've thought about my offer?"

"I have."

"And?"

"Let's talk after the lunch rush. I'll come back to the office."

Ginger's phone notification went off, and she glanced at the screen. Distracted, she excused herself. "That'll work. I need to get this first anyway."

"Everything okay?"

"I'm sure it will be. See you in a bit." Swiping the accept button, she hurried toward the office.

Ginger disconnected the phone call to the bank. Her heart sank over the discussion with the loan officer. She felt squeezed like the sandwich generation, except her child wasn't an unruly teenager but a business on the verge of collapse. That very source of tension wasn't something to turn her back on, despite her threats to the contrary. It put food on their table and a roof over their heads. Her eyes fell on the letter in front of her, demanding she catch up on her payments or risk foreclosure.

She filled her cheeks with air and blew out slowly, attempting to calm her racing thoughts. The same thing she had done when she was abandoned by her fiancé then found out he had a ring on some other girl's finger within a month. The betrayal had sent her to a counselor as she adjusted to life in Preston Hill alone. Another breath. She eventually moved on, and like that incident, this too would pass. But when?

"Lord, I could use a bit of help." Someone cleared his throat and she startled. Swiveling her chair, she saw Mike standing at the door. Relief washed over her seconds before she felt herself close off. She couldn't burden Mike with this. Could she?

"Sounds like I stopped by at the right time. What do you need help with?"

Ginger struggled with her decision. Since the day at the river, she had avoided thinking about what could be with Mike. What she knew he wanted. She made a show of straightening her desk. And even though the idea of having help sounded alluring, her heart wanted to go the default route. Close everyone else out in typical fashion. Go hide. Eat chocolate. Then face it on her own.

Mike sat down in the chair next to the desk and held her hands. "I know you're used to being independent and have always counted on God to help you, but don't you think that one of the ways He does that is to send someone else to be His hands and feet?"

She recoiled at her audacity to refuse God's offered help through those around her. But people left people. People disappointed people.

Was that preferable to simply never knowing hope or shared strength? The truth was it wasn't preferable. She wanted to hope. She gripped his hand as though, if she hung on tight enough, he wouldn't let her slip.

He turned her face until their eyes met. Cupping her cheek, he caressed her skin with his thumb. "Let me help you. This is a part of being open to 'us.'"

"Why are you so patient with me when I keep pushing you away?"

"Let's see. You feed me delicious chocolate concoctions, straighten me out when I need it, you're fun..."

Ginger laughed. "Fine, I get the message. I'm new to letting others know what my needs are. I mean, the surface stuff—that's easy enough. 'I need volunteers for Christmas brunch' is easy. 'Betsy, I need you to help waitress.' But letting you in to see what stresses me—or that I'm stressed in the first place—or how I'm struggling emotionally, that's different. You might have to point me in the right direction."

He squeezed her hand. "I'll do better than that. I won't let go."

She remembered his strength as he pulled her up on the rock. She could trust him. "Thank—"

"Ginger?"

She looked up.

Rachel stuck her head in the door, saw the two of them sitting there, and gave them an approving look. "I can come back later."

Ginger withdrew her hand from Mike's. "Come in. Mike was offering to help me." Her face heated again when Mike grinned at her.

Rachel looked back and forth between Ginger and Mike. "Give me ten minutes, and I'll be ready." She turned and hurried away.

"So, tell me what's going on."

Thankful Mike had dived right into a businesslike approach, Ginger closed the office door and handed him the letter from the bank. She watched as he opened and read it. When he looked up, she filled in the gaps of information.

"When I came back to Preston Hill after my dad died, I found out he was carrying quite a bit of debt. I took out a thirty-year mortgage on our house to pull us out. We were getting close to paying that off when, about four years ago, I took out a second mortgage on the house to make necessary repairs and updates to keep the Jukebox open. It's been tight for a few months as business has declined.

"A couple months ago, I couldn't make the payment on the second mortgage. The bank extended a three-month grace period due to our history with them since my great-grandparents first bought the place, but I'm afraid it won't make a difference. Next month is the last month of grace. I can't sell the café because that's our income, and I can't sell the house because that's where we live." She looked away. "This is all we have."

"Does Walter know?"

"No."

"Have I ever told you that I minored in accounting at college?"

"No."

"Would you give me access to your books so I can look things over?"

"Yes."

Taking her hand again, he bowed his head. "Lord, Ginger has a great need here. I believe You sent me to help her. Show me how. Open my eyes to options she might not have seen yet. Provide for her every need. In Jesus' name, Amen."

"Thank you." She grabbed a tissue with her free hand and wiped away the dampness on her face.

"I can come back later this afternoon to look through the numbers. Would that work?"

"I'll make it work anytime that works for you."

He grinned. "I like this."

"What?"

"Helping you. The feel of your hand in mine. Do I have to let go?"

A knock sounded on the door.

"I think that's your signal."

He let her hand slip from his. "If I must." With a grin stamped on his face, he rose and opened the door without taking his eyes off Ginger. "See you later." He nodded at Rachel as he left and strode through the kitchen to the back door.

Rachel watched him go then looked back at Ginger.

"What?"

"Nothing." Rachel smiled. "I'm ready to talk about the job if you are."

CHAPTER TWENTY-EIGHT

Ginger watched from outside the office door as Mike worked at the computer. He had been in her life for so long. Friend. Pastor. Fellow chocolate eater. She was glad he was the one had God sent to help her.

And then there was Rachel, now the manager of the restaurant. The girl had taken the job fully understanding the financial bind they were in. Willing to pitch in whatever way her skills and talents would lead to. Already, the lettering on the window had pulled in new customers. People who videoed her in the process of lettering had shared on social media, bringing in even more new faces. People passing through on their way to the city noticed the café now and stopped to eat then they talked about the food. Word was getting around, and the travel blogger hadn't even posted yet. Would Rachel's other ideas to create a website and social media accounts for the Jukebox, get new menus, and make other improvements around the place be enough to grow the business to the point where Ginger wouldn't end up losing all she had?

"Penny for your thoughts." Mike spoke without turning around.

Ginger chuckled and went into the office. "How did you know it was me?"

"That would be telling." He spun the chair around.

Ginger planted her hands on her hips.

He held his hands up. "You wore the perfume I like."

Ginger bit her lip and glanced away. She wasn't used to this type of attention. But she had to admit it felt good. "I'm hoping you'll find some solution I didn't think of."

"We could go out on a few dates."

"I'm talking about the finances."

"Oh." Mike attempted to plaster an innocent look on his face. "Is that pie slice for me?" He lifted his chin toward the plate in her hand.

She handed him the pie and sat next to the desk. "Find any windows of opportunity? With the finances."

He laughed. "I think the best opportunity you have is Rachel. She's great at marketing this place." He swiveled his chair to look at her. "Ginger, you've done a great job with the books, and you're frugal with your budget, but in a small town like ours, sometimes business shrinks."

"Unfortunately."

"I think her marketing will build that back up. And there might be a couple places we can tighten up if needed. But let's wait and see what happens in the next few weeks." Mike linked his fingers behind his head and stretched his back. "Did you hear what Walter and his crew are planning?"

"No telling."

"They want to lay a trap for the local vandal."

She raised her eyebrows. "Is that a good idea?"

"Don't worry. I'll keep an eye on them. They recruited me for the mission."

"That ought to be interesting."

"It's actually a good idea. I'm going to tell the sheriff, so the police don't get freaked out by a bunch of old men running around town at midnight."

"And maybe to provide a bit of backup?"

"I have a feeling it's some kid and that won't be necessary. Josh is going with us, too." He held up his hand, stopping the protest on the tip of her tongue. "We got permission from Megan and Greg."

"And that makes it better to take a young teenager out late at night, on a catch-the-criminal mission no less?"

He reached over and took her hand. "Trust me?"

She relaxed at his touch and nodded.

"It will be fine. This is Preston Hill, not New York City."

"I know I'm being overprotective."

"Yeah. I hear a 'but' in there."

"Grandpa's all the family I have."

"I know. Will it help if I promise to bring them all back in one piece?"

"I'll shut up now."

"But I like your voice. Talk about other things."

"How's the bake sale coming along?"

His eyes lit up when she changed the topic, and he took his hand from hers. "I'm sure you'll be accosted at church to provide more than you have already promised. Feel free to say no." He turned back to the computer and closed the open programs. "Want me to turn off the power?"

"Absolutely. I'm done with that stuff for the day."

"Go on a walk with me?"

"I'll let Rachel know I'm headed out. Give me five minutes."

"Not a second longer."

Rabbit raced toward Ginger and Mike as they walked the perimeter of the park. Mike waved as Walter headed their way with Bo and Eugene.

Ginger scratched Rabbit behind his ears. "One thing about having this dog, Grandpa is getting more exercise. Maybe Rabbit is partly why he's been skipping some of your chess games."

"Makes sense." Mike turned to Walter. "We could bring our chess game to the park."

Walter brightened. "Where's your chess board? There's no time like the present."

"I can go get it." He checked the time on his phone. "Be back in half an hour."

"We'll be at the picnic table in the middle. Be ready to lose, young man."

Mike laughed as Walter returned to where they had been playing with Rabbit. He whistled and the dog ran after him.

"Quite the pair. Want to come with me to get the chess set?"

"Lead the way. I just need to be back to the café for supper."

Mike stuck his hands in his pockets. "I was thinking…"

"Yes?"

"There's another outdoor movie in Kearney this weekend. Any interest in going with me?"

Ginger had hung out with Mike at events before, but not with the acknowledgement of things changing between them. Although she liked the change, her first thoughts about going to a movie with Mike were to turn tail and run from anyone else seeing them together as more than friends.

"No pressure." Mike shrugged. "Thought it sounded fun. Especially with you."

"It does sound like fun. Especially with you. I'm…not ready."

Mike nodded. "Then we'll leave that idea for another time."

CHAPTER TWENTY-NINE

Painting day at the Jordans' ended up being more fun than stressful. She glanced down at Mike, the reason she was enjoying herself. Working on one side of the house by themselves, they had no one to intrude on their banter, making it easy for Ginger to relax.

She stretched her arm and dipped her paint brush into a bucket hanging on the ladder next to hers. Her balance wobbled, and she squealed when the ladder left the surface of the house. Her arms flailed.

"I've got you." Mike caught her before she hit the ground.

She looped her arms around his neck and looked up at his face. "That could have been bad."

Mike chuckled. "Glad to be of service, ma'am."

Suddenly feeling awkward, she giggled.

"What's going on here?" Grandpa used his gruffest voice, the one that came out when he didn't like what was happening.

Mike set Ginger down. "Caught her before she went splat, sir." His shoulders lifted up and down moved as though he was holding in a laugh.

"Hmph." Grandpa got in Mike's face. "I'll be watching."

"Yes, sir."

"Carry on." Grandpa glanced at Ginger and, using the hand that Mike couldn't see, gave her a thumbs-up.

Once Grandpa was out of sight, Ginger and Mike looked at each other and busted out laughing. Mike led the way to a shade tree where ice water waited. He lowered himself to the ground and patted the space next to him. "Join me?"

She lowered herself to the grass and took a long drink of water. "Sorry about Grandpa."

"He's looking out for you."

She rested her arms on her knees. "It feels good to be out here instead of in the café."

"And I finally get to spend time with you."

She elbowed him. "I really have given you a hard time these last several years, haven't I?"

"She admits it."

Avoiding his gaze, she became fascinated with an ant hill. Picking up a stick, she poked at it. This new thing between them still made her uncomfortable when they talked about it. They were being open with each other and letting things become what they might be. They had fallen into a new dimension of their relationship that seemed to have been waiting for them a long time. She didn't want words to get in the way of what this was. She knew her tendency to bolt when cornered.

He reached over and turned her face toward him. "What's going on in that mind of yours?"

She shrugged, not sure what to say, and poked some more at the ant hill. She heard him gulp down more water and felt him watch her. The sun peeked through the branches of the tree and warmed her skin. She and Mike had something she had never experienced with her fiancé. With her fiancé, she had what she liked to call gooey feelings that everyone expected with being in love. But with Mike, there was a belonging, like...like chocolate and pie belonged together. She smiled. Gooey feelings didn't promise a happily ever after. They didn't even promise to get you to the altar. But this—this could last a lifetime if she gave it half a chance.

A shudder ran up her back. What she lost when her fiancé chose not to stay with her didn't compare with what she would lose if Mike was out of her life. Had love crept up so quietly over the years that she hadn't noticed? She glanced at Mike from under her lashes. Butterflies danced in her stomach at the idea of what this might be. Fear of calling it by name almost sent her running.

"Are you doing okay with us?" Mike leaned back on his elbows.

"What is us?"

"Does it need a name?"

"I suppose not." She glanced at him and smiled.

"Then let's not call it anything for now. I'm enjoying being around you. Helping you. Being a part of what you do." He reached for her hand. "Doing this when I can sneak it in." He kissed the back of her hand. "You, letting me." He grinned. "Let's see where it goes."

She nodded. "I hope the ladies at church stay out of it."

"I understand. But let's not allow whatever they do to interfere with whatever this is."

Silence surrounded them again until Josh's voice could be heard from around the house calling everyone for lunch. Mike stood and offered Ginger a hand up. When Josh came into view, Mike dropped his hand and bent down for his water bottle. Appreciative that he wasn't going to add fuel to the fire of any gossip about them, she followed him to the backyard, where food was being served. They joined the line of about twenty people from church who had showed up to help with the house repairs today.

Mike filled everyone in on the details of her almost landing on her backside, and several offered her advice on how to not get hurt while painting the house.

"Guys, I wasn't even a full story above ground."

Barking from over the hill behind the Jordans' house caught Ginger's attention. "Is that Rabbit?"

Those around them quieted. Ginger shielded her eyes as Rabbit bounded toward them. "Where's Grandpa?"

Mike jogged toward the dog. Rabbit danced on his feet in front of him then bounded toward the hill with Mike close behind.

Ginger jogged after them. She topped the hill and saw Grandpa lying on the ground near where the hill leveled out. "Grandpa?" She caught up as Mike knelt beside him.

"Walter?"

Grandpa opened his eyes. "What took you so long? Help an old man up, would you?" He held out hand to grasp Mike's.

"Let's make sure you're okay before you move."

"Dagnabbit. Nothing's broken. I tripped over the uneven ground, and it's hard to get up."

Mike looked up at Ginger. "I think he's okay."

"Of course I am." He grabbed Mike's hand and pulled himself to a standing position. "See? I'm fine." He started walking up the hill.

"What if you hadn't been?" Ginger walked close to Grandpa.

"I'll be fine, missy." Grandpa marched ahead of them as though he didn't want to acknowledge that he needed help or that he could have been hurt. Rabbit stayed close to Grandpa.

"He needs his independence as long as possible. It will be easier now that he has Rabbit. He'll watch out for him." Mike took held her hand as they walked up the hill.

"I know. I really try not to hover."

"You're doing good."

They walked in silence till they reached the top of the hill when Ginger let her hand slip out of his. As they neared the food tables, Megan ran up to them. "I need to tell you something. Mike, hold her spot." She led Ginger away from the food. "We found Josh's brother."

"That's great news. Where was he?"

"He made it all the way to Omaha. Got hooked up with some bad influencers and landed in juvie. But as of the latest, they're going to place him with us."

"What does Josh think?"

"We're going to tell him next week that we've found his brother, but we want to surprise Josh with his arrival. We're hoping by Josh's birthday."

"Isn't that coming up pretty soon?"

"Last week of the month. Can't wait to see Josh's face when he sees his brother. Will you be there?"

"Absolutely."

Arriving back at the café after painting all day, Ginger and Mike passed the sink filled with pots and pans. The dishes were piled next to the dish washer. "We haven't had this many dishes since..."

Ginger hurried to the swinging door between the kitchen and dining hall. Harry was focused on dishing up a line of plates. She pushed the door open partway and glanced out. The dining hall was full, and people stood in line waiting to be seated. Bridgette and Rachel bustled from one table to another.

"It's a beautiful thing, isn't it?"

Ginger looked over at Harry. "How?"

"Remember that travel blogger? His post released yesterday. One of the major networks picked it up on their travel tips section. Evidently, he gave our place such a write up, everyone in the surrounding counties wanted to give us a try." He nodded toward the dining hall. "Rachel has taken it all in stride. She's perfect for this place. But you might need a new dish washer."

They looked back at the pots and pans where Mike was elbow-deep into the suds. After a long day of painting, he was still willing to pitch in. A greater affection for Mike grew in Ginger's heart.

The back door swung open, and Grandpa and his buddies hurried through the kitchen out to the dining hall, then promptly returned.

Each one grabbed an apron from the hook near the door. As they passed Ginger, they grinned. "Saw the crowd and thought we would make good on that offer to help in the dining hall." They marched out and she watched through the window as they took on the duties of busboys.

She grinned. They might keep the restaurant after all. "Harry. Put me to work. What do you need me to do?"

After the crowds had gone, Ginger and Mike sat at a table across from Rachel listening to her plans to advertise for another waitress. She brought out her laptop and showed them the new designs for the menus and the website she was in the process of building.

"If I can get this website up, we can take advantage of this uptake in business."

"This is beautiful, Rachel." Ginger clicked on the zoom to see more detail.

"Thanks." She looked down sheepishly. "I know money is tight, but do you think we could get fifty menus printed?"

"Absolutely. What do you think, Mike?"

"Menus would be a good investment. Let me double check the numbers first thing in the morning."

Feeling a tiny bit like a kid in school, Ginger reached for Mike's hand under the table. Having Mike help her with the Jukebox finances was already lightening her load.

CHAPTER THIRTY

Ginger placed the pan of her Jukebox cinnamon rolls in the church fridge. She would have to scoot out of service early to get them in the oven so they would be done in time for lunch. She used to make something from her home kitchen for the church's potluck Sunday but gave up when everyone always requested the rolls. It made life simpler.

Ginger entered the sanctuary as the church started singing "It is Well with My Soul." Allowing her mind to linger on the words, she slipped into the back row. She knew it was well and that God was taking care of her, so why didn't she feel it? She glanced over at Grandpa sitting ramrod straight near the front on the left-hand side. *Lord, help me believe that all is well even when I don't see it.*

A couple more songs and the congregation sat. Mike took his spot behind the podium. He talked a bit about his time in the Marines. About being able to fall asleep anywhere to catch rest on the go as they were able. He told on some of his fellow Marines and the places they found themselves sleeping and soon had the whole congregation in stitches. She remembered that, when he first came to Hillside Community Church, his rough Marine exterior was a put-off to some. Now they enjoyed the perspective it brought to their community.

He led into the sermon with a verse from the Psalms. "Truly my soul finds rest in God." As he looked out over the audience, his gaze landed briefly on her, then moved on across the auditorium. "Rest isn't about binge-watching TV or sports or video games. Trust me, I've tried all of it. Even in the Marines, before I knew Christ—you've heard my story—I tried more illicit ways of escape. That is not rest. Rest isn't about distraction. It's about slowing down and remembering that God is in control and that we can trust Him. In the book of Matthew, we're told that God cares for the sparrows and that he cares for each of us even more."

The words of the sermon rolled over in Ginger's mind as Mike continued his teaching. She savored their sweetness as the idea of rest, like water on parched ground, quenched her soul.

Mike's laugh from the front pulled her back to his sermon. "Sometimes the most spiritual thing we can do is take a nap." Soft laughter rippled across the auditorium and a few "Amens" came from the crowd.

As the closing hymn started, Ginger slipped out and hurried to the kitchen to put the rolls in the oven. After double-checking that all the plates and plasticware were set out, she found a place to sit until the crowd made its way down.

They were still singing upstairs, so while waiting she pulled out her notebook and doodled the word "trust," then an arrow pointing to the word "God." Was she self-reliant to the point of doing things in her own strength instead of trusting God? Is that why she felt near burnout?

Adding the word "rest" to her doodles, she thought about what rest might look like for her. For someone who was on the go from sunup till sundown? Everything in her life had a purpose that couldn't be ignored.

Ginger let out a frustrated breath. What could help her feel rested and put God in first place at the same time? Stopping always felt selfish but trusting God would allow her to better care for others. One thing she knew, something had to change.

"Hey." Mike sat next to her. "You look deep in thought."

"Taking advantage of the quiet." Ginger stuck her notebook back in her purse and checked her phone timer. Still another fifteen minutes on the rolls. The noise of conversation filled the dining hall. "Your sermon got me thinking."

"I hope that's a good thing."

"I think so." Ginger smiled at him.

"Want to talk?"

She shrugged. "Maybe later."

"You know where to find me. How's Rabbit this morning?"

"Ha. We could hear his whining from outside when we left. I hope he doesn't tear up the house."

"Ginger. There you are. Just the person I needed to talk to." An older lady with graying hair stopped in front of her and Mike. "We need someone to host the women's tea next month and felt like you would be the perfect person. Can we put you down for the second Tuesday of the month?"

"I'm not sure that—"

"We're pretty certain it's your turn."

While the woman rambled on about all the reasons Ginger should host the tea, she visualized her full calendar. It felt as though someone had taken her stress, anxiety, and dread about her life, wrapped them up together around her, and then squeezed. How could she add one more thing to her schedule? She took a deep breath.

Mike gave Ginger a smile, then stood and put his arm around the older lady. "Why don't I help you find someone else who can host next month?"

Grateful for the save, Ginger went to the kitchen and pulled out the cinnamon rolls. She added them to the table, which was filling quickly with dishes ranging from fried chicken and mashed potatoes to tofu and sushi. Lillian must be there. She always brought something a bit out of the ordinary.

Grandpa walked up next to her. "What's that?" He pointed at one of the more interesting dishes of food. "That doesn't look edible."

"Shh. Then don't eat it if you don't want to. There are plenty of other things you like."

Grandpa huffed and crossed his arms. "Don't shush me."

Ginger raised her hands in surrender. "Fine." Sometimes the best approach was to ignore Grandpa. She walked back to the kitchen to get a spatula for serving up the cinnamon rolls.

After Mike said a prayer for lunch, Ginger grabbed a plate. She thought about the sermon as she stood in line.

Maggie smiled at her from across the table. "It's about time." She reached for a roll, almost spilling her plate of fried chicken into a dish of coleslaw.

"What?" Ginger reached over and leveled out Maggie's plate.

"Thank you, dear." Maggie pointed her finger at Ginger. "You and Mike are a good team. We heard from the Drakes who helped with the painting day at the Jordans' that you two are dating."

One of Maggie's friends standing next to her nodded. "Besides, we're running out of people to set him up with. A pastor needs a wife."

Ginger opened her mouth to talk as another woman standing behind Ginger edged closer.

Leaning forward as though listening, the woman jumped into the conversation. "Are you dating Pastor Mike?" Her voice rose and a couple people looked their direction.

Ginger felt cornered by others' expectations and wanted to crawl inside a hole and hide. "We're just—"

Betsy wedged in between the ladies. "What she means to say is that when there's news, you'll know. Until then, mum's the word." She gave them a teacher-reprimanding-students look and moved her fingers across her lips as if she was zipping them.

"Oh." Maggie lowered her voice to a whisper. "We can keep a secret. Right, ladies?" She looked at each woman involved in the conversation.

They all nodded, but Ginger knew that by nightfall most of the women in Maggie's Bible study would be talking about Ginger and Mike's future. She really didn't need the pressure, but what had she expected? She expunged a pent-up breath.

Betsy patted her arm. "You're way too serious about this. Keep enjoying whatever is going on."

Ginger placed a spoonful of coleslaw on her plate then whispered close to Betsy's ear. "This town will have Mike and me married by the end of the day. I'm supposed to relax about that?"

"Is that such a bad thing?"

Ginger stuck the spoon back in the dish of coleslaw. "Not you, too."

"Relax, girlfriend."

"I don't like being pressured about this." Ginger dropped a mound of mashed potatoes on her plate.

Betsy held her finger up to her lips. "I'll be quiet now."

Ginger closed her eyes and counted to ten. "I'm sorry I snapped."

"I get it, girl."

Ginger nodded and stepped out of line. No longer hungry, she found an empty spot at a table to the side of the dining hall. Within minutes, Mike sat next to her. She glanced up. "I can't believe some of these women."

"I've heard. To clear the air, I had nothing to do with what they're saying."

"I know." She smiled. "You're not the issue."

"Maybe I can preach a sermon on gossip." He made his Groucho Marx face, eyebrows bopping up and down.

She chuckled. "Somehow I think it would only fan the flames of their curiosity."

"Speaking of curiosity..."

She glanced to the side where Mike was looking. A couple women turned from her gaze and whispered together. "I think that's my cue. I'm going to take my pastor's advice and do something spiritual with my afternoon. I'm going to go home and take a nap."

CHAPTER THIRTY-ONE

Grandpa marched up to the table laden with sweets where Ginger worked. "I want to know what you are doing to find my wife."

Had he already forgotten the conversation they had yesterday about her progress? She caught Mike's attention where he stood checking over the set-up of tables in the church's fellowship hall. He hurried toward her.

"Walter. Can I get your opinion on something?" Mike led Grandpa toward another table.

Breathing a sigh of relief, Ginger finished the display of goods for the bake sale. Between what the café had contributed and the baked goods the ladies of the church provided, it promised to be a successful event. She checked the time on her phone. Another hour before they opened.

"Need to get off your feet?"

Ginger smiled up at Mike. "That would be heavenly."

He led her away from the volunteers and into the sanctuary. "The only quiet place today." He sat in a pew, and she followed suit. He slid his arm around her, and she leaned against him. This was something her soul had needed for a long time. Someone who brought rest into her life.

Grandpa forgot about a conversation he and I had about his wife the other day. Of course, I forget things, too. How do I know when his forgetting is more than just forgetting?"

"I don't know. When is his appointment with the doctor?"

"Next week."

"You okay?"

She took a deep breath. "I will be."

Mike kissed the top of her head and began humming the melody to "It is Well." For a few minutes, she let go of the demands that waited for her right outside the doors.

"Pete, the vendor from Mountain Home Flea Market, sent me an email." Ginger moved away by a few inches so she could see his face.

"Did he have anything helpful to add to your collection of clues?"

"He verified that the box was one that his grandfather made in the thirties. According to his records, his father repurchased it from someone in Mountain Home near the end of the war."

"That seems to jive with what Walter told you about his family getting rid of Irene's things before he returned from the war."

"I know they weren't happy about the two of them marrying so young, but why would they do that?"

"I don't know, Ginger. Sometimes parents do crazy things to protect their kids."

She leaned her head back on his arm stretched along the back of the pew, but startled when the doors to the sanctuary burst open, banging against the wall.

"Come quick. It's your grandpa." Josh motioned for Ginger to come.

Mike and Ginger jumped up from the pew and hurried after him. Ginger could hear Grandpa before she saw him. The anger in his voice caught her off guard, and she stopped short when she saw him standing toe to toe with Betsy. If there wasn't so much ire in his manner, she would have thought it comical.

"I tell you what, missy. That is no way to treat your elders." He stood with his hands on his hips. His eyes bore into Betsy's.

"Grandpa." Ginger looked from him to Betsy. "What's going on?"

Betsy shrugged. "No clue."

"Likely story, young lady."

"Grandpa? Want to go on a walk with me?" Ginger touched his arm. He pulled away.

Mike whispered in her ear. "Want some help?"

She nodded.

"Trust me?"

A crowd was gathering along the edges of the fellowship hall. She nodded.

Mike stood in front of Grandpa and looked him in the eye. "Attention."

Grandpa snapped to attention and saluted.

"Return to your barracks. We need to discuss our mission."

"Yes, sir." Grandpa headed out of the building.

Mike motioned Grandpa's buddies to go with him then turned to Ginger. "You want to go with Walter? Maybe Betsy can take your place today?"

"What's happening to him?"

"Age is catching up. Hey. Where's my brave girl?"

Tears trickled down her face. "I've been pretending all this time."

"I know for a fact that isn't true. You're one of the bravest people I know."

Ginger glanced around the room, suddenly self-conscious, but everyone milled around not paying them any attention. "Can you arrange things with Betsy?"

"Sure. I'll stop by this afternoon." He gave her hand a squeeze then scooted her out of the building.

Grandpa was sitting in the easy chair by the window when Ginger arrived back home. "I'm sorry about the bake sale."

She hurried over and sat on the couch close to him. "It's okay."

"No, it's not. Sometimes I get confused, or I don't remember things. I get frustrated and say things I don't mean."

"I still love you."

He patted her hand. "I know. But it's hard on an old man used to being independent."

"How can I help?"

He inhaled a deep breath and let it out. "Even if I can't remember, don't forget me." Tears trailed down his wrinkle-lined cheeks.

She went down on her knees and wrapped her arms around his neck. The thought of him not remembering her grieved her heart. What would she do without Grandpa? "I will always remember you."

"Thank you, child."

She wanted desperately to change the topic. This time she was the one needing distraction. "Want some pie and coffee?"

"Depends on what kind."

"I can run across the alley and grab one of your favorites."

"Two pieces?"

"You got it."

Rachel stopped Ginger in the bakery area. "Do you know anyone renting an apartment or even a room? Beth told me that she is moving, so I have to find a new place by the end of next week. That's not much time."

"I'll ask around and let you know."

"Thanks."

Ginger decided to take a whole pie. Mike might want some when he stopped by later.

When she arrived back at the house, Grandpa had stretched out and fallen asleep in the easy chair. She set the pie in the kitchen and grabbed a book. She settled into the couch and lost herself in the world between the pages. Deep into the story, she didn't hear the knock or the squeak of hinges as the door opened.

She jumped when Mike spoke her name. "You scared me."

"Must be a good story." He glanced at the book she held.

"It's the one we were going to read for the book club but never got into it."

He chuckled. "You looked cute sitting there unaware then jumping when I said your name."

"Ha." She threw a pillow at him, which he caught and tossed back at her. "Want some pie?"

Mike lowered his voice when he noticed Grandpa asleep in the chair. "I was hoping you would have something. I had to be around those baked goods all morning without taking one bite. Drove me crazy."

He followed her into the kitchen where she dished up a piece for each of them. He grabbed a fork and joined her at the table. "How is he?" He tilted his head toward the living room.

"Ask me yourself, young man." Grandpa came in and joined them at the table. "Well? Do I get any pie?"

Ginger slid her piece across the table to him then got another one for herself. Grandpa's mood was shifting all over the place. She met Mike's glance and raised her eyebrows. He shrugged and they ate in silence. He reached across the table and placed his hand on top of hers. Grandpa smiled as though he had a secret and kept eating. Go figure. Even in his agitated state, he seemed to approve of Mike.

"Tell me what you've found out so far about my wife." Grandpa pointed his fork at her.

"The box was first purchased in Mountain Home."

"I could have told you that." Grandpa scooped up another bite of pie.

"But you didn't."

"Hmph." Grandpa ate the bite balanced on top of his fork.

"The great grandson of the man who made the box is the one who sold it to Beth."

"Pete?"

Ginger glared at Grandpa. "You knew his name, too?"

He nodded. "I'm not an idiot."

"Is there anything else you haven't told me that you would like to now?"

"You read the letters?"

She narrowed her eyes. "Yes."

"Then now you know what I know."

"Can I read the letters again?"

"I don't know what good it will do you. I've read them hundreds of times. Nothing changed."

"Grandpa."

"Nope."

"You sure have a lot of expectations of me without being willing to help."

"You watch your tone, young lady." Grandpa pointed his fork at her again.

Glaring at him, she shut her mouth. It wouldn't do any good to argue. She pulled her hand back from Mike's. "I need some space." After grabbing her phone, she left the house and walked. Frustration fueled her, and the pace left her a bit out of breath.

By the time she arrived at Center Square Park, her mind had begun to clear, and she headed to Betsy's house. Her phone's notifications alerted her to a text from Mike. She ignored it. Everything in her wanted the calm she found when Mike was beside her, helping her. But on the flipside, it scared her not to take care of things herself. How did she balance independence with the need for another person? She marched up the steps to Betsy's back door.

"I saw you coming girl, swinging those arms like you have something on your mind." Betsy opened the screen door and let Ginger in. "And talking to yourself, too. Must be a doozy. What's got you tied up in knots? Is it Mike?"

Ginger rolled her eyes. "I'm not here to talk about Mike."

"Far be it from me to want to know how my friend is doing." Betsy lifted her chin.

"Don't go all Grandpa on me."

"Tell me what's bothering you."

Ginger paced the kitchen floor and let out an exaggerated breath. "Everyone's expectations. That's what. I'm feeling squished, but I know that if I lay out a plan to get it all done, I'll be fine." Ginger grabbed a napkin and a pen lying on the table and started writing.

Betsy watched her for a moment, then placed a hand on top of Ginger's and halted her hurried doodles. "Stop. All this will get done. Or not. But right now, you're weary and hurting."

A notification alerted Ginger to another text from Mike. She flipped her phone upside down on the table.

Betsy looked over at Ginger's phone. "Why are you ignoring him?"

"I'm such a mess right now."

"I don't think that matters much to him."

The doorbell rang, and Betsy got up. "And if I'm right, that's for you." She went to the front door.

Ginger heard voices, then quiet. A hand rested on her shoulder. Mike had come.

He sat in the chair next to her and placed a stack of letters on the table. "Walter sent the letters and this." He pulled a locket out of his pocket and set it on Ginger's palm. "He thought you might want to wear it."

She opened the locket and stared at a tiny image of Irene. "Thanks."

"Tell me what's going on."

She grabbed a tissue and blew her nose. "My thoughts and feelings are all jumbled up. I've been holding them in so that I don't hurt people, but I feel like I'm about to spew them out like hot lava. I don't want to say things I'll regret."

"I can take it."

Ginger shook her head.

"You can trust me."

She looked into his eyes. He didn't waver.

Grandpa expects me to find Irene. The ladies at church expect me to be on every committee that gets formed at church. The bank expects me to pay the bills. You expect me to be able to slide into this new aspect of our relationship without any struggle. I'm feeling squished. I can't do it all. But most of these are legitimate expectations. I can't not pay the bank." She looked down to avoid his gaze.

"You've also placed a lot of expectations on yourself."

"To meet my responsibilities." Her defenses rose.

"To do everything for everybody. I rarely hear you say no."

Ginger squirmed at his accuracy.

"You insist on doing everything yourself."

She whispered, "I've already disappointed you."

"No, you haven't. And to clear the air, I don't have a list of expectations for you to meet in order to make me happy. This sounds like fear talking. What are you afraid of?"

Ginger grabbed a tissue. "Mostly, that I won't be enough. That I'll be too needy. That you'll walk away." She got up and paced in front of the table.

"I'm not leaving."

"How do you know?"

Mike looked down at the floor, then back up into Ginger's eyes. "Because I love you."

The truth of what she hoped for took her breath away—to have love returned. But what if it didn't last? She opened her mouth then closed it. How did she respond?

Mike stood and drew near to her. "I'm not expecting you to say anything at this point. I want you to know my heart. When you're ready, I'll be waiting. Please, don't give up on us."

CHAPTER THIRTY-TWO

Ginger stacked the last of the pots in their rightful place. Mike hadn't been in for coffee this morning, but maybe he would come by later. Making a mental note to talk to Rachel about further training needed for the new dish washer, Ginger went back to the office.

Sitting at her desk, she let out an audible sigh and closed her eyes for a moment of stillness before busying herself with the next task of ordering supplies. She turned on the computer and waited for it to warm up. A new computer would be a great idea, too. This one was a dinosaur. It was a good thing Rachel had her own for her digital designing.

With all the new business, they would need to order more than usual this month, and she hoped the funds were there. Her first instinct was to try to take care of the books herself, but Mike already had a system figured out. She didn't have to do everything on her own.

She paused at the thought of calling Mike. She missed him. That was the truth of it. Two days ago, after Mike told her he loved her, she asked for time to think things through. She still hadn't figured anything out and already a part of her was missing. What was there to figure out? He loved her and, though she hadn't admitted it out loud, she loved him. She pursed her lips. She wasn't ready to go where that admission would take her. That was the problem. It was her, not him.

Church had been awkward yesterday trying to avoid the gossip mill and being cornered into more commitments. Betsy had schooled her on saying no and made her promise not to take on any more without getting a second opinion.

Ginger made a neat mess of the piles stacked haphazardly on her desk and gave herself a lecture. "Get it together, girl. Even though I want space to think this through, he said he wasn't leaving. Pick up the phone and ask him to come over and help." She straightened the last stack and startled at a knock on the office door. She looked up to see Mike grinning at her.

"Came to look at the books for you before you sent the bat signal up. Is this a good time?"

Grateful he brought humor into the situation, she relaxed at seeing him. "I need to place an order, so would half an hour or so work?"

"Can I get some of your chocolate pie while I'm waiting?"

She laughed. "Help yourself. Have Rachel make you some fresh coffee, too. The rush is over, so she should have time."

He started to go, then turned back and closed the door. "Are you doing okay? I watched you in church on Sunday and you weren't yourself."

She lifted her shoulders and laughed under her breath. "I was trying to avoid being cornered about us or more commitments."

"Makes sense. Anything else?"

Ginger looked down at his hands holding hers. She would be a fool to push him away. "What happens if we disappoint each other?"

"When we disappoint each other—and we will from time to time, because that's just a part of living—God is still faithful. If we keep hanging on to Him, we'll get through it intact."

Ginger nodded. His words made sense. Hopefully reality would hold the same truth. She tugged her hand from his. "I better place that—"

"Ginger."

The frantic call came from the kitchen. She jumped up from the desk and hurried past Mike to where Harry stood holding his hand wrapped in a towel.

"Need to get to the clinic. I cut myself."

Ginger nodded and called back to Mike. "I have to run Harry to the clinic. Go ahead and look through the numbers—I'll place the order later."

Rachel came through the swinging doors and took in the situation. "I can do the order."

"Thanks." Ginger was glad she had shown Rachel how their ordering system worked. "Call me with any questions. Come on, Harry." She grabbed her purse from the office and they headed out to the car.

Two hours later, Ginger and Harry returned to the café. The cut ended up being smaller than the blood had first made it appear. After a few stitches, Harry was good to go.

Ginger watched Mike as he focused on the numbers. She waited till he looked up. "Did you get your chocolate pie?"

"Two pieces. I could use a break, though. Join me for coffee?"

She hesitated for only a second. "That sounds nice." Despite her uncertainties about herself, she wanted to spend time with him, so she led the way to the dining hall.

"I have news about our Catch the Vandal Mission." Mike filled a mug and handed it to Ginger.

"And?"

"Walter's idea to plant cameras in the area where the vandal seems to be showing up worked. Last night we finally got the vandal on tape. Turned it in to the sheriff this morning. We have proof now that it wasn't Josh. Looks like a kid, though. The sheriff said he would go out and tell the Jordans and apologize directly to Josh for not giving him the benefit of the doubt."

"It's about time. What will happen to the vandal?"

"Probably land in juvie, unless we show grace. I talked to the sheriff, and this week I'll talk to the victims about dropping charges and pushing for community service."

"Like painting over their work?"

"That would be good option." He leaned against the counter. "The gift we ordered for Josh's birthday was delivered. What time do you want me to pick you up on Saturday?"

They had made plans to ride together before she felt the need to take some time to think through their relationship. Likely it would be unfair to Mike to carry on as though she had made a decision in favor of moving forward.

"I know that look."

"What?"

"Debating about whether riding with me is fair to me or not."

Ginger tilted her head. "How do you do that?"

"I know you better than you realize. With that being said, I would like it if you rode out to Josh's party with me. Regardless of where you are with us. Will you?" He offered her a lopsided grin.

"Yes, I'd like that. Let me check with Rachel and make sure the café is covered." Bridgette was usually more than eager to work.

"What do you need to check with me on?" Rachel draped an arm around Ginger's shoulders.

"Josh's birthday party this weekend. You think Bridgette will be okay on her own?"

"Betsy offered to help her. I think they'll be fine. Want to ride with me? And what about Walter?"

"Greg will pick Grandpa up early that day and bring him back. I've got a ride."

"Of course you do." Rachel palmed her forehead and laughed at what must have been an embarrassed look on Ginger's face.

Mike leaned over and whispered, "Don't add this to your list of cons about our relationship."

She swatted his arm then turned to catch Rachel as she left. "Now that we're in the same spot for half a minute, I have a proposition for you."

"Sounds intriguing."

"How would you like to move into my house?"

Rachel's eyes grew wide. "Really?"

Ginger nodded. "We have plenty of space."

Rachel tilted her head. "What's the catch?"

Ginger laughed. "No catch. You have a place as long as you need."

"What's the rent?"

"Think of it as part of your benefits. Our guest rooms are sitting empty, and it's one way I can pay you what you're worth here. At least until the Jukebox gets back on its feet. We can re-explore rent when I can give you a raise. You game?"

"Give me some time to think about it." Rachel grinned. "Of course."

"When do you want to move?"

"End of the week work?"

"Perfect." Ginger gave Rachel a hug. "I'm glad you'll be at the house."

Ginger came home weary from the day and headed back to her room to change into comfy clothes for the evening. Rachel had things well in hand to close the restaurant.

Ginger's gaze fell on her Bible sitting on the bedside table. How long had it been since she had spent more time in quiet spaces with God than it took for a quick prayer for help and reading a short verse between running from one thing to another?

Picking up the beloved yet neglected book, she sat on the edge of her bed. She opened to the Psalms and thumbed through the pages until her eyes fell on a favorite verse, which she had underlined. "Why, my soul, are you downcast? Why so disturbed within me? Put your hope in God, for I will yet praise Him, my Savior and my God."

Closing her eyes, she told her soul to hope in God, like the psalmist had. After taking a few deep breaths, she cried out to God about her frustrations and anger over Grandpa's dementia. She slipped to the floor next to her bed. "Lord, keep those days far in the future. Help me to find Irene and give Grandpa good years with her. Give me grace when dementia steals him away from me." Tears overwhelmed her as she acknowledged her grief.

Grief spent, her thoughts turned to Mike, and she smiled. "God, what are your plans for us? I'm better with him at my side. Thank you that one of the ways you help us is to send someone with skin on. I need his strength. Help me to bless him as much as he blesses me."

Grandpa slammed the front door on his way inside for the night. Her soul at peace, Ginger slipped under the covers and prayed until she fell asleep.

CHAPTER THIRTY-THREE

The midday sun glared off the hood of Mike's truck as they drove to Josh's party. Mike's willingness to wait on her still astounded Ginger and she resisted the urge to reach for his hand. "Didn't see you at the café this morning. Sneak in while I was over at the house?"

He looked over and smiled. "One of my elderly neighbors was sick and needed a ride to the doctor. Besides, I knew I would get to spend most of the day with you."

"Thank you."

"For what?"

"This. Being okay with not rushing me."

"It's best for now. But you know what I want to do sometimes?"

"Do I want to know?"

"Sometimes I want to throw caution to the wind and tell the world how I feel about you. I want to remind you over and over until you believe that we'll be okay."

She sucked in a breath.

"No worries. I'll keep it slow and easy. For now." He kept his focus on the road.

Ginger watched the passing scenery out the window. She didn't deserve Mike. She remembered her prayer last night and chided herself for not just telling him how she felt. It was past time she let go and enjoyed whatever their future held.

"Think Josh will like what we got him?"

"What? Oh. I have it on good authority he'll make good use of that toolbox."

"Where were your thoughts?"

"Us."

"Hmm. I like your voice."

"Hey, you better watch the road."

"There's a much better view sitting beside me, but I suppose." He made a big show of pouting while watching the road.

Trying to ignore the feelings he stirred in her didn't change the truth. She liked his attention.

"Does Josh have any clue yet about his brother?"

Thankful for the safe topic, she relaxed. "He knows they found him and that they are trying to bring him into their family, but he doesn't know his brother will be at his party. The social worker agreed to bring him around three. She warned them he hasn't been cooperative so not to expect too much."

"Being with Josh will make a huge difference. Especially once he gets to know the Jordans."

"How long has it been since the boys were separated?"

Mike scratched his chin. "I think it's been about four years. If more people would be willing to take in siblings and keep them together, things like this wouldn't happen."

Mike pulled down the drive to the Jordan farm and parked in the grass with two other vehicles. He grabbed their gift from the back of the truck then let the tailgate down for Rabbit to jump out. His phone chirped. A quick glance at the number and Mike huffed.

"Everything okay?"

"My ex-wife."

"I thought you hadn't kept in touch."

"She found me. Remember those calls from California? That was her. She finally left a message and said we needed to talk."

"About what?"

He shrugged. "I guess I should call her back and find out."

"Ginger, Mike." Megan's enthusiastic greeting interrupted and hurried them along. "Everyone is around back. Come on."

The cake sat on the patio table. Betsy helped with bringing out food, and Grandpa chatted with Josh. The other kids scattered around the yard. Mike left Ginger to her own devices while he added their gift to the present table.

Megan walked up beside Ginger. "I approve."

"Of what?"

"Girl, I've been hearing speculation about you and Mike for years. You must have very bad hearing, or you've been ignoring the rumor mill. Besides, it's obvious that things are changing between the two of you."

Fine, God. I get the hint. I talk to him today.

Mike came back with a bottle of water and offered it to Ginger. "What did I miss?"

Megan laughed. "I'm staying out of that one. I need to go out front and watch for the social worker." Megan whispered to Ginger, "I hear your grandpa has a bet going with his buddies about you two."

Ginger spewed water out of her mouth. "What?"

Megan waved and took off, grinning at the disbelief on Ginger's face.

Ginger narrowed her eyes at Mike.

He shrugged. "What?"

"Did you know about the bet?"

He held up his hands as though in surrender. "I can't stop the talk, or your grandpa betting, but I did ask people to keep their suppositions to themselves. I didn't want them to ruin any chance I have with you."

Ginger wanted to get mad, but she supposed it was funny. And for her to not have heard anything? A laugh started deep inside her. She offered a lopsided grin. "I wonder how high the bet is."

"I wonder who's betting against us. Because they're going to lose." He took hold of her hand. Ginger's gaze locked onto his. It was time to let go of her fears. She could trust what God was doing. "I think maybe—" The crunch of gravel announced the arrival of another car. Distracted, she looked over as the gray sedan parked, then turned back to Mike.

He grinned. "That we need to talk?"

Ginger nodded.

"On the way back to town?"

"That works." The sooner the better.

He grinned as they turned to watch Josh's upcoming encounter. Mike slipped his arm around Ginger's shoulders.

Grandpa kept Josh occupied in conversation while others drew closer to the patio, anticipating Josh's surprise. Mike pulled out his phone and tapped on the camera app.

Megan came around the corner. "Josh, we have a surprise for you."

Josh stepped closer to Megan but stopped when he saw his brother. "David?"

The two stared at one another.

"Hi, Josh." David hooked his thumbs through the belt loops on his jeans.

Josh walked toward David and hugged his younger brother. Hands hanging at his side, David stood quietly while Josh hugged him. Josh stepped back. "What's wrong, man?"

"Looks like you landed a nice place."

"And now it's your place, too."

"Whatever." David shrugged. "It never lasts long."

"Megan and Greg are good people."

"We'll see. So, what's out at the shed?" He headed toward the outbuilding, and Josh followed, the two boys leaning their heads together in conversation.

Mike disappeared around front with the social worker and Greg. After a few minutes, they came out of the house. David and Josh wandered back to the house. Greg took the boys inside, and Mike headed Ginger's way, grabbing a handful of popcorn as he passed the food table. "We took David's stuff inside, and Josh is showing him where everything is. David is one angry kid. I'm afraid they have quite a road ahead of them."

Charlie from the garage showed up as people began to leave. Even with his duck dynasty beard, Charlie couldn't hide his fondness toward Josh behind his rough exterior. "Where is the birthday kid?"

Megan shook his hand. "Glad you're here. It will mean a lot to Josh. He's really enjoyed working at your garage. I'll have Greg go find Josh."

A few minutes later, Josh ran up to Charlie with his brother right behind. "Hey, Charlie."

"Got something for you."

Josh took the box Charlie held out to him. He shook it, a puzzled look on his face.

"Open it."

Josh grinned. David watched over his shoulder as he tugged off the lid. Inside was a set of keys attached to a ring. Josh held them up. "What are these for?"

Charlie cleared his throat. "Know that old car out back you've been eyeing for the last several months?"

Josh's eyes widened.

"It's yours. It'll take a lot of work to get her running, but I figure you're gonna need a car to get to your new job."

"New job?"

"It's part time for now, but seeing how you like cars and how good you are with 'em, I want you to learn the ropes real good, then we'll talk full time once you get that car going."

Josh threw his arms around the big man. "Thank you. I'll work hard. You'll see."

"See you next week." He nodded at Megan then hurried around to the front.

Josh turned to his brother. "Can you believe it, man?"

David shrugged and walked away.

"Wait up." Josh caught up with his younger brother.

Ginger thought about how Grandpa would feel if they found Irene. She imagined them walking hand in hand as they rediscovered one another. Hopefully Josh and David could make their way back to what they once had as well.

An hour later, her stomach full of birthday cake and party food, Ginger took the hand Mike held out to her and followed her to the truck. Rabbit stayed behind with Grandpa. Ginger focused on the feel of her hand in Mike's. Where should she start?

He kissed the back of her hand then whistled the rest of the way to the truck.

Something new entered Ginger's heart. Confidence in what God was doing. The days ahead held promise.

Mike's phone rang as he opened the door for Ginger. He held up his finger as he answered the call. Deep concern lined his face as he listened. "I'll be right there. I'm at the Jordans'. Give me twenty minutes." He disconnected the call. "I'm sorry, Ginger. That was Maggie. Millie fell and she's been taken to the hospital. Maggie needs a ride and someone to be with her until they know what's going on. I can still drop you off on the way through town."

"I understand." Ginger climbed into the cab. It didn't stop the disappointment, but this was the life of a pastor.

He climbed behind the wheel and started the truck. "I'll call you later, and we'll figure out a time to talk."

CHAPTER THIRTY-FOUR

Ginger didn't get a chance to talk to Mike after he helped Maggie and Millie the day before. He was at the hospital till late then had to take Maggie back home. By the time he was done, Ginger had already left him a message that she was headed to bed and for him to call her today.

This morning, between the breakfast rush and lunch, Ginger and Betsy were getting Rachel moved in. She didn't have much since she had only come to Preston Hill for the summer. They each made two trips from the car to the guest room Ginger had set aside for Rachel to have and they were done. Rachel took a few minutes to situate things where she wanted them.

"Ginger, you need to decorate her room. It still looks like something from the sixties." Betsy traced her finger along the flowered pattern of the wallpaper.

"Maybe because it is from the sixties." Ginger laughed.

"I'm serious, girl. This room will give Rachel a headache."

"You don't need to redecorate on account of me."

"You'll change your mind after a week in here." Betsy led the small troupe back to the living room.

"I'm happy to have a place to live. I still can't believe you're letting me live here, Ginger."

"Believe it. Ginger is one of the most thoughtful people you'll meet." Betsy sat on the bed and bounced on the edge.

"So, are you serious about letting me help you with the search for your grandma?" Rachel put the last of her clothes in the closet.

"I need all the help I can get." Ginger led the way back to the living room. "Anyone for something sweet?"

"Where's Irene?" Grandpa rushed into the house. The evening sun sent dancing shadows through the front window.

"It's just us beautiful ladies." Betsy fluffed her hair and made an exaggerated pose like a model.

"But I saw her come in the house."

Ginger pulled Grandpa close. "She's not here."

He edged away from her. "I can see that." He stomped out of the house. The door slammed shut behind him.

"Well. That was interesting." Ginger worried about his insistence that he'd seen Irene here and other places about town. She would add that to the list to ask the doctor at the appointment in a couple days. "Anyone up for that break?"

"I need to get back to the café in about half an hour. I have till then." Rachel sat on the couch with her feet underneath her.

"A breather sounds great. Is chocolate involved?" Betsy sat in the easy chair and pulled the leg rest up.

"Chocolate coming up." Ginger hurried to the kitchen and back. "How's brownies?" She passed out the napkins.

"I'll take the pan." Betsy served herself a double-sized piece and passed the pan to Rachel.

Rachel dug out a piece for herself. "Have the DNA results come back?"

"Nope. Not sure we can count on that to help us." Ginger took a bite of her brownie.

"Too bad." Betsy licked her fingers covered with gooey chocolate. "These are great. Something new for the menu?"

"Have to keep a few recipes for myself." Ginger wadded up her napkin.

"True that." Rachel laughed and looked at her watch. "I better scoot. See you later."

CHAPTER THIRTY-FIVE

Ginger thumbed through the magazine to distract her mind from the upcoming doctor's appointment. Dropping it in her lap, she gave up as her thoughts turned to Mike. Over the last couple days, they had barely had time to do more than say hi in passing or leaving each other voice mails.

Grandpa stood. "Dagnabbit. Can't they turn that noise down?" He glared across the waiting room at the receptionist who was on the phone. Grumbling, he sat back down.

Ginger was thankful that only the two of them and the receptionist were in the area. "That's beautiful classical music."

"Hmph." He picked up a magazine and flipped through the pages, then tossed it down. "How long do we have to wait?"

"Grandpa."

"Don't scold me. I'm not a child."

Ginger remained silent. It wasn't easy knowing that his age was catching up with him. She anticipated bad news from the doctor.

"You mad?" Grandpa got up and paced.

"What?"

"You're awfully quiet for someone who usually talks all the time."

Ginger shook her head. Couldn't win for losing. It wasn't him that made her mad. She was mad at this whole dementia thing and what it was taking from them.

"You need to quit avoiding Mike." Grandpa sat back down.

She turned in her chair to face him. "Excuse me?"

"I've seen you two. You're good for each other. Don't know why in the world you're messing around wasting time. You never know when it'll run out. Here I am fighting to remember the one I love while you're choosing to forget the one you love."

"We're working on it."

"He's a good man. He won't let you down."

Grandpa was right about that, and even though she was determined to move forward, she still had doubts about herself. "I know. But what if I let him down?"

"When you love someone, you see it through. Even when you let each other down on occasion."

"Who said anything about love?"

He raised his eyebrows. "Going to play it like that, are you?"

She looked away. She wasn't going to deny how she felt, but she hadn't even told Mike.

Grandpa patted her arm. "The scariest part is standing on the diving board debating if you ought to jump. Not so bad after you're in the water."

"Walter Gipson." The nurse stood at the doorway leading to the examining rooms and waited.

"Your Mike isn't going anywhere anytime soon. He's patient and determined. But you're wasting time." He rose and headed toward his appointment.

Ginger gathered her purse and book and followed. She had almost forgotten how perceptive her grandfather was.

After another fifteen-minute wait in the examining room, the doctor showed up and apologized for the delay. "Had a bit of an emergency with a young patient." He sat behind his desk and pulled Walter's file in front of him. Glancing through the notes, he nodded at Ginger before focusing on her grandfather. "How are you doing today?"

"Fine. Give it to me straight, Doc."

The doctor nodded then glanced at Ginger, pulling her into the conversation. "First, I don't want you to get discouraged. Walter, you're ninety-eight years old, and your general physical health is good for your age."

"The bad news. Don't mince words." Grandpa sat up, his posture rigid.

"I'm sorry, but everything from your tests and from what we've covered in your appointment points to early stages of dementia."

Ginger gasped. Grandpa reached over and took her hand.

The doctor walked around to the front of the desk and sat on a chair across from them. "You caught this early instead of ignoring it. That's good. It means that, with the drugs available, we can slow the process down. You could still have good years ahead of you." He spent a few minutes going over the medication, its expected benefits as well as the side effects. He went back to his desk and made a note on his computer.

"Continue eating a healthy diet and incorporate exercise into every day to keep your body strong. We'll be here to help every step of the way. Walter, listen to Ginger. She's looking out for you. Don't fight her."

Tight lipped, Grandpa crossed his arms.

"Walter?" The doctor crossed his arms, too, and stared at Grandpa.

"Fine. But I don't have to like it."

Ginger bit her bottom lip to keep from saying something she would regret. *Lord, I'm going to need your help.*

The doctor addressed her. "The receptionist can set up that appointment for you. Do you have any more questions?"

"I'll probably wake up with a million of them tonight." Tendrils of fear about the days ahead wrapped around her mind.

"That's normal. And we'll help you find the answers you need. Make a follow-up appointment next month, and we'll see how the meds are doing." After Grandpa left the room, the doctor stopped Ginger on her way out. "I'm sure you're already experiencing the effects of having a grandparent with dementia—the stress, the worry, and fear. It would be a good idea to find a counselor and support group. Even though he could still have good years ahead, dementia is a long journey. One best not traveled alone."

Ginger watched Grandpa from the corner of her eye. He hadn't said a word after they left the doctor's office. She couldn't imagine being told that one day your memory might all be gone. Even though that was what they had expected, to hear the doctor confirm it brought them face to face with their fears. She had them. She knew Grandpa must. *Lord, make the day he can't remember far away. I don't want him to forget me. I don't want to be alone.*

A verse she had read that morning came to mind. "Have mercy on me, my God, have mercy on me, for in you I take refuge. I will take refuge in the shadow of your wings until the disaster has passed." Her heart cried out to God for refuge, and an image came to mind of Mike in her office reminding her that one of the ways God helps us is to send someone else to be His hands and feet. Pulling into the alley behind the café, she acknowledged her needed for Mike.

"Ginger?"

Sadness filled her as she faced the man who had raised her and loved her through every difficult part of her life so far.

"Find Irene before I forget. And quit running from Mike. Love is worth the risk." He looked down at his hands. "I don't want you to be alone when I'm gone."

Ginger hugged her greatest hero. "Okay."

He nodded. "I'm going to rest now."

"Need me to come in?"

He shook his head. "Go to him."

Ginger sniffled as she turned onto Mike's block. An unfamiliar car sat in front of his house. Ginger slowed the car. Mike sat on the porch swing with a beautiful woman with long dark hair, talking and laughing. It didn't look like his sisters, not from what she remembered from pictures in Mike's place. Ginger pulled into the drive, and Mike looked her direction. He headed off the porch.

An old feeling revisited her from the day she'd seen her fiancé with someone else wearing Ginger's ring. But Mike wasn't like her fiancé.

The car door opened, and Mike knelt next to her. "Walter?"

She nodded. "It's dementia." A torrent of tears flooded her face. She had no words for the deep sadness in her heart. She rested in Mike's strength as he enveloped her in a hug.

After a few minutes, Ginger looked up. "I better go."

"Come inside."

She glanced over at the house. "You have company."

"That's just my ex-wife, Jackie. I can talk to her later. She'll understand."

"I'm confused."

"Me, too. It's a long story for another day. Right now, you're most important."

CHAPTER THIRTY-SIX

The late afternoon sunlight came through the lone window in the attic, and Ginger took solace in the quietness. After she cried on Mike's shoulder, she returned to the house. Grandpa was sitting by the window. She knelt next to the chair and leaned against him. They shared their grief for a few minutes before he scoffed at her concern and encouraged her to go do something else. He left for the café, and she sought sanctuary in this space filled with memories of her family.

Interrupted only by Rabbit's occasional barking at the bottom of the ladder, she embraced the attic's invitation to reminisce, leave the present behind, and forget the future for a few moments. She allowed herself the distraction of searching for clues and poking through boxes long forgotten.

To the left of the ladder, everything imaginable was stored from more recent years. Her dad's things, which she had brought up after he died but never sorted through, Christmas decorations, and seasonal clothing. To the right was a treasure hunter's delight. Old trunks from her great-grandparent's era. Furniture that promised the telling of family history. Framed photos of ancestors long forgotten. Stacks of boxes holding untold stories of life in earlier days. And dust. She coughed.

The musty fragrance reminded her of stolen childhood moments when she hid among the mazes of treasures, pretending to be an adventurer. But that was before she turned eleven. Before her mother died. Since then, she'd avoided coming up here except for the rare unavoidable search for things lost or bringing up one more thing to add to the piles. And now, another unavoidable search lured her forward to discover the truth.

Brushing the dust off a box, she opened the lid. Recipe books. Those would be interesting to go through later. She set the box aside. Somewhere in this place was a small chest full of her mother's things. A memory surfaced of the Christmas Eve when she and Mike had hunted for Christmas decorations to bless the Jordan family. In this dusty old place, they began a lasting friendship. Why had she allowed her fears to dictate their relationship for so long? Sitting in the waiting room at the doctor's, her grandfather saw the truth of what she held in her heart for Mike.

"Girlfriend, you up there?" Betsy's voice traveled up the stairs, followed by her appearance. The familiar jangling of bracelets sang a calming song to Ginger's soul, and she fell into Betsy's open arms.

"I've got you." Betsy murmured calming phrases until the sobbing ceased.

"Did Grandpa tell you about the doctor visit?"

"Mike told me."

"I'm going to miss Grandpa. He's always been there for me." A fresh wave of tears drenched her face.

Betsy patted her back. "You cry all you need to, girl. Let that grief out."

After a few minutes, Ginger's eyes slowed their downpour. "Thanks for checking on me."

"That's what friends are for. Now, what can I do for you and your grandfather?"

"Help me keep the promise I made to him. I need to find Irene while he can still remember her. That means I need to find a small chest of my mother's things up here somewhere."

Betsy nodded. "Then I better pull up my sleeves. What are you hoping to find?"

"Something to lead us to my grandmother or her grave. Grandpa needs to know what happened to her while he can still understand."

Footsteps coming up the ladder preceded a head poking up through the floor where the steps deposited visitors to the attic. Rachel hoisted herself up. "Now I know why you stay here so long. It's not easy getting up."

"Thanks for taking care of things at the Jukebox."

"Sure. I had an idea. I was thinking about checking with Sunrise about hiring another one of their residents."

"Good idea. Bridgette's worked out well. Relief surged through Ginger that the weight of the café was lessening even more under Rachel's management.

"So..." Rachel looked around the haphazard arrangement of things. "I'm sorry about Walter. Anything I can do?"

"Keep taking care of the Jukebox. That's going to allow me time to find Irene. Even though the doctor said it could be a slow-progressing dementia, and he might still have good years ahead of him, we don't know for sure. I'll be there when I can, but I don't know how much time this will take."

"You got it. You'll let me know if there's anything else?"

"I will." The attic darkened. Ginger glanced out the window. "Looks like a storm brewing." Thunder rolled and lightning lit up the shadowy space around them. "The weatherman was right." She brushed off her jeans. "This will have to wait for another day. I'm hungry. Time for lunch."

CHAPTER THIRTY-SEVEN

Ginger relished the gentle sprinkles on her windshield instead of the recent downpours. The sun held dominance in the sky for now, but according to the weatherman more rain was moving in. It was going to be another gully washer. She parked her car at Charlie's and looked around. Mike's truck wasn't here yet.

She walked around to the back of the garage to see the progress on the plane while she waited on Mike. "Hey, Charlie."

The big man waved and pointed his thumb toward the plane. "They're making progress."

Ginger leaned against an old car sitting in the back lot and watched the War World II vet and two lanky teenagers at work. This was good. Heads together, the boys listened as Grandpa pointed to various spots, explaining each part and what it did. He was a good teacher. He'd done a lot of that with her growing up, teaching her how to change a flat tire, how to change the oil and spark plugs. This would keep his mind working and off the dementia. Staying connected was important.

Grandpa straightened and headed to the toolbox. The boys followed.

The light fragrance of Mike's cologne accompanied his appearance at her elbow. He slid his arm around her shoulders and pulled her close.

She relished the strength she found when she was next to him. "They're doing a good job on the plane, but David is so angry. It comes out in everything he does."

"Give him time. He's been through a lot." He looked down at her. "How's my girl doing?"

She nestled back against him. "Better than yesterday."

Mike tilted her chin up. "My sweet Ginger. What I would do to ease your pain."

"You're doing it." She offered a slight smile.

"How's Walter doing?"

She shrugged. "He's either accepted it or is denying it. He's been acting as though everything is fine."

"Sometimes, knowing what you're facing can take away a lot of the fear that actually makes things worse."

"Maybe."

A clatter brought their attention back to the trio working on the plane. Josh's younger brother threw a ratchet on the ground next to a socket wrench. "This is stupid."

Grandpa got in the boy's face. "You will respect the tools, young man. Pick those up and put them in the box where they go."

The two glared at each other. Josh stood to the side with a smirk. No doubt he remembered when it had been his turn a few months ago to receive a tongue lashing from Grandpa. He had come a long way.

"Fine." David picked up the tools and placed them in the box with an exaggerated motion. "That good enough for you?"

"For now." Grandpa looked up at the sky. "We better close things up."

"Why? Scared of a bit of rain, old man?"

Josh poked his younger brother in the chest. "Enough. Let's help."

David let off a stream of curse words but lent his energy towards putting tools away.

Ginger turned to face Mike. "So, tell me about what's going on with your ex."

Sprinkles turned to lush fat drops, falling here and there, leaving behind their footprints on the pavement.

He tucked a strand of her wet hair behind her ear. "We had to take care of some things that caught up with us."

"Like?"

The raindrops crowded together, dowsing Mike and Ginger. Lightning flashed, followed a few seconds later by thunder, making it impossible to hear. Rain unleashed in full measure from the sky. Lightning lit up the space around them, striking a nearby tree. She jumped. He grabbed her arm and pulled her toward the garage where they sheltered inside with the others.

Charlie urged everyone to head elsewhere while he closed the doors. "Weatherman says a tornado was spotted west of here. We need to find better shelter. This old place will blow away if a tornado rips through town."

Mike spoke in Ginger's ear. "We'll talk tomorrow after I do the books." He turned to the men. "Josh, you and your brother come with me." He tilted his head toward his car.

"You can't tell us what to do." David crossed his arms.

Josh elbowed his brother. "Come on, dude. You really want to make it an issue?" He pointed up at the darkening sky. Lightning flashed nearby.

"Fine." David stomped to the car.

"Let's help Walter and Ginger to her car first." Mike took Walter's arm, the rain falling in sheets as they hurried to their vehicles.

By the time Ginger made it home, Rachel had closed the café and waited for them at the door to the house. "I was hoping you would get back. I didn't want to be here by myself." Rabbit paced around, almost as if he was in a hurry for them to head for safety.

As fast as Walter's pace allowed, they hustled down to the basement where they would wait out the storm. Half an hour later, they breathed a sigh of relief as the storm passed without a tornado. The phone rang.

"Everyone okay?" Mike's voice soothed her nerves.

"Coming out of our hole now. How about over there?"

"Josh and David weathered this like pros. I'm going to take them out to the farm and then check on some of the older congregants. Need anything? Did Walter do okay?"

"We're good." She glanced at Grandpa. "He weathered it like a pro, too. Thanks."

"See you tomorrow."

CHAPTER THIRTY-EIGHT

"You sure you don't mind helping?" Ginger scooted another box out of the way. After work was the only time Rachel had to pitch in with her search for Irene clues.

"Absolutely. Wouldn't miss this adventure." Rachel snapped a few pictures. "These images would be great for my blog. Can I use them?"

"Don't see why not. Help me with this stack of boxes. The chest I'm looking for might be in the area behind here."

Rachel and Ginger alternated grabbing boxes and stacking them a few feet away. A path cleared, and Ginger entered an area set up almost like a little bedroom. To her right, a wingback chair upholstered in a floral pattern sat next to a small table with lamp on top. Across the space where the pile of boxes stood, a dresser braced the wall. Books piled on top leant weight to there being a strong reader in the family.

To the left of the dresser, a wooden room divider stood, splitting the seating area from the rest of the attic. Ginger opened the drawers and discovered piles of faded linens. She promised herself she'd revisit this spot and uncover the history she had allowed to remain hidden all these years. History that Grandpa was sure to enjoy.

She closed her eyes. Where had she put that chest? She must have come up here more than she realized over the last several years. Hugging herself against a chill in the air, she meandered around the attic. She skirted Rachel, who was intent on taking pictures.

At the point of giving up, her foot caught on an old rug, and she sprawled onto the floor. Rachel hurried over to help her. From her vantage point on the floor, she looked up at the tall shelves lining the wall and tapped her forehead with the palm of her hand. "There it is." Ginger laughed. "Right where I left it."

Taking Rachel's hand, she pulled herself up, then found the step stool and retrieved the chest. "Now, to see what my mother had to say on the matter."

Setting her phone to the side, Rachel joined Ginger in the middle of the area rug Ginger had tripped over. She reached into the box and pulled out an old leather-bound book. "This is amazing."

"My mother's diary." Ginger took it and flipped through the yellowed pages, stopping to read a few sentences throughout the book. "Looks like she wrote a lot of this when she was a teenager. Oh,listen...

"*I started having these dreams lately. My grandparents ignore me when I talk about them. Dad...well he's always preoccupied. I dream about a young woman. I'm a toddler and she's reading to me. I feel warm and safe. Could I be dreaming about my mama? No one will tell me about her. Maybe my heart will remember what my mind has forgotten.*"

Ginger held a hand over her mouth. Did she finally hold the answers in her hand?

"Keep reading." Rachel pulled Ginger's arm to direct her to the couch.

Ginger lowered herself, her gaze intent on the words in the diary.

"What does it say?"

She flipped the page. "She's talking about her mother's jewelry box." Ginger skipped a few lines down.

"*I dreamed about that box again. According to my dad, I was a toddler when she left. Could I really remember that far back? In my dream I asked my grandparents about the box and the next day it was gone.*

"She writes that it was the last thing she had of her mother's."

"How sad." Rachel looked over Ginger's shoulder at the journal.

"Maybe that jewelry box Grandpa found really is my grandmother's. There's more." Ginger ran her finger down the text, skimming the diary for more information. "Here."

"*Another dream. I woke up crying. My pillow was wet with tears. Mama hid a note to Dad in the bottom of the box. In my dream I watched as Mama put the note inside, then glued the edges of another bottom she put on top. She was singing a song the whole time she worked. It's the song I remember most. But what use is remembering this now? The box is gone.*"

Ginger touched the pages where water marks marred and blurred words here and there. Possibly the tangible evidence of her mother's grief. Her hands shook as she touched the pages. They were getting close but still had no idea where Irene was. Ginger lowered her face to her hands.

Rachel's touch on her shoulder reminded her she wasn't alone. "You have the box now."

"Do we?"

"Only one way to know." Rachel smiled. "Let's go test it."

"You're right." Tucking the diary under her arm, she pulled the chain turning off the light and headed for the exit.

Downstairs, Ginger pulled the box close and opened the lid. Using a nail file, she dug at the edges of the bottom. It was stuck tight. "How do we get it out without ruining the note?"

"Could we get the glue wet?" Rachel leaned closer to look inside the box.

"Maybe." Ginger got a dropper she had saved from an old medicine bottle and filled it with water. Carefully, she dropped water along the edges. "Let's wait a bit and let it soak."

Rachel giggled. "This is kind of fun."

Ginger felt almost numb. Could the answer have been this close the whole time?

After a few minutes, Ginger went back to work with the nail file. Bit by bit, the edges came up. With Rachel looking over her shoulder, she pulled up the bottom she had loosened. Underneath was a neatly folded piece of paper. Ginger stared at the piece of paper. What had Irene revealed? Would it be enough to help them find her?

"I'm almost afraid to read the note." Ginger took a deep breath and took it out. "Here goes." She flattened the yellowed page on the table.

> *Dearest Walter,*
>
> *My one and only love - now and always. I've been living with my parents, but they want to move out by Brainard, near Lincoln. My father is afraid of my mother and me being interned or being treated badly during this awful time. Things are supposed to be better near Lincoln and my parents are making me go with them. You know how they are. Supposedly we have friends in the area willing to help us.*
>
> *They promise to bring me back to you, to let me write letters, but I'm not sure they intend to do that. Come find me if I don't return. I refuse to steal our daughter away from you. Love her enough for both of us and don't let her forget me. I will do everything in my power to make it back to you. I promise.*
>
> *Forever loving,*
> *Always loved,*
> *Your beloved wife, Irene.*

"Wow." Ginger leaned back on the couch.

"Time for a road trip." Rachel touched the pages in the diary. "Something so familiar about these pages. Worn as though broken down by time and grief. Every family's story at some point in their history."

"Speaking from experience?" Ginger laid a hand on Rachel's.

Rachel shrugged. "It dredges up a longing for a connection to the past that I didn't realize was there. Strange, right?"

Ginger pulled the younger woman into a hug. "Then we're both strange."

CHAPTER THIRTY-NINE

Later that day, before meeting with Mike, Ginger stopped in at the café to check on the new waitress.

"Table four up," Harry called out and slid three plates onto the pass-through window.

The new waitress that Rachel had hired from Sunrise took to her job as if she was born for it. Apparently, before she hit her current rough spot, food service was her forte. She and Rachel made a good team.

Ginger turned over the food prep to the young chef's assistant who arrived for his shift, then checked on the customers. She stopped to talk to a few friends and welcome travelers passing through on summer vacation. Rachel's marketing at work. Wanting to see Mike, she went back to the office where he worked. He promised to tell her about his ex-wife saga and then she hoped they would finally have their talk.

"Any news?"

Mike looked up to where she stood in the doorway and smiled. "You can write a check to the bank that should hold them off. Keep up this pace and by next month you'll be caught up. The Jukebox will be in the clear. And with the new revenue coming in now, you'll be fine."

"How can I thank you enough?"

He reached for her hand. "For starters, go on a walk with me." He grinned and led her toward the back door. "Harry, do you need Ginger?" He held tight to her hand.

"Nope."

Rachel came through the swinging doors in time to catch the exchange. "Me neither."

Mike led Ginger down the alley toward the park. "You ready for this story?"

"Absolutely."

"You met my ex, Jackie. She was in town to pick up our daughter Rose."

Ginger stopped and pulled her hand out of his. "Daughter? I thought you didn't have any kids."

"That's what I thought. Apparently, Jackie was pregnant when she left."

"Okay. I guess. That would make Rose how old?"

"Twenty or twenty-one by Dad math." He ducked his head. "Jackie was back and forth between me and the other guy for about a year. Each time she walked through the door she would tell me she wanted to work things out. I fell for it every time. Then one day, she was gone, and I never saw her again. So Rose is probably more like twenty." He scratched the back of his neck.

Considering Mike's lifestyle back then, that made sense. "So, why was your daughter here?" Ginger started walking. "This is getting crazier by the minute."

Mike fell in step beside her. "Tell me about it."

"Keep going." She picked up her pace.

"I was a jerk when Jackie and I were together. So, her not telling me? That makes sense from her perspective. She wasn't a lot better, though. Carrying on an affair with the man she is now married to while I was deployed. I was clueless. Anyway, she was reasonably sure the baby was mine but, since she was seeing both of us for a while and not wanting to risk her new marriage, she never said anything or had any tests run."

"Then how did Rose find out?"

"She was helping clean out their garage and came across some things from when I was married to Jackie. A box of memorabilia from the good times including a bunch of pictures. According to my ex, Rose doesn't look much like her dad, but something in one of the pictures of me reminded her of herself." Mike ran a hand through his hair.

"But how did she get from a few pictures in their garage to knowing you were her father and then arriving in Preston Hill?"

"Jackie kept her journal from back when we were married. She had written all kinds of things in there about how much of a jerk I was and how she planned to leave. She wrote about the pregnancy and how the baby could be either mine or her husband's and that she didn't plan to tell her new husband."

"That would do it."

"Rose's behavior changed overnight. Usually a quiet artist who did life under the radar, she started acting out. Even though she was enrolled in college, Rose lived at home. When the dean's office called her parents to let them know she was failing two classes, they confronted her. That's when trouble became her new middle name. Sulky all the time, she developed quite the mouth. New friends began showing up at the house bringing a wild element to Rose's life. This went on for almost a year, but when the kid who swore she would never get a tattoo showed up with one and her head half shaven, they knew there was more going on than she was telling them."

"How did she get from there to here?" Ginger slowed her pace as they crossed the street to the park.

"She's very resourceful. With a bit of online research and the help of social media, she found me. As far as she was concerned, I had abandoned her."

"But it was Jackie who decided not to tell you."

Mike shrugged. "Who knows what went on Rose's mind."

"I'm guessing that very resourceful young lady came looking for you."

Mike pointed at Ginger. "You got it. She has her own car, and she left a note to tell them she was safe. Of course, she didn't tell them she knew where I lived. Jackie and her husband were beside themselves. They scoured Rose's bedroom and found Jackie's memory box. She knew what Rose had found out. Jackie called up a couple my old Marine buddies, and they pointed her in the right direction."

"Wow."

"There's more." One side of Mike's mouth lifted in a grin. "Rose is the graffiti artist."

"You're kidding me."

"Nope. Rose targeted places of importance to me with her art."

"What will happen to her now?"

"Everyone agreed not to press charges. That's what I was doing the last couple days. Talking to all the recipients of her artwork. She'll do community service."

"Can I meet her?"

"You want to meet her?"

Ginger nodded. "She's your daughter. Of course I want to meet her."

His grin broadened. "I'm sure I can arrange something while she's still in town doing community service. But you've seen her. Remember hoodie girl at Sunrise?"

"That's Rose?"

"Hiding in plain sight." He glanced at his watch. "I'm supposed to meet her in about half an hour."

"Want to stop by for coffee and pie afterwards?"

"Want to? Absolutely. But I'm not sure how long this will take."

"You do have a lot of catching up to do."

"Indeed. I have a daughter. That sounds so foreign to me."

"Better get used to it."

After a couple hours of sorting out her office and the storage room, Ginger made her way to the dining room for coffee. She hoped Mike had time to stop by after his meeting with Jackie and Rose. She'd forgotten to tell him about the letter hidden in the jewelry box and wanted to fill him in on what she had learned.

She sipped on her coffee. If Mike went with her to Brainard, they would finally have plenty of time to talk. An image of Rose as hoodie girl entered her mind, and she shook her head. Mike had a daughter. A young adult daughter. Life sure could change in an instant. The thought sobered her as she recalled Grandpa's diagnosis. Those two facts could drastically affect their relationship. Was Mike willing to stick around for the long haul? If his past persistence was any indication, then he was.

"What's got you looking so serious?" Rachel stopped next to her table and warmed up Ginger's coffee.

"Thinking about Mike finding out he has a daughter and about Grandpa's diagnosis."

Rachel sat in the chair opposite Ginger. "Loss and gain in the same breath. That's a lot for anyone. Are you doing okay?"

Ginger smiled at Rachel. "I have great friends to support me."

"And Mike."

Ginger looked down at the table. She wrapped her hands around her mug and took a sip of coffee. She had Mike to count on. The thought warmed her.

Rachel chuckled. "You have it bad."

"What?" Ginger looked up. "Oh." She laughed. "I'm acting more like a schoolgirl than a woman my age."

"You're allowed when you're in love. No matter the age." She got up from the table.

No turning back now.

Lightning lit up the sky. Thunder rumbled nearby. "This year's been bad for storms." Rachel headed over to the coffee machine.

"Ginger." Harry called from the kitchen. "Tornado watch."

"Let's close early." Ginger gathered her things and helped Rachel lock up before they headed over to the house.

Grandpa and Bo were enjoying a mug of cocoa at the kitchen table when Ginger and Rachel got to the house. Rachel excused herself to call family, and Ginger headed to the kitchen as she hummed a random tune.

"How's the storm, Ginger? Bo's thinking about heading home." Grandpa served himself a piece of her chocolate pie.

She glanced out the window. "Looks like it's easing up. I'm headed to bed. Bo, do you want me to make up one of our extra guest beds, so you don't have to go out in this mess?"

"That would be great."

After fixing up the guest room, Ginger closed her bedroom door and called Mike. At the tone, she asked if Mike wanted to be her sleuthing partner on the day trip to Brainard.

Shadows moved into the house as the sun fell lower in the sky. Ginger turned on the overhead light and closed the curtains. She stared at the jewelry box on her dresser as she sank onto her chair and contemplated her next move. The note from the bottom of the jewelry box rested on her leg and she pressed it flat. Would Irene or the evidence of her having lived near Brainard still be there? She reviewed what Grandpa had finally told her he had done to find Irene over the years. Brainard hadn't come up. The note mentioned it was near

Lincoln. She opened her laptop and typed the name into Google Maps, then waited while her computer brought up the location. How close was this to Mountain Home where Grandpa and Irene lived when they first got married?

Given enough time, Google Maps showed Brainard to be north of Lincoln—the opposite direction from Mountain Home—about a two-hour drive east of Preston Hill. She went down the hall and checked to see if Rachel would be okay if Ginger took the next day for a bit of sleuthing. Disappointed that she hadn't heard back from Mike, she called Betsy. Always eager for an adventure, her friend jumped at the chance to ride shotgun.

CHAPTER FORTY

Ginger waited for the coffee to drip. At five in the morning, she needed caffeine before she and Betsy headed out to Brainard. She opened the windows to hear the early morning sounds. Birds chirping in the pre-dawn darkness reminded her of the verse from Mike's sermon on rest. "Look at the birds of the air; they do not sow or reap or store away in barns, and yet your heavenly Father feeds them. Are you not much more valuable than they?"

God was looking out for her grandpa and his crazy determination to find his wife. And He was looking out for her. They would be okay.

"See you later." Grandpa and Bo rushed past the kitchen doorway.

"In a hurry?"

"Things to do. We'll get breakfast at the café." The two men left her to guess what they were up to. Probably work on the airplane.

Her phone rang from the bedroom, and she hurried to pick up. Mike. It stopped ringing as she swiped to answer. "Drats." She tried to call back, but he didn't answer, so she opened her voicemail.

"Hey, Ginger. Miss me already?" He chuckled.

She blushed even though no one was around.

The message continued. "I have to miss the day trip, though I would have enjoyed having you to myself all day. Long story, but here's the short version. My visit with Rose went well. You'll like her. On the way to see you, I helped Charlie get someone out of the ditch and then I gave them a ride to Omaha where they live. While there I decided to look up a couple Marine buddies for dinner. Ended up staying overnight since it was late. I have a meeting later this morning with the church board. Call me when you get back from Brainard and we'll have that coffee and pie."

Ginger set her phone down. Her heart warmed toward the man she hoped to spend the rest of her days with. The buzzer went off on the coffee pot, and she hurried back to the kitchen and poured a cup, then opened her mother's journal, which was lying on the table.

Turning the page, she sat back in surprise. The image attached to the page was faded, but the script below indicated that her mom had found the picture of Irene while snooping in her grandparents' room. This looked to be in better focus than the one Grandpa had. She held the image closer to the light. Could it be? She pulled out the magnifying glass that she kept handy for the tiny print on ingredient labels and examined the image. No way. She walked back to her room and looked at herself in the dresser mirror and then at the picture. The hair was different, but she looked like Irene. That explained why Grandpa kept thinking he saw his wife.

"You ready to go?" Betsy's voice shook Ginger out of her discovery.

Not wanting to share what she had found yet, she closed the journal. "Let me put this away and grab my phone." She tucked it under her mattress. *Lord, tell me if I'm crazy.*

Ginger grabbed the report from the genealogy site and tucked it with the note from Irene into her purse. She felt like she had in college while watching for the casting sheet after play tryouts. Knowing she'd gotten the lead, yet not knowing. "Let's go."

Two hours later, they drove into the tiny town of Brainard. With no idea where in the area Irene had lived with her folks, they headed to City Hall. Inside, they found the county clerk and within a few minutes, using her parents' names, had a location for a house. Unfortunately, there were no longer any buildings on that section of land.

"What now?" Ginger slid into the front seat of her vehicle and waited for Betsy to buckle up.

"What about stopping by some of the churches in town?" Betsy rolled down her window.

"That's a great idea." They started with a church on Main Street. The office was closed, so they drove through town and stopped in on several others.

"This is frustrating." Ginger pulled into the parking lot of another church and they got out of the car. "How many does this make?"

"Five or six, I think. But the day isn't over yet. Have a little faith." Betsy bumped Ginger shoulder to shoulder. "We'll find something."

They entered the front door and followed the signs to the office. The lights were on and the door was open, but nobody seemed to be around.

"Yoo-hoo. Anyone here?" Betsy's call didn't rouse any response.

After a couple minutes, an older woman came down the hall. Thin, she initially looked frail, but her steps and voice were strong. Her gray hair had strips of purple peeking out in several places. "Sorry ladies, I'm the only one here today." She scrunched her shoulders. "I needed a break." She covered her mouth and giggled. "My name is Jolene. How can I help you?"

Ginger grinned. She couldn't resist the woman's joy. "I'm Ginger and this is Betsy. We're looking for someone who used to live in this area."

"Not sure that I'll be much help. Did you check with the town clerk?"

"That was a dead end."

"Hmm." The woman tapped her foot. "When did you say they lived here?"

"Would have been around the end of World War II."

Her eyes lit up. "Why didn't you say so?" She walked around her desk and grabbed a ring of keys. "There's someone you need to meet. My brother knows everything about everyone."

The woman locked the door behind them and headed out at a fast pace. "My family has lived here since before the war. We took in boarders during the depression and the war. As a matter of fact...what did you say the family name was?" She stopped in the middle of the sidewalk and waited for their answer.

"Hutton." Ginger's hopes took a jump forward at the expression on the woman's face. "Daniel and Regina Hutton. They had a daughter Irene."

Jolene looked up at the sky as though the answer would be written there. After a moment, she held her finger up. "Hutton. Hutton. Wait. Did she go by Grace?" The woman looked about to burst with anticipation.

"That was her middle name."

"Did she have a son?"

"She had a daughter, but she wouldn't have been with her."

"That doesn't make sense." The woman headed down the block and stopped at the corner. "Change of plans." She did a U-turn and headed back the way they came.

Ginger wanted the answer now but didn't want to interrupt the woman's progress toward someone who could give them the information they needed, so she kept her mouth closed. She looked over at Betsy and grinned.

"Here we are. If your Irene is our Grace, then Mary Sue will have answers for your quest." She knocked on the door. "It takes her a while to get to the door." She clapped like an excited child. "This is fun."

The woman who answered the door sat in a wheelchair and looked like she was about the same age as Grandpa. She smiled up at Jolene. "Did you bring me visitors?"

Jolene nodded. "Ginger and Betsy." She swept her hand toward the woman in the wheelchair. "This is Mary Sue."

Mary Sue waved them in then backed up her chair so they could get past her.

"They're looking for information on an Irene Hutton. Said her middle name was Grace."

"My Gracie?"

Jolene shrugged. "Maybe. I'll go make some tea."

Ginger and Betsy sat on the couch across from where the woman parked her wheelchair.

"I had a best friend in 1948 named Grace Hutton. I called her Gracie. She was the sweetest woman. We found jobs in Lincoln that were close to each other so we could ride together." Mary Sue rolled to a shelf a few feet away. "Let's see, where is that?" She pulled a photo album down and rolled back to the couch. "Here's a picture." She handed the album to Ginger.

She looked into the face of the same woman who was in the picture from her mom's journal. Ginger stroked her face. "That's Irene."

"Well, I'll be." Betsy leaned over to get a view. "She looks like you."

Ginger handed the album back to Mary Sue. "When her husband came back from the war, she was gone. He's always believed that she was still alive."

"She never made it back to him? Oh, that poor dear. She said her parents would prevent it. So, he doesn't know about William?"

Ginger tilted her head. "William?"

"Her son."

She felt as though she had been punched in the gut. Irene didn't have a son when she left and didn't mention one in her letters. That could only mean one thing.

"Honey. Don't worry. William was her husband's son. She was pregnant when she left. I almost forgot. I've got something for you. Wait here." The woman rolled into the other room.

Jolene came in with a tray of tea and served them. "I'm going to head to work. It was so nice meeting you. Can you make it back on your own?"

Ginger assured her they could.

A few minutes later, Mary Sue rolled back in. "She left these." She handed Ginger a box. "She said if Walter ever came looking for her to give him these."

Ginger opened the box and gasped. The box was full of letters. "These are all for Walter?"

Mary Sue nodded. "They all came back to her. I tell you, she loved that man something fierce, but she couldn't get to him without help from her parents. Didn't have easy access to people like we do today, what with the internet and such." The woman shook her head. "Such a shame. When you find her, tell her Mary Sue said hello."

Ginger hurried across to the Jukebox from the house. She thought about the letters from Mary Sue she had tucked away in her room. She didn't know what the letters contained and didn't want Grandpa caught off guard with news about his son. She and Betsy hadn't been able to figure out the DNA information, so she planned to follow up on those results first, then talk to Mike once he got back before she decided what to do.

She peered up at the darkening sky. The weather report indicated a severe storm with a history of tornados moving into the area within the next couple hours. She needed to close the café soon and send folks to shelter just in case.

Ginger clutched the DNA papers and hurried into her office. She called the number supplied on the genealogy site to clarify whether she understood the test correctly or not. She was surprised not to be put on hold. After a few minutes of questions, they confirmed what she thought she understood. There was a high probability that she did have family out there. She felt giddy, like a schoolgirl waiting for her first date to pick her up, and she wanted to shout it to the world.

Harry knocked on the doorframe. "The weather service has just issued a tornado warning. They spotted one about fifty miles west of here."

"Thought that wasn't due in for another two hours." Ginger stuffed the tests into her pocket. "Let's get everyone over to the basement at the house." They hurried into the dining hall where a handful of people were enjoying a meal. Rachel urged the guests out through the kitchen and across the alley. Harry shut all the open flames on the stoves. Ginger locked the front door and followed them across the alley as the tornado siren went off. Grandpa held open the door so they could scoot inside and down the stairs with Rabbit close on their heels. They hunkered down under the central beam and waited.

Grandpa tuned in the radio and they listened to the progression of the storm through the static. "If you haven't taken cover, do so now. A tornado has been spotted on the ground headed directly into Preston Hill, and it doesn't show any indication of slowing down. It's leaving plenty of damage in its path. Head to cover now. I repeat. Head to cover now."

Ginger checked her messages for one from Mike. Nothing. From his message this morning, she thought he would be back in town already. She had left a message as soon as they got back from Brainard. Why hadn't he dropped by already? Where was he? *Lord, keep Mike safe. I can't lose him now.*

Rachel scooched close to Ginger. "I don't like these storms."

"We'll be fine down here."

"Where's Mike?"

"Safe. I hope." Inwardly, Ginger feared the worse, but didn't want to alarm Rachel.

The wind wailed angrily as debris and rain pounded against the house. Ginger put her arm around Rachel and looked at the group huddled together in various stages of fright and concern. One of the men had his phone out recording the noise. When he attempted to go video the storm, Grandpa wouldn't allow him up the stairs. The roar of the tornado increased.

"Sounds like it's right overhead." Rachel's breath shuddered.

A crash shook the house. Ginger and Grandpa exchanged glances. What part of the house had just become collateral damage? Ginger thought about all the research upstairs and hoped it didn't blow away. Was Mike out in this storm? There was so much she needed to say to him.

The roar moved away from their location, and the wind began to calm. After about twenty minutes, the siren went silent as the weatherman came on and reported that the warning was over for their area.

"I'll go check things out." Harry took the lead. Grandpa looked ready to fight over it, but he glanced toward Ginger and didn't argue.

After a few minutes, Harry called them up. "It's a mess, but we're safe."

The group clustered on the porch and took in the damage around them. Debris lay everywhere, including the top half of a neighbor's tree that had fallen close enough to the house to knock into it. Ginger studied the roof closely. No holes.

"I can't wait to post this." The young man who had wanted to video the storm grabbed the hand of the girl with him, and they took off down the alley, phones in hand, presumably to take pictures to share with the world.

Another couple waved and went to check on their car. With Rachel close behind, Ginger walked across the alley to check on the Jukebox. In the kitchen, all seemed well. The dining room was another matter.

Some of the windows and the door had been shattered by flying debris, and the place was soaked from the rain that had been pouring only moments ago. Ginger let out a pent-up breath of relief, glad they had all gotten out when they did.

Rachel peered out the front windows. "The other side of the street made out worse than we did."

Rather than crunch through the broken shards lying across the floor, they went the long way around through the alley and down the sidewalk to check on their business neighbors. One by one, they made their way to the sidewalk. They called out to check on each other then took stock of the damage. *Mike.* She pulled out her phone and dialed his number. When he didn't pick up, she left a voicemail to let him know she was okay.

"I can't reach Charlie. I need to check on the airplane." Grandpa's voice startled Ginger.

"I'll take you over after we cover these windows."

He nodded. "We've got those boards in the garage. Think Mike could help us?"

"Can't reach him."

"I'm sure he'll be checking on you." Grandpa patted her on the arm.

"Sorry about all your work on the window, Rachel."

She shrugged. "It can be redone. I need to call my family and let them know I'm okay."

"Take whatever time you need. We won't be opening for a few days at least." Ginger watched Rachel leave. What would this damage mean to the café? Mike had said they were close to being caught up with payments. But how long would it take to get the café back open? She turned and almost ran into Greg and his boys.

"We got here as soon as we could. What can we do?"

"You didn't have to come. I'm sure you have your own mess to clean up."

"Everything is fine at the farm. You know how tornados are. One house is blown away while the one next door has no damage. Now put us to work."

"Then follow me." Ginger smiled and led the way to find Grandpa.

A couple hours later, Greg and the boys nailed the last board in place and went across the street to help others with their cleanup. Ginger tried calling Mike again and, after no answer, loaded Grandpa in the car and drove to Charlie's.

"You worried about Mike?"

"Starting to be."

"He'll be okay."

Ginger nodded. She hoped he hadn't been caught in the storm.

Coming into view of the garage, Walter let out an audible breath. The tree that used to stand at the corner was gone, but the garage looked unscathed. No sooner had she stopped the car than Grandpa got out and hurried around back. A shout of excitement suggested that the plane had not been damaged. The grin on his face when he came back confirmed it.

Charlie pulled into the parking lot and got out of his tow truck. "Should have called you earlier, but it got a bit crazy checking around town for anyone needing help."

"No worries. How bad is it?" Ginger held her breath.

"Main Street got it the worst. But time will tell when all the reports come in."

Grandpa climbed back into Ginger's car. Rabbit was close behind. "Stop by Mike's?"

Ginger didn't need any more encouragement. Debris littered the yard. His truck wasn't in the drive and there was no sign of Mike when she knocked on his door and peeked in the windows. On the way back home, she and Grandpa stopped to check on several people from the church to make sure they were okay. Maggie and Millie needed to be calmed down, but other than a few branches in the yard and loose shingles flapping on the roof, they were fine. Lillian and Randy were at Betsy's helping with debris and a broken window. Other members were assisting their neighbors. Along the way, they picked up a stray dog and took it to the vet. Daylight was fading by the time they pulled up behind the café. News reports were rolling in about the damage along the tornado's path.

After Grandpa went to bed, Ginger prepared a snack of cheese and crackers along with a pot of tea for her and Rachel. "You ever been in a tornado before?"

Rachel shook her head. "That was terrifying."

"I've seen worse."

An hour later, Ginger's phone rang. The number unknown, she picked up.

"Is this Ginger Moreland?"

"It is."

"I'm calling from Immanuel Hospital in Omaha. Mr. Thompson was in an accident, and you're on his phone as a local emergency contact."

Ginger grabbed Rachel's hand. "What happened? Is he okay?"

"I can't speak to that, ma'am. I'm not his doctor. I'm just making notifications. Would you like his room number? You could find out more information from the nurses or his doctor on morning rounds."

"I'll be there." Ginger didn't just want to know how Mike was doing, she wanted to see him for herself. She took down his room number and approximate time of rounds the next day before hanging up the phone. She turned to Rachel. "Mike's been in an accident."

CHAPTER FORTY-ONE

Ginger lingered in her car in the hospital parking garage. Questions swirled in her mind about whether Mike was okay or not. If he could have, he would have called himself. How bad were his injuries? "Stop it, Ginger Maria Kelly Moreland. This isn't doing yourself or Mike any favors. Just. Go. In." She grabbed her purse and headed to the elevator.

After an awkward ride up in an elevator full of doctors, Ginger disembarked on the fifth floor and followed the nurse's directions to Mike's room at the end of the hall. She knocked before entering.

He lay resting in semi-darkness, the shades still closed. Hooked up to monitoring wires and an IV, he looked vulnerable. The machine beeped a steady rhythm. She stopped next to his bed and reached out to push a lock of unruly hair off his forehead. Her fingers paused on a bandage near his temple. What had happened? He was always joking about being able to drive anything. After all, he could drive a Humvee in the desert. She laughed softly, remembering that first Christmas when he so gleefully let everyone know he could handle driving in their winter weather. She sobered as she thought about what he might not have been able to handle this time.

Someone knocked, and Ginger jumped. A woman's voice spoke into the quietness. "I'm Mike's physician, Dr. Miller. You must be Ginger, his emergency contact. Are you family?"

"A good friend."

She flipped through her papers. "Has anyone filled you in on what happened?"

"I just got here."

"There was a multi-car pile-up on 680 here in Omaha. First responders got him out as quickly as they could, but he was cut by shattered glass. He had bandaged it to stop the bleeding before he passed out, but he lost quite a bit of blood. Must have some training."

"He's an emergency medical responder."

"It's a good thing. He was unconscious when the paramedics got to him. He also has a concussion and a couple broken ribs. We ran some tests and there's no internal bleeding. He's been coming in and out, but he's on pain meds, so give the man some slack. He may be a little out of it when he first comes around." The doctor smiled.

"He'll be okay?"

"Because of his concussion, we need to keep him a few days to be sure. But with plenty of rest, I'm sure he'll be good as new.

Mike's medicated voice broke the tension. "I'm not new. I've lived here for...how many years...let's see...would somebody get me a hamburger?"

Ginger patted Mike's arm. "I'll ask the nurses about that hamburger."

"Are the nurses pretty?" He opened his eyes. "You're pretty." He grinned a lopsided grin. "Come here and kiss me."

Ginger's cheeks warmed.

"You're on your own with that one." The doctor left the room.

Ginger laughed to ease her embarrassment. An urge to kiss him filled her heart. She cleared her throat and looked away from Mike.

Mike grabbed her hand. "Ginger?"

"I'm here."

"I'm going back to sleep." He closed his eyes. After a few minutes, soft snores told her he had succumbed to sleep.

Leaning over, she kissed him on the cheek, then pulled her hand out of his. She needed to find out where his phone was so he could call his sisters. They needed to know what had happened.

Ginger found a quiet place in the hospital to call Mike's sister, Laura. The phone rang four times before she picked up. "Hey, Mike. Why didn't you call back?"

"Laura? My name is Ginger. I'm a friend of your brother's—"

"Is he okay?"

"He's okay, but he was in an accident."

"What happened?"

Ginger relayed what the doctor had told her.

Laura let out a heavy sigh. "Thanks for being there for him."

"Absolutely. If it weren't for the tornado ripping through Preston Hill, I'm sure there would be others here."

"I heard about that. How did the town fare? Your café? Mike says it's the best place in town."

Mike had told his sisters about her? What, exactly, had he said? She shook her head and brought her attention back to the conversation at hand. "I headed to the hospital before I heard the full extent of the damage in town. But from what I saw, nothing was completely leveled. I'll find out more when I go back tonight."

"Preston Hill has been good for Mike. He's made a lot of good friends there."

"He's been good for the town, as well."

"I need to call our sister and let her know what happened. Would you keep us updated?"

"Sure thing."

"It sounds like he's being taken good care of. And Ginger?"

"Yeah?"

"He's better with you in his life." Laura's voice broke on the other end of the line. "Please, don't let him go."

Ginger was stumped for words. Mike must have told his sisters a lot. She looked up at the ceiling as though searching for the right words, but there was only one thing to say. "I won't."

Ginger placed the phone back in the drawer next to Mike's bed. A glance at the clock explained the growl in her stomach. She picked up her purse, said a quick prayer over Mike, and slipped from the room.

Betsy and Grandpa were exiting the elevator as she came down the hall.

"How is he?" Grandpa leaned on his cane more heavily today. "Mike missed our chess game." He sounded agitated.

Ginger knew that probably indicated worry over Mike, but it was hard to bite her tongue. "A bit battered and shook up, but he'll be okay. Still hooked up to the wires and an IV, but the doctor thinks he'll head home within a week."

"Good." A sigh escaped Grandpa's lips and his shoulders slumped. Tears rimmed his eyes when he met Ginger's gaze. "Now, if you gals want to have lunch, I'll sit with Mike. This body needs to rest a spell."

Ginger hugged Grandpa. "He's not quite ready for a game of chess, but you might have an interesting conversation with him while he's under the influence of the pain meds. He's all the way at the end of the hall on the right." She watched Grandpa hobble past the nurses station.

"They'll be okay." Betsy pushed the elevator button.

The realization of how much Ginger needed both Grandpa and Mike in her life almost knocked the breath out of her. Grandpa's health had begun declining while Mike took on new importance. God in His goodness providing for her needs. And then there was her newest discovery. "Betsy. Have I got some news for you."

Half an hour later, they settled in the hospital café over soup and sandwiches.

"Hmm. This is good. You should have this on the menu at the Jukebox." Betsy took another bite of her roasted red pepper soup. "Now, out with it."

"I called the genealogy site about the test results. According to customer service, the high centi— Ugh, something I can't remember. Anyway, that high match centi-thingy means he's a close relative. A second cousin or closer. But they don't reveal which line. So, everything has to be confirmed with some sort of paper trail."

Betsy set down her spoon. "Mary Sue had to have been right about Irene."

"If I'm understanding this right."

"And you're sure that Walter didn't know?" Betsy sat forward in her seat.

"He would have said something if he did. All I know is that I have family." A shudder traveled up Ginger's back as she contemplated the possibilities.

"What now?"

"I need to get into my online profile and see if my suggested match has responded to my request to connect. Get this. The family requires potential matches to go through their lawyer."

"That's intriguing. And exciting."

Ginger started to take a bite of her grilled cheese sandwich, then set it down. "I hope Irene is still alive and whoever my match is wants to meet us."

"If Irene is alive, I can't imagine her not wanting to meet you."

"I hope you're right." Ginger pushed down the fear that her grandmother might have moved on with someone else.

"When are you going to tell Walter?"

"I'm going to wait until I know more. I don't want Grandpa to get excited about what might turn out to be nothing, especially if they decide they don't want to meet us."

Betsy gave her a mock salute. "Let me know how I can help."

"Help with what?" Megan and Greg joined them at the table.

Ginger got up and hugged Megan. "I wasn't expecting you. Thanks for coming. I should have called someone to pass the word around about Mike. I'm sorry."

"Want me to make some calls while you guys talk?" Betsy pulled out her phone.

"That would probably be good. Thanks."

"And since we're here, what can we do?" Megan gently elbowed Ginger.

"The doctor thinks Mike will go home in several days. Not sure there's anything." Ginger shrugged. "Wait. Greg, can you check on Mike's house and clean up the debris from the storm? That would be helpful."

"Already done. A few other men from church helped, too."

"What about checking on the rest of the congregation?"

Greg nodded. "We checked on everyone and helped where we could."

"I know that will mean a lot to Mike. He'll be worried about everyone, I'm sure." Ginger sat back down. "Have you had lunch yet?"

"We grabbed something on the way. Right now, we're going to go up to his room for a bit then we'll see you back in town. Lillian lined up some sitters for us, but we don't want to leave the kids too long." After getting quick directions, the couple headed upstairs.

Ginger picked up her forgotten sandwich, dipped it into her tomato soup, and took a bite. Her stomach quit yelling, and she let out a groan of satisfaction.

Betsy laughed. "That good?"

"That hungry." Ginger took another bite. Her thoughts moved into better focus.

"You realize you're going to make a great pastor's wife."

Ginger almost choked on her food. Her eyes wide, she shook her head at Betsy. She swallowed then took a gulp of water to wash the bite down. "What are you talking about?"

"The way you made sure things were taken care of with Mike unable to. Just saying."

"Betsy. What are you...don't...argh..." Betsy could be so frustrating. Although denial was the first thing out of her mouth, her heart danced at the idea of a life together with Mike.

"I assume you aren't planning on letting him go." Betsy's eyes twinkled with mischievousness.

Ginger squinted her eyes at her friend.

Betsy laughed. "Okay. I'll stop." Her eyes continued laughing long after her voice quieted.

Ginger rolled her eyes. Did the whole world know?

CHAPTER FORTY-TWO

As Ginger drove back from Omaha, the damage on the outskirts of Preston Hill threatened to overwhelm her.

A verse she had read recently in Psalms filled her heart. "Praise the LORD, my soul; all my inmost being, praise His holy name. Praise the LORD, my soul, and forget not all His benefits."

She could choose to be thankful and remember what God had done, despite the damage and Mike's being in the hospital. So far there had been no fatalities reported from the tornado. Mike was alive, and the doctor felt certain he would be fine. People were pulling together to help each other. Her soul rested in the fact that God did care.

She began singing, "...It is well, with my soul, it is well..." Even if family members she discovered through the genealogy site wanted nothing to do with her or Grandpa, she would be okay.

By the time she pulled up to the back of the café, she felt at peace and knew that God was in control.

A news crew on the sidewalk near the Jukebox Café filmed a segment for the evening report. Many of the store owners on Main Street observed the activity from their establishments.

Rachel watched with Ginger from in front of the café and, after a few minutes, the reporter walked their way.

"Can we interview you?"

Ginger held up her hand, intending to decline, but Rachel nudged her forward. Ginger looked over at Rachel then nodded at the reporter. "Sure."

The cameraman moved around to an angle that framed her with the reporter, the Jukebox behind them.

The young woman wrote down Ginger's name and business, then held up her mic. "We're coming to you from Preston Hill, a small community about an hour north of the city. Today, I'm visiting with Ginger Moreland, owner of the Jukebox Café, which sustained damage—as did most of the buildings down Main Street—when the tornado touched down. The damage was minimal considering what it could have been, as you'll see when we show you a video a local photographer caught on film. Ginger, what's the general mood here?"

"Grateful no one was hurt. Everyone is helping their neighbors. We're going to be okay."

The reporter faced directly into the camera. "Preston Hill is a beautiful little town, with a beautiful spirit in its residents."

Ginger watched the reporter head across the street toward other shop owners. How long would it take for things to return to normal? She shook off the unknowns. "Rachel, were you able to get hold of the insurance company?"

"They'll be out tomorrow morning about nine. They have several customers in the area they will be visiting."

"What about the glass?"

"Measured and priced. Ready to order once insurance approves it."

"I'll stop in at the bank before it closes today. I think that's it for café business."

"How's Mike?"

Ginger laughed. "Under the influence of drugs."

"Did he say anything incriminating?" Rachel's eyes gleamed with mischief.

"Fortunately, only the doctor was in the room with us."

"You telling?"

Ginger's heart warmed at the thought of Mike asking for a kiss. "How's Rabbit doing?"

"Fine. I'll let it drop. For now. But don't think you're off the hook." Rachel laughed. "Rabbit is doing fine. If you don't need me, I'm going to check on our neighbors and see how we can help."

"You go ahead. I need to take care of a few things then I'll join you." Ginger wanted to check her profile on the genealogy website to see if they had responded yet to her request to contact them. She wasn't sure what it indicated that she had to talk to their lawyer, but the sooner she heard back the better.

Excitement and anxiousness blended in her mind. This mystery had shrouded their lives since Grandpa returned from the war to find his wife gone, and they were finally on the verge of finding answers. She wished Mike was well enough to walk her through this.

There was no news on her profile about being contacted. Disappointed, Ginger left her phone in the office and wandered through the café assessing the damage. *Lord, please let the bank extend grace on our payments.* She warred against the thoughts that wanted to consume her peace right now, reminding herself that God still cared for her in the middle of this upset. Many people had sustained worse damage than the Jukebox Café had.

Her phone rang and she hurried back to the office. The number was unfamiliar. Ginger tapped on the message icon and listened to the voice mail. It was from her possible match's lawyer.

"I'm calling to set up a phone appointment with Ginger Moreland. This is concerning the DNA test she recently took and the suggested family match with David Hutton she received. Before direct contact can be made with the family, you will need to go through an interview with me. Please call at your earliest convenience to set up an appointment with my secretary." The woman left the name of her firm and a number before ending the message.

A lawyer. Betsy was right, this was intriguing. Why did she need to go through a lawyer? Was the lawyer even legit? Probably a good thing she hadn't made any of her information public on the site. Ginger tapped her finger on the desk. "Ginger Moreland, you're being paranoid. Stop it." But nothing wrong with checking the lawyer out. Lillian's husband would be a good one to call. She dialed the number for his law office. He took down the name of the firm and the number and promised to check it out. Within half an hour he called her back.

"The firm is legit. As a matter of fact, I went to law school with one of the partners. The lawyer who called you does work there. They only handle large accounts, so they're probably wanting to make sure anyone who calls is sincere in their search for family. Call me if you run into any issues, but you can trust her." Randy ended the call with a promise to help out if the need arose.

With shaking hands, Ginger pulled out her phone to make an appointment. This was what she and Grandpa had hoped to find, but she was still nervous. She could hardly stand the suspense until she knew for certain that her relatives did want to connect. Instead of getting the secretary, the lawyer in question answered the phone and suggested they go ahead and have the interview. Ginger agreed and closed the office door.

The woman sounded kind. "So we have a few questions that should confirm your relationship. Do you have any other family?"

"Walter Gipson is my grandfather."

"Is your grandmother still living?"

"We don't know. That's part of the reason I had my DNA tested. She disappeared soon after Pearl Harbor, after my grandfather went to fight in the war. Her name was Irene."

"Really?" The interest level in the woman's voice went up a notch. "Do you know her full name, including her maiden name?"

"Irene Grace Gipson. Hutton is her maiden name."

"Do you have a picture of her you could scan and send to me?"

"Sure." Ginger sat on the edge of her seat. "You know."

The woman's gentle laugh soothed Ginger's doubts. "I'm not at liberty to say. But I can tell you that the family wants me to wrap this up as soon as I can. Only a couple more questions. Do you have a copy of Irene and Walter's marriage license?"

"Yes." A knot formed in Ginger's throat. The lawyer wouldn't be asking that if this wasn't her family.

"Scan that and send it along with the picture. Do they have any children?"

"Patricia, my mother. She died in 1986."

"I'm sorry for your loss, Ginger. I have one last question. Do you know what Walter gave Irene for their first anniversary?"

"A locket."

"That should do it. I'll call the family and let them know about the interview. You should hear back from someone in the next couple days. Hang in there, the waiting will be over soon." The smile was evident in the woman's voice.

Ginger swiped her phone screen to disconnect the call and headed over to the house to find the documents. By the tone in the lawyer's voice, Ginger felt sure she would be meeting family before too long. She paused inside the door when she overheard Grandpa's animated conversation with Bo and Eugene.

"That granddaughter of mine went into my room and took all of Irene's stuff out. Can you believe it?"

Her mouth gaped open. She had moved Irene's things from the kitchen table to the guestroom, because he wanted her to have those things. Sure, later she went into his room but hadn't even thought about taking things out. A knot tightened in Ginger's gut. She slammed the door and headed to the guest room. She tried to remind herself that this kind of thing was a part of dementia, but she felt attacked.

Grandpa and his suppositions. And here she was working to find Irene. She needed a few moments to clear her head. After closing the door to the guest room, she dug out the documents the lawyer wanted her to send. For good measure, she would add the picture of the jewelry box and the letter that was inside. She stopped and sat on the edge of the bed to collect her thoughts. *God, forgive me. I know taking things out on him won't help.* He didn't even know what he was doing. She hoped the drugs did kick in soon and that they would help. Life might be able to find some sort of routine.

Ginger slipped into the back of the room about fifteen minutes into the meeting. After the most recent episode with Grandpa and her reaction she'd decided it was time to check out the support group. She needed Mike, that was for sure, but she needed others who were going through this a bit ahead of her. People she could gain wisdom and understanding from. She watched for a few minutes until the one who was leading the meeting looked her way. "We have a new face. Come on in."

Ginger made her way to the only empty seat in the circle. She glanced around at the women as they welcomed her, then one by one they shared their names and who they were a caregiver for and how far into the journey they were. She was touched by their honesty and transparency and knew she had found a good support group.

"I'm Ginger Moreland. I just found out last week that my grandfather has dementia. It's been me and Grandpa for so long. And the other night I was so ugly about something he couldn't help." A knot formed in her throat. She squeezed her eyes closed, but the tears seeped out anyway. She covered her face with her hands. The women on either side of her placed their hands on her back. She began sobbing, unable to contain the sorrow over losing Grandpa to dementia any longer. She heard prayers being said on her behalf around the circle as they stopped their meeting to meet her need.

When Ginger began to calm, the leader spoke. "This is why we're here. Does anyone want to share with Ginger about the early days of your journey with dementia? Maybe some thoughts on how to get through this?"

For the rest of the meeting, the women shared about their own ongoing grief. About the need to find those who not only listened, but could help with their loved one's care. And they all encouraged her to take care of herself along the way. At the end, their leader took prayer requests and they closed the evening by praying for each other. Ginger left worn out but hopeful. She was ready for the next day. Like Mike had encouraged her, one day at a time.

CHAPTER FORTY-THREE

When Ginger arrived at the hospital to pick up Mike, he was sitting up in bed, dressed to go home.

He grinned. "You are a sight for sore eyes. Did you bring me some strawberry rhubarb pie?"

She smiled at his much-improved countenance. "Sorry. No pie. Has the doctor been by?"

He pointed to the doorway where the doctor stood. She nodded at Ginger then shifted her focus to Mike. "I hear you've been listening to the nurses."

"I know how to follow directions."

"Well, as long as you can promise to take it easy, I'm going to clear you to go home."

Mike did a fist pump in the air. "No offense, but once you eat this lady's cooking..." He pointed at Ginger. "You are spoiled for anything else. Especially hospital food."

The doctor laughed. "I usually pack my own lunch. I get it." She signed a few papers. "No driving for about a week. No climbing ladders or the like. In general, take it easy."

"Yes, ma'am."

"Make a follow-up in about a week with your regular physician to get the all clear to resume your regular activities." She handed him a sheet of discharge information before she left.

The nurses went through their checkout procedure then helped Mike into a wheelchair.

Ginger looked through all the drawers to be sure Mike had

everything. "Do you have all your personal effects?"

He held up a manila envelope. "I'm ready to go."

Ginger walked alongside as the nurse rolled him out of the room.

"Tell me about life outside of this place. Have you heard anything from your family yet?" Mike reached over and grabbed her hand while they waited for the elevator.

"No. It's only been a couple days, though."

He chuckled. "I can feel the nervous energy in your hand. It's like you can't keep still."

"Would you be able to keep still in my position?"

"Fair point. How about we make an escape?" He glanced behind him at the nurse then back at Ginger. "If we make our plans quietly, no one will know."

Ginger took her hand back as the doors slid open. "After you." She moved out of the way as the nurse rolled his chair into the elevator. "Where did you want to go?"

"I want a piece of strawberry rhubarb pie."

"Fine. The Jukebox isn't officially open for business, but we can stop by for pie." Ginger laughed and left him at the curb with the nurse while she went to get the car. Life felt more normal now that Mike was getting out of the hospital.

Once on the road, Mike asked about the efforts to find Irene.

"I heard from the lawyer representing my possible matches on the genealogy site."

"Lawyer?"

Ginger laughed. "Right? It sounds like something from a novel. I guess I'll find out why when they contact me. The lawyer thought I would hear back within a couple days. And that was two days ago."

"Have you told Walter yet?"

"I want to be sure what the situation is first. I don't want to stress him out."

He kissed the back of her hand. "How are repairs on the Jukebox coming?"

"Hopefully the windows will be in within a couple weeks."

He kissed her hand again. "We never did have that talk."

She glanced over at him.

"Maybe we should wait till we're not on the road." He winked.

"I think that would be a good idea." She pulled her hand out of his. "You're very distracting."

"And very tired." He closed his eyes.

Within minutes a gentle snore told Ginger that he had fallen asleep. She let him rest until they pulled into town. "Mike? Still want to go to the Jukebox?"

He sat up. "If it's with you. I've missed being around you."

"Me, too." Ginger parked in back of the café, and they went in together.

Grandpa came over after they sat down. "Mike. It's about time you got out of that hospital."

"I agree."

"You've missed our chess games."

"Do you want to play now?"

Grandpa's face lit up. "I'll go get my set. You going to be here awhile?"

"Till someone takes me home." Mike looked over at Ginger.

"You two making googly eyes at each other again? When are you going to ask her to marry you?"

Mike spewed the water he had been drinking out of his mouth. He glanced at Ginger.

"Grandpa." Ginger hid her face behind her hand.

Mike laughed. "Are you trying to throw me off for the game?"

"Ha. Did it work?"

"Not a chance. I'm ready when you are."

"Fine, you whippersnapper. I'll be back." Grandpa turned on his heel and marched out of the Jukebox.

Mike smiled at Ginger. "He knows how to get to the point."

"If that's what you call it." She laughed.

"At this point in his life, he's likely to say pretty much anything. We might as well laugh it off."

"True. I'll try and keep that in mind. I'm going to get your piece of pie." She went to the kitchen and pulled a pie out of the cooler. Her phone rang and an unfamiliar number popped up in the notifications. She set the pie on the counter. "Hello?"

"Is this Ginger Moreland?"

"Yes."

"This is David Hutton. Your cousin."

"Oh." The tears came before she had a chance to process.

"Ginger? Are you okay?" His deep voice had a hint of Grandpa in it.

"Yeah. Just give me a minute." She took a shuddering breath. "I need to go somewhere private. I'm going to put you on mute a minute." She stared down at the pie as if it would give her the words to say to her cousin.

Rachel stopped deep cleaning the counter space. "What's going on?"

"Family. I have family."

Rachel's eyes grew wide. "Need me to take care of that?" She pointed at the pie.

"It's for Mike. Let him know about the call, but don't let Grandpa hear. I'll be out in a bit." Ginger headed to her office. She closed the door and took her phone off mute. "I'm here."

"I'm sure you're anxious to know what I have to say, so I'll tell the short version first. The lawyer is confident that you are indeed our family. We want to connect. I don't think Grandma and Walter, uh...Grandpa want to waste any more time."

"I can hardly believe that I have family. It's been just me and Grandpa for so long."

David laughed.

"Your laugh reminds me of Grandpa's in his younger days."

"Grandma has always said I reminded her of him."

"I can't wait to meet you. Is it just you and Irene? I mean Grandma? What about William?" Ginger explained about their trip to Brainard and Mary Sue's claim that Irene had a son.

"There's a whole slew of us. William had three kids, and we all married and have families. But I don't want to overload you with names over the phone. We were thinking you and Grandpa might like to come and visit. As far as what happens after that, we'll figure it out. But one thing you need to know is that you are family. We want you both in our lives."

Ginger grinned. "That's music to my ears, but there's something I didn't mention when I talked to the lawyer. Grandpa has recently been diagnosed with dementia. It's in the early stages, and they've given him drugs that will help slow it down. But..."

"We don't want to waste time. Or do anything to make it worse. So let's keep it small the first time we meet up. We can arrange it sooner, because we won't have to wait for a time when everyone can make it. Plus, Grandpa won't be confused by meeting all the family at once. We're in Renegade, Nebraska. Where are you located?"

Who had mentioned Renegade recently? "I'm in Preston Hill, Nebraska. I run the Jukebox Café in town."

David laughed. "You're that Ginger?"

"What?" The pieces fit into place as she recalled Rachel mentioning her grandma lived in Renegade.

"Rachel is my niece."

"How did we not connect the dots?"

"She and her parents have only recently reconnected with family. She probably doesn't know the whole back story like most of the family does. Speaking of which, do you have any questions you're dying to have answered before we move ahead on this?"

"What was the lawyer all about?"

"Sorry about all the rigmarole. Dad, William, has made some great investments over the years, and our family lawyer suggested we direct inquiries to the law office in order to protect ourselves. It took a couple weirdos calling up because of the last name and some distant possible DNA connection for us to see her point of view. They tried to weasel their way into the family once they found out we had money. We immediately put her suggestion into action."

"Makes sense." Ginger laughed. "I hope you don't think we're weird."

"Hey. I resemble that remark." His laughter reassured her that what he said about wanting them in the family was the truth.

CHAPTER FORTY-FOUR

Ginger sat in her chair and reviewed her conversation with David. She needed to process this before she told the others. She laughed. Rachel was family. God had been moving them toward finding Irene before Grandpa ever showed signs of dementia. Gratefulness filled her heart. While she had been crying out for family, God had already been on the move. "God, You are good. Thank you for the rest you have given our hearts."

She and David had agreed on a couple things. They needed to reunite Grandpa and Irene as soon as possible. And it was up to Irene to tell Grandpa about William and the fact that he had a large family. Which included Rachel. Rachel was going to flip.

Ginger tapped a pen on the desk. What they hadn't decided was how to bring about the meeting. She wanted Mike's thoughts on this. Once they had that part figured out and she had told Rachel separately, it would be time to tell Grandpa. Ginger couldn't wait to see the look on Grandpa's face.

A knock at the door brought her mind back to the present. Mike slipped in and closed the door behind him. "Thought I would come back and see how things were going while Walter is taking a break from the game."

Ginger jumped up from the chair and gave Mike a hug.

"What did I do to deserve that?" He kept one arm loosely around her as he wiped away her tears. "What's this?"

Ginger laughed. "Happy tears. Mike, I have family. And guess what?"

"No clue."

"Rachel is related to me. She's my second cousin I think."

"No way."

"That news is straight from David. He's my cousin."

They sat down and Ginger relayed everything that David had told her. "What do you think about taking Grandpa to see Irene or Irene coming here?" Ginger laughed. "I need to start calling her Grandma."

Mike chuckled. "Walter's been pretty clear headed lately."

"I don't want him getting confused."

"Which environment would be calmer and more controlled?"

"From the way David described their place, probably there."

Mike held his hand out with his palm up. "That's what I would recommend. You could manage his input better."

"That make sense. Unless Grandpa objects, that's what we'll do. Do you have an appointment yet to get the all clear for resuming your activities? I'd like it if you came with us."

Mike took her hand. "I'd like that too. I'll call tomorrow and see if I can at least get cleared to ride shotgun. Do you want me with you when you talk to Walter?"

"That would be nice."

A knock interrupted, and Rachel stuck her head in the room. "Walter's looking for you, Mike."

Mike let Ginger's hand slip out of his. "Let me know when you want to talk to Walter. I'll be there." He grinned. "The church is insisting I take a week off to recuperate, but somehow I don't think that will look like they think it will look." He laughed as he headed back out to play chess.

Rachel dropped into the extra chair in the office. "Out with it. I want to know all."

Rachel reacted to the news that she was family like Ginger expected. With a squeal. Followed by a happy dance. The hardest part had been convincing Rachel to not tell Grandpa until he knew about his son William. But she finally understood and promised not to tell anyone. She had plenty of family in Renegade to talk to if she felt like she was about to burst with the news.

Ginger followed Rachel out of the office and made her way to the dining room. She walked over to where Grandpa and Mike were concentrating on their game. She didn't dare interrupt. Now would be a good time to visit Betsy and fill her in. She let Rachel know where she was going then stopped by the house for Rabbit.

Two days later, Mike, Ginger, and David schemed about the trip. They had tried setting up a video chat, but in the end settled for a phone call. Mike had been cleared to travel, and they arranged with David to come to Renegade on Friday. David, an officer in the Air Force, had taken a month of his leave so he could be available.

David laughed when he learned the name of Grandpa's dog and insisted that they bring Rabbit with them. He understood Rabbit would calm Grandpa, besides David wanted to meet a dog with such an unusual name. Mike and Ginger planned to tell Grandpa all of the news tomorrow.

In between the planning and getting to know each other, David filled in the why's of Irene's story. "Her disappearance came down to her family's Japanese descent. Even though President Roosevelt's executive order hadn't directly affected them, they were afraid. The distrust of the Japanese after Pearl Harbor was rampant. They were not treated well."

"Even in Nebraska?"

"Some places weren't as bad, but it was everywhere." David's voice grew in intensity. "So many Japanese families were torn out of their homes and lost most of their belongings. Including businesses. It's understandable they were afraid."

"Why did they move to Brainard?"

"Irene's grandma, who was a first-generation Japanese immigrant, lived in California. She was detained and moved to an internment camp. That fueled Irene's parents' fear and determination to distance themselves. That's why, when they moved to Brainard, they didn't allow Irene to tell Walter's parents."

"Why did she leave my mother behind?"

David sighed. "Fear makes people do irrational things. Irene's parents had convinced her they were in danger, and she couldn't bear the thought of Patricia going into one of those camps. She was young and had no reason to distrust her own parents."

Ginger fought back tears. "But she took William."

"In the end she couldn't let go of both of them. William was her one connection to Walter."

Mike held her hand. "I can't imagine being in that position."

Ginger battled a knot in her throat. She focused instead on her hand in Mike's and felt her tension ease. "You mentioned New York. How did they end up there?"

David continued the story. "Irene's grandma had been relocated to New York City, so eventually the family joined her there. Irene didn't make it back to Nebraska until William established his own law practice here twenty-seven years later. That was still ahead of the internet and ease of access to public documents. So, even though Irene attempted to find Walter, his family had moved and hadn't left a trail. It's hard to believe they lived so close and never found each other. Of course, since her parents had her going by her middle name and her maiden name, it confused the search."

Ginger sat back in her chair. For thirty years they had lived in the same state. It took Grandpa developing dementia to motivate them to push through till they found Irene. Of course, without the DNA test, which was a much more recent addition to the tools available to find people, she wasn't sure they would have been able to find her. Ginger decided to count finding family as a blessing that came out of something hard. She planned to look for more. It's the way God seemed to work, and it would help her to get through the days ahead. She squeezed Mike's hand as she looked into the face of another one of those blessings.

Ginger nestled under Mike's arm as they waited on the couch for Grandpa and sipped their coffee in silence. Ginger rubbed damp palms on her jeans. How would Grandpa respond? Probably demand they load up the car immediately.

Grandpa thumped into the room. He narrowed his eyes when he saw Ginger and Mike. He sighed and his shoulders slumped. With shuffling movements, he shuffled to the chair across from them. "Is it too late?"

"For what?" As soon as she asked, she knew what Grandpa was thinking.

"Irene."

Ginger glanced at Mike then set her coffee down. She crossed over to Grandpa and knelt in front of him. "No, Grandpa. We found her. She's been waiting for you."

Tears ran down Grandpa's cheeks. "When do I get to see my Irene?"

"Tomorrow."

"Is she coming here? Where does she live?"

Ginger smiled as life came back into Grandpa's eyes. "She lives in Renegade, and we are planning to go there. Is that okay with you?"

"I can't believe it. Thank you." Grandpa looked over at Mike. "Are you coming, too?"

"I wouldn't miss this for anything."

"Good. Now can I have my breakfast? I need to get a few things done before we go."

Ginger laughed. "Breakfast coming up."

CHAPTER FORTY-FIVE

"You sure you're up to this?" Ginger waited while Mike got into Mike's SUV. They decided to take his vehicle to give him more space to stretch out during the trip. He winced as he settled into the front passenger seat. "I want to be there with you."

"That wasn't the question."

Rachel chuckled. "Okay, you two."

Mike glanced at Rachel. "I think she likes fussing over me."

"He'll be fine. Now hurry up. I have a date." Grandpa let Rabbit jump into the car then climbed into the back seat behind Mike and slammed the door.

Ginger crossed her arms and stared at the three of them. "I'm concerned. Mike got out of the hospital a week ago after being in a wreck, sustaining blood loss, a concussion, and broken ribs."

"It's okay. I like you fussing over me."

Ginger smiled. This new openness between them had its benefits, even though she sometimes felt awkward when others were around. She pulled her hand out of his and walked to the back of the car to toss in their overnight bags in case their visit ran long or Mike wasn't up to the trip back on the same day. Aware of his gaze on her, she climbed behind the wheel.

"To answer your question, yes, I'm up to the trip." Mike grinned as he buckled the seatbelt. "We're not climbing any mountains, are we? My doctor cleared it as long as I take it easy. I can even help drive."

Ginger chuckled. Of course, he would want to help drive. Probably itching to get his independence back. She could understand that. She lowered her window. "Rachel, thanks for taking care of the Jukebox repairs while we're gone."

"We'll be fine. Enjoy the—"

"You forgot my snacks." Grandpa opened the car door and told Rabbit to stay. He hurried into the house as fast as his shuffle allowed and back out. He climbed back into the car with his bag of food. "Now I'm ready."

Ginger looked in the rearview mirror. Grandpa was looking toward Mike. "You sure you're not eloping with my granddaughter, young man?"

"Grandpa." Ginger sunk down in her seat as if she could hide.

Rachel covered her mouth as a chuckle escaped.

"We're leaving." Ginger raised the window and backed up.

Mike whispered to Ginger. "You know, it's not a bad idea."

"Should I drop you off at your house?"

"I'll behave. This is going to be a great day."

Ginger tapped the steering wheel.

"Hey, beautiful." Mike roused from his nap.

Ginger glanced over at the passenger seat and smiled. Over the last week, since Mike had gotten out of the hospital, they had spent quite a bit of time together, and he claimed a spot in her heart that could never be taken away. Her love for him was growing at a rate she hadn't anticipated. "Either of you want to stretch your legs?"

"That's probably a good idea. I am feeling a bit stiff. Besides, I'm getting hungry. What about you, Walter? Want to stop?"

A loud snore sounded from the back seat, and Ginger laughed. "I guess that's a yes."

"How far are we from Renegade?" Mike sat his seat upright.

"A couple more hours. There's a town coming up in about ten miles."

"Perfect." He looked back at Grandpa then lowered his voice. "This is nice." Mike reached for her hand.

Ginger grinned. Her heart had been waiting for her brain to catch up.

He kissed her hand then let it go as they entered the town. She decelerated and crawled down Main Street at twenty miles per hour. On the north side of the downtown, several eating establishments lined the road.

"Fast food or sit down?" Ginger peered at the signs.

"Let's get out of the car and sit. That diner looks promising."

In the back seat, Grandpa stirred. "Are we there?"

"Making a stop."

"It will take too much time." Grandpa's voice rose in intensity.

Ginger pulled into a parking spot. "Mike is getting a bit stiff and needs to move around a bit. Besides, I'm hungry."

"Fine." Grandpa got out of the car. "Crack the windows for Rabbit. Good thing it's not a hot day. What would you do then?"

Ginger ignored his irritable attitude and complied. She looped her hand through Mike's arm as the three of them walked up the steps of the building. They found a booth next to the window where they could keep an eye on Rabbit. Grandpa slid in on one side with Ginger next to him, and Mike sat across from Ginger. Within minutes an older waitress brought over water and menus. "Be right back to get your order." She smiled and headed to another table.

Mike opened the menu and slid his finger down the list of food. "This sounds good."

Ginger looked across the table at the dish he pointed to. "Grilled trout. Nice. I think I'm going for the grilled cheese and roasted red pepper soup."

"You get that quite a bit."

"I'm thinking about adding the soup to the menu."

"I have a new menu item for the Jukebox." He set the menu down.

"What's that?"

"Mom's turtle pie."

"Really?"

"It's about time, don't you think?" Mike kept his focused attention on her.

"What?"

"Can't a guy admire the view?"

"Mike." She looked around for anybody seeming to pay attention to them.

"Yeah, Mike." Grandpa perused menu.

"I don't care if the world knows how I feel. Including you, Walter. You might as well get used to it."

Grandpa grinned. "Good." He went back to studying the menu.

Ginger swatted both men with the menu. "Behave."

"Must I?" Mike offered her a puppy dog look.

She gave him a playful glare.

"Fine. I'll play nice."

"Okay. I'm back." The waitress stood at the side of their table. "I'm Katrina, and I'll be taking care of you. Do you know what you're ordering?" She looked over at the door when a bell jingled. "Be right with you folks." She turned back and waited.

"Grilled cheese and red pepper soup."

"Bowl or cup?"

"Bowl, please."

"I want some chocolate pie." Grandpa handed his menu to the waitress then elbowed Ginger. "I need to go to the men's room." She got up and let him out.

Mike ordered his meal, then turned his attention to Ginger after the waitress had gathered the menus and walked away. "How's Rabbit doing?"

"Now that the tornadoes are past, he's doing great."

"Tornados can be overwhelming to the animals."

Ginger moved the condiments around on the table and began organizing them. Mike placed his hand on top of hers. "You're not at work, you know."

She scooted everything to the side with one swipe of her arm. "Better?"

"Absolutely. Now you can give your attention to me."

Anybody listening would think they were being corny, but this level of their relationship was new, and being able to say all those stored-up things was refreshing. She smiled. "You still haven't told me how your meeting with Jackie and Rose went before you ended up in the hospital."

The waitress set Mike's trout meal and Ginger's grilled cheese on the table then hurried to get their coffee and Grandpa's pie. "Y'all holler if you need anything."

Mike took a few bites of his fish. "It was mostly a get to know each other time. Jackie did make it clear to Rose that I never knew about her, so I think that helped. A little mad at her mom, but they're talking. I think Rose is old enough to understand."

"Does Rose want a relationship with you?"

"As a matter of fact, I was going to ask you about something."

Ginger tilted her head and narrowed her eyes. What did this have to do with her?

He set his fork down. "Rose wants to stay in Preston Hill the rest of the summer. Jackie is okay with it, but I told them I wanted to check with you first. What do you think? Are you okay with it?"

Ginger took a drink of water. "I think it would be good for both of you. It will probably be a challenge, but now that the truth is out, I know you'll want to be a part of her life."

"That doesn't answer my question. Are you okay with it?"

Ginger laughed. "She's a part of your life now. That means…" She lowered her gaze as she caught her next words. They seemed presumptuous.

"She'll be a part of your life, too. I know what I'm asking."

Ginger was grateful that her thoughts weren't racing ahead of his. "I'm okay with it."

"Okay with what?" Grandpa approached the table, and Ginger stood to let him slide across the seat just as the waitress brought his pie and their coffee.

Mike pulled around the circle drive of the large estate. "This is impressive."

"I had no idea. Grandpa, what do you think?" Ginger unbuckled after Mike parked near the front door. She took a deep breath and touched the locket around her neck. "I can't believe we found family."

A man in an Air Force uniform stepped outside. He lifted his hand to acknowledge them then clasped his hands behind his back and waited. He reminded her of Grandpa's younger pictures.

Mike squeezed her hand. "You ready?"

"I don't know. It feels surreal."

The man walked down the stairs.

"It's now or never." Ginger opened the car door.

Mike came around and stood next to her.

Grandpa remained in the car and stared up at the big house.

"You must be Ginger." The man stepped forward.

She nodded.

"I'm David." He rubbed his hand across his face. "You remind me of Grandma."

"You remind me of Grandpa." Ginger laughed as she wiped the tears streaking her cheeks. She was grateful for Mike at her side.

"Grandma always believed Walter would find us someday."

"I can't stand this. Can I give you a hug?" Ginger moved toward her cousin.

He folded her into a warm welcome. "Hey, cuz. I can't believe you're here." He held onto her a moment before letting go. "Who's this?" David pointed over at Mike.

"This is Mike he's ...a good friend."

"Thanks for coming." David shook Mike's hand then looked back at Ginger. "That Grandpa?" He lifted his chin toward the car.

"Yes. I think he's a bit overwhelmed." She looked over at Mike.

"I'll talk to him." Before Mike reached the car, Grandpa exited the vehicle, let Rabbit jump out, then slammed the door. Rabbit ran circles around them and barked before he raced off onto the grounds.

"Where's Irene, young man?" Grandpa marched up to David.

David looked at Ginger over Grandpa's shoulder. They had decided not to tell him yet about William and that he had other grandchildren. That part of the story was for Irene to tell. David had to wait before he could greet him as a grandson would greet his grandfather. David's eyes looked watery. "I'll take you to her, sir."

After all this time searching, they would finally meet the woman who had held Grandpa's love all these years. Ginger felt giddy like a school kid.

CHAPTER FORTY-SIX

They followed David inside the house. The foyer was simple and classy. Ginger's gaze landed on family pictures that lined the wall to her left. Drawn like a magnet, she moved that direction. The reality of the size of her family caught her off guard. "I'm not alone." Realizing the family pictures might confuse Grandpa, she started to move away from the photos.

Grandpa walked over and stood in front of a two-by-three-foot framed painting of him and Grandma. Ginger joined him.

David came up behind. "The original photo was small and worn. Irene managed to keep it with her even when her parents wanted her to shed her entire past. On what would have been your fiftieth anniversary, this painting was commissioned from that photo."

Ginger reached up to touch the frame. She trailed her fingers along the words. "Forever loving, always loved." The same line Grandma had used in the letters. Ginger examined the woman's face in the painting. "Where is she?"

David inclined his head to a nearby doorway and motioned for them to follow him. She and Mike let Grandpa enter the room in front of them. Near the front picture window sat a beautiful, gray-haired woman with wrinkled complexion. She covered her mouth with her hand.

David stopped and moved out of the way. Grandpa made his way closer to the woman. "Irene? Is that really you?" He stopped in front of her. She opened her arms. In slow and what must have been pain filled motion, he knelt next to her chair and leaned into her arms. Sobs poured out of him. She stroked his hair. "You found me, my love."

"I always believed." Grandpa lifted his head and cupped her face in his hands. With the patience of a man who had waited for years, he kissed his wife.

Ginger longed to know the warmth of her grandmother's embrace. But this was Grandpa's moment. Feeling as though she was intruding, Ginger glanced over at David and gestured toward the door. She started to leave the room.

"Ginger?" Grandpa's voice stopped her.

She faced her grandparents. Grandpa now stood to the side as Grandma opened her arms for her granddaughter. She hurried to Grandma and collapsed into her embrace. Comfort seeped into Ginger's soul. Grandma rubbed her back. "There, there, child. You're with family now."

After what seemed like a precious amount of forever, Ginger sat back on her heels. "I have something for you." She reached up and took off the locket and held it out.

Grandma held the locket between her fingers. "I still remember when Walter gave me this. Our last Christmas together." She looked at Grandpa with deep love in her twinkling eyes. "Walter and I have a lot to talk about, so I'm going to let David give you two the tour. But first I want to talk to you, young man." She pointed at Mike.

"Me?" Mike pointed at himself.

"Quit being smart and come here." Grandma laughed.

Mike sat on a nearby chair.

"I see the way you're watching my granddaughter. You love her?"

He looked at Ginger. "I do, ma'am."

"Don't ever let someone talk you into letting her go."

"No, ma'am. Wouldn't think of it."

"Smart man. Now scoot. David, I'll have Helen come get you when it's time for you to return."

David motioned for Mike and Ginger to follow him out of the room. He led them to a terrace overlooking the grounds. Rabbit ran up and plopped down with a groan onto the cool cement. David stared out toward a pond at the far end of the property that he explained was part of their land.

Ginger walked up next to him. "Thank you."

He rested his arm across her shoulders. "Thank you. So, what's the story with Mike?"

Ginger watched the man she loved bend down and rub Rabbit's stomach. How could she capture their story in a few words? She smiled. She hoped to have the same kind of love that Grandma and Grandpa had. But, at this point, that hope was for her heart alone. "Time will tell."

"Fair enough." David walked to the door. "Helen, could you bring some of your lemonade?"

A few minutes later an older woman dressed casually and wearing an apron brought each of them a tall glass of lemonade. David introduced Helen as the housekeeper and cook before he led the way to a patio table. "The tour was an excuse to get us out of the room. You're free to explore the house and grounds at your pleasure. Let's just relax and get to know each other."

Over the next hour they swapped grandparent stories and laughed until their sides ached. David attempted to tell them about the family but gave up when Mike and Ginger grew confused about who was who. There would be enough time for introductions face to face another day.

"David?" Helen came out onto the terrace. "Your grandmother is ready for you."

He set his glass down. "Make yourselves at home. Helen can help you find anything you need." He looked at the time on his phone. "You have a few hours. Grandma likes dinner served at six. I'll see you then. Enjoy yourselves."

Left to themselves until dinner, Mike and Ginger strolled the grounds. Hand in hand, they walked the perimeter down to the pond and found a gazebo hidden behind a stand of trees.

"This is a beautiful spot." She climbed the stairs and stood at the railing that overlooked the countryside.

Mike came up behind her and encircled her waist with his arms. "I could get used to this."

"Me, too." She enjoyed the stillness the day had brought to her soul. This quest to find her grandmother had brought answers to so many prayers.

"Ginger?"

"Hmm?"

"I meant what I said to your grandma about never letting anyone talk me into letting you go."

Ginger smiled. "That's good, because if you do, I'll come hunt you down. I'm pretty good at that."

Mike laughed. "That you are."

Rabbit chose that moment to catch up with them. He barked as though he had treed a squirrel as he danced around them. They laughed and climbed down from the gazebo. Mike found a stick and threw it far up the hill. Rabbit bounded after it.

"Ginger. Mike." A woman's voice called for them.

They looked around. A woman waved from the top of the hill, so they headed back to the house. Time to meet more family.

They still hadn't gotten back to that conversation about where they were in their relationship. Although, Ginger didn't need words to know where Mike stood. She hoped he knew her heart as well.

Grandpa and Grandma had eaten dinner together in the great room the night before. Mike and Ginger had enjoyed their meal in the

271

breakfast nook with David and his wife Tracy. She was the one who had called them back from their exploration. Helen served lasagna with a hint of something different that Ginger couldn't put a name to. Would the woman supply the recipe? It was delicious. Talk had gone late into the night and left no time for a heart to heart conversation between Mike and her.

After consulting with Grandma and Grandpa, they decided that Grandpa would stay at the house for a while so that he and Grandma wouldn't have to be separated another day. They would take one day at a time to see how he adjusted. They planned to introduce Grandpa to the family one or two at a time so as not to overwhelm him. He had been delighted to find out that Rachel was his great-granddaughter, and she had enjoyed calling to tell him. Decisions about the future would be made down the road.

Since he had Rabbit to calm him, they all hoped that the unfamiliar territory and people wouldn't be a problem. He seemed more at peace than he had for a long time. Unless Grandpa needed her sooner, Ginger planned to return at the end of two weeks and take him back for his follow-up doctor's appointment.

This morning they enjoyed a light breakfast with the family. Toward the end of the meal, Grandpa and Grandma excused themselves. They were like high schoolers discovering first love and the joy of being together.

"Grandma dreamed about Walter last night." Tracy grinned. "Love is the air." She glanced at Mike as he got up and headed to the coffee pot. "In more than one place, I think."

Ginger took another sip of her coffee.

Tracy placed her hand on Ginger's arm. "You're cute. Have you ever been married before?"

Ginger shook her head.

"He seems like a good man." She watched Mike as he approached the table. "So, when are you headed out?"

Ginger smiled at her cousin-in-law, thankful for the change in subject.

"The bags are in the car." Mike walked up behind Ginger where she stood on the terrace and wrapped his arms around her. "You ready?"

"It's weird leaving Grandpa here. I've never lived in that house without him. And I've gotten so used to Rabbit, the house will feel empty."

Mike turned her around to face him. "I'll only be a phone call and a short walk away."

"I know. It feels strange, though. I think I'm a bit uneasy not knowing how he'll adjust."

"You told me you could see the hand of God working before Walter even started showing signs of dementia. God knew today would come, and He's not going to abandon your grandfather or you."

She allowed him to hold her. She needed Mike. That was a fact she could no longer deny. She sighed and rested against him. His heartbeat calmed her rushing thoughts. After a few moments, she backed out of his arms. "I guess it's time to say bye." She took his offered hand, and they went back inside to where Grandpa and the others were gathered in the great room.

After a round of hugs and more than a few tears, Ginger and Mike loaded into the car along with a basket full of food for lunch on the trip home. Ginger watched her grandfather till he was out of sight. *God, take care of Grandpa. Surround him with your peace and love. Don't let him be afraid or feel abandoned.*

CHAPTER FORTY-SEVEN

The road noise lulled Ginger into a light sleep until Mike pulled off the main highway. Ginger opened her eyes and looked around. She rolled her window down and enjoyed the feel of wind whipping through her hair. "This is nice. Thanks for driving. How far are we from home?"

"Not far. But I thought that first we would take advantage of the picnic lunch Helen packed for us." He reached for her hand. "I like having you to myself."

"It is rather nice." Ginger smiled and held her right hand out the window. Air ran between her fingers. "This is feeling familiar."

"It should."

She looked around. They were near Maggie and Millie's land. "Another picnic by the river?"

"The girl gets the prize."

She laughed. "You are in a mood today." She slapped his arm playfully.

"It's a good day."

"That it is."

Mike brought his SUV to a stop near the same place he had stopped their first visit here. Ginger opened the door and hopped out. Mike stopped her before her forward momentum carried her down the slight incline.

"Thanks."

"My pleasure." Mike grinned and pulled the basket from the back seat. He handed the blanket to Ginger then took her hand in his as they made their way to the picnic spot.

"This might not be such a good idea. You shouldn't be climbing yet."

"Um...there may or may not be another way up."

"Why you..." She pulled her hand out of his and swatted him with the blanket. "You made me crawl up there when I could have strolled around?"

"We going to fight or eat?"

"You have a point. But this time, take me around the easy way, mister."

He held his hand out in front of him, indicating a faint path she hadn't noticed before. "After you."

A mere few yards and they were on top of the rock. She held out her arms and lifted her face to the sun. "This feels nice."

Mike spread out the blanket. She sat next to him while he opened the basket and pulled out their lunch. Helen had prepared chicken salad sandwiches, sweet potato fries, strawberries and blackberries, and a can of whipped cream. Ginger helped dish up the food, then sat back to enjoy. Mike raved over his sandwich. "Think you can get the recipe from Helen?"

"She already sent it to me."

"It's a winner." He popped a strawberry into his mouth then picked up the can of whipped cream. "Want some?"

She held out her finger and he sprayed a pile on top. It jiggled all the way into her mouth and then she licked her finger. She stopped when she realized Mike was staring at her. "What? Do I have whipped cream on my face?"

He shook his head. "You're cute."

"Well, you have whipped cream on your face." She reached over with a napkin and wiped off the spot.

He caught her hand. "These last few months have been good."

"Even with all my uncertainties over Grandpa's dementia? And when I pushed you—"

"Shh." He put a finger on her lips. "Rough spots don't make it bad."

"True." She furrowed her brow at his expression. "You look serious."

He got up and led her to the side of the rock overlooking the water.

"Remember when we came here the first time?"

"Yeah."

"Remember what it felt like?"

"I was scared."

"I felt hope. For the first time since I'd known you, I felt hope that today might actually get here."

She tilted her head in question.

He held her hands in his. "You know I want to spend the rest of my life with you, right?"

Ginger nodded.

He grinned his crooked grin. "Ginger, will you marry me?"

She took one hand from his and covered her mouth. "Yes." She grinned. "Yes. I'll marry you."

He drew her into his arms. "I will love you forever, my sweet Ginger."

At the touch of his lips on hers, Ginger melted into his arms, as though by a mere kiss she could return the love to him that he had poured over her these last few years.

She pulled back and took his face in her hands. "I never thought it possible to move beyond the hurts and fears from the past and learn to trust someone with everything that goes on inside of me. But you kept loving me until I could trust your heart. I promise to give the same to you through all of our tomorrows. I love you, more than I can put into words." She lifted her face to receive the tender expression of his love. His kiss was like honey drenching her soul.

He pulled a breath away from her. "One more thing." Keeping her close, he reached into his shirt pocket then held up a ring.

Ginger gasped and held out her hand so he could slide it onto her left ring finger. "It's beautiful."

"If you want something else—"

She put her hand over his mouth. "I love it."

"Good. Because it looks perfect on you." Mike pulled her close.

"You actually brought this with you on the trip?"

"I was hoping we would get around to finishing this conversation." Once again, he claimed her mouth with his own.

CHAPTER FORTY-EIGHT

Ginger opened the journal Mike had given her for their first anniversary last week. He suggested she write down their story. Like her mother had. Ginger tapped her lip with the clicker end of her pen. "Where do I start?" After a moment of reflection, she began to write.

Grandpa and Grandma will be living at the big house in Renegade as long as health allows. So far, the drugs are helping with his symptoms of dementia and they are enjoying their time together.

Mike and I were married after a four-week engagement. Short by some peoples' measure. But not for us. We had waited long enough. Grandma insisted that we have the wedding and reception at the big house. It ended up being a double wedding. She and Grandpa renewed their vows. They were adorable. The wedding was incredible. The whole family was there. My family.

Rose is back for another summer. This year, she's staying with Rachel over at the house. She said it was because she wants to be close to the Jukebox where she's going to work. But I think it's because she wants to give Mike and me some space. I don't mind that one bit.

Rachel. I still have a hard time wrapping my mind around the fact that she is family. She runs the Jukebox like she was born to do it. I think maybe she was. She's been getting frequent visits from the travel blogger. I guess I called that one.

Rabbit is loving his new home. He is such a blessing to Grandpa.

From the corner of her eye Ginger saw Mike cross the floor toward her. He stopped behind her and kissed the back of her neck. Shivers ran up her spine. She never got tired of this.

"You ready?"

She looked up at him. "That's a loaded question."

"Having doubts?"

"Are you kidding?" She closed her journal. "It's about time I did this, don't you think?"

Mike grinned. "Letting go looks good on you."

Ginger laughed. Over the last few months Mike and Ginger had made the decision that she would officially step down from the Jukebox Café. She wanted to focus on her life with Mike and work with him in the church. She also needed the freedom to be involved in Grandpa's care as needed.

Rachel was ready to take the reins. The café would remain in Ginger's name for now, but eventually that would change as well. After all, the Jukebox Café needed to stay in the family. Today she was turning over her keys. The Jukebox Café would be Rachel's to run as she saw fit.

Ginger stood. "It looks good on me, because you'll get me to yourself more often."

Mike pulled her into his arms. "I'm not going to lie. That is the absolute truth."

Acknowledgements

Foremost, I want to thank my family who bore the brunt of all the long hours, piles of unfolded (although clean) laundry, leftovers and shortcut meals, and a full calendar that came with writing and editing this book. To my husband, Kevin, you were a constant support and never entertained the word quit. To my daughter Elizabeth, you are my ever ready brainstormer. To both of you for patiently listening to all my ideas for stories. Again, and again.

To my early readers and critique partners. You graciously gave of your time to read and gave feedback to improve my story.

To my editors, Lesley and Sara, who helped fine tune my story. You helped me see the forest when the trees were getting in my way. I couldn't have done it without you.

A huge thank you to RJ Thesman, the author of the *Reverend G* series and *Sometimes They Forget*. You offered invaluable information and feedback about the aspects of dementia in the story as well as suggested changes that greatly impacted the flow of the story. *This Side of Yesterday* would not have been as complete without your attention.

Thank you to the authors in The Mosaic Collection. Your support, guidance in this journey and ready answers to questions invaluable. It's an incredible blessing to be a part of you. Without you *This Side of Yesterday* wouldn't have seen today.

Most of all, I thank my heavenly Father. The one who provides rest in our most challenging seasons. The one who loves us even when we bring him our darkest days.

About the Author

Angela D. Meyer began writing in junior high when she scratched out poetry in her journal. She eventually penned inspirational non-fiction pieces and children's stories. In 2008 when a critique a partner challenged her to put more detail into her children's story, she wrote her first draft of a full length novella. In 2012, she published her first book, Where Hope Starts followed in 2015 with the second book in the series, Where Healing Starts. Both books were published with CrossRiver Media. Angela is in the process of planning to re-release these books in addition to the third book in the series, Where Joy Starts.

Angela currently lives in NE with her husband of 28 years. They have two children, both of whom they homeschooled and graduated. Lucy, a green eyed, orange tabby, who loves popcorn rounds out their family. In addition to teaching her own children, Angela taught children's Bible classes for over 35 years and now co-leads a women's Bible study at her church. She currently serves on the leadership team of her local Christian writers' group. Learn more about Angela at www.angeladmeyer.com.

Let's Connect!

Find Angela online at www.angeladmeyer.com and on Facebook and Goodreads.

For news and encouragement about upcoming books, contests, giveaways, and other activities, sign up for Angela's monthly newsletter.

If you've enjoyed *This Side of Yesterday*, please consider leaving a review. Your words bring hope and encouragement to the author as well as to other readers.

Other Books
BY ANGELA D. MEYER

Where Hope Starts
Where Healing Starts

Coming soon to

THE MOSAIC COLLECTION

Lost Down Deep by Sara Davison

She is the only one who can tell the police who attacked her in her home. If only she could remember ...

Summer Velasquez is on the run from a man she has no recollection of after an attack she can't recall.

Every face in the crowd is a potential suspect, so how is Summer supposed to know who is a threat to her and who isn't?

After fleeing her assailant and the parents who lied to her about what happened, she changes her name and seeks refuge in Elora, Ontario. The small town feels familiar, although she has no memory of ever having been here.

Even in what should be a safe place, she can't shake the feeling that she is being watched.

When Ryan Taylor strolls into the Taste of Heaven Café where she works, Summer is immediately drawn to him. However, he may not be who he says he is either. As her suspicions grow, Summer prepares to run again.

But at least one person is determined to stop her. Permanently. And if she can't remember who he is, this time he may succeed.

ABOUT SARA DAVISON

Sara Davison is the author of the romantic suspense series The Seven Trilogy and The Night Guardians. She has been a finalist for eight national writing awards, including Best New Canadian Christian author, a Carol Award, and two Daphne du Maurier Awards for Excellence in Mystery/Suspense. She is a Word and Cascade Award winner. She resides in Ontario, Canada with her husband Michael and their three children, all of whom she (literally) looks up to. Get to know Sara better at www.saradavison.org and @sarajdavison.

www.ingramcontent.com/pod-product-compliance
Lightning Source LLC
Chambersburg PA
CBHW020241180626
46810CB00006B/2300